W9-BTM-933

ALSO BY JULIÁN RÍOS

Larva: Midsummer Night's Babel

Poundemonium

Kitaj: Pictures and Conversation

LOVES THAT BIND

LOVES THAT BIND

JULIÁN RÍOS

*Translated from the Spanish
by Edith Grossman*

ALFRED A. KNOPF   *New York*   1998

THIS IS A BORZOI BOOK
PUBLISHED BY ALFRED A. KNOPF, INC.

Translation copyright © 1998 by Julián Ríos

www.randomhouse.com

Originally published in Spain as *Amores que atan o belles lettres*
by Ediciones Siruela, S.A., Madrid, in 1995.
Copyright © 1995 by Julián Ríos
Copyright © 1995 by Ediciones Siruela, S.A.

Library of Congress Cataloging-in-Publication Data
Ríos, Julián.
[Amores que atan]
Loves that bind / by Julián Ríos ; translated
by Edith Grossman. — 1st ed.
p.   cm.
ISBN 0-375-40058-3 (hardcover : alk. paper)
I. Grossman, Edith.   II. Title.
PQ6668.I576A8613   1998
863'.64—dc21   97-49473
                              CIP

Manufactured in the United States of America
First American Edition

C O N T E N T S

LOVES THAT BIND

ngels?
the round-cheeked brunette in the white blouse with dots as blue
as her eyes said in English, leaning forward at the next table
beside the slender Amazon with gray hair cropped very short
who had just unfolded—with heavily freckled hands—a tourist
brochure from Nice, and she nodded and read in French with a
Yankee accent: the Bay des Anges, though it sounded like des
Singes, and both leaned their heads even closer over the
unfolded blue, where I could make out tiny dark wings high in
the sky. It's high, very high, I repeated, perhaps aloud. As if I
were high in the clouds in that French sky, or rather on the
moon still almost full (was it the moon the day before last, alas,
that made you run away?) and shining so decoratively, like a
streetlight through the branches outside these windows that
face King's Road, and not simply in one of our two pubs at this
far end of the world, The Man in the Moon, where I have come,
impelled perhaps by a lunatic impulse or by the presentiment
that if you were in London I could probably find you here
tonight. The man in the moon. I look at him with curiosity (a
tall lanky fellow with black hair and beard, round black glasses
like John Lennon's, a black coat, and a satchel strapped across
my chest) as if my sad countenance (the Ugly Knight of
Gloom, you laughingly called me) were not the one reflected in

the mirror framed in bottles behind the bar. The J-shaped scratch beneath my left eye alters my face somewhat. I saw you so often in that inebriated mirror, leaning on your elbows beside me. It was not the memory of you, however, but the one of the earlier Fugitive that came to me first, summoned by the angels of temptation. Then I recalled with rancor the phrase in your language that you were so fond of, "Ah! tu me mets aux anges . . . ," or, as we would say in mine, you take me to seventh heaven, to glory, through all the spheres of heaven and circles of jealousy! Oh God, she never cried out to me, those words were only for the girl from the laundry, a laundress who lances my soul! and perhaps, too, for Andrée and Elisabeth and Esther and Léa, for her intimates, for all her frolicsome friends, though she would deny it with her usual brazenness no matter how the blush on her cheek plainly belied her words. But at times her lies disguised themselves as truth, and vice versa. With her I was never certain of anything. Not even of her deceptions. I see her again, curled in my bed, rolling, purring, playing with me like a cat, sniffing at me with her little pink nose. And in a sense her friend Andrée also played cat and mouse with me, always, first affirming they had never had intimate relations (in the mirror of my memory they both are reflected, pressing very close, breast to breast, revolving slowly in the casino at Incarville, Andrée with half-closed eyes kissing her on the neck), that this was simply play, the innocent effusiveness of friends, only to acknowledge much later, when she was in my arms, that my prisoner liked those ladies of Gomorrah, those girls at the beach, as much as she did . . . Ah, libertine! not caring about the agonies I suffered searching incessantly for my lost inferno. But Andrée, too, lied as easily as she breathed and probably made her confession to arouse me, for I had asked her to do with me what she did with her fondling female friend. According to Andrée, my passionate one found pleasure not only with her but with a handsome boy named Morel. Was that an invention, Morel? A youth who offered himself as bait to fishwives, laundresses, working-class girls, and shared them with her on a remote beach. For fear of losing him, their seducer, each one came to accept the supplementary caresses of her, the intruder, and, by the same token, had little opportunity for second thoughts because everything began all over again when they traded partners. Variety is the spice of life. Once they even took one of those poor unwary girls to a brothel in Couliville and shared her with four or five volunteers. But then, according to Andrée, she was consumed with remorse. She tried to overcome her vice, and according to Andrée, I was the burning straw she clutched at to keep from falling into the flames of her passion. A straw man, a slave, burning in the same hell. And she knew that if she left me she would return to her old life. Why, then, did she go? Or why did she never say to me, these are my inclinations? I would have accepted them with humility, allowed her to go on satisfying them, and sealed our pact of love with a kiss. And to think that only three days before she left she swore to me she had never had relations with the amie of a certain mademoiselle of my acquaintance, and hers, not realizing that when she turned tomato red she was professing her persistent perjury.

She turned red so often. She always had! Several years before, for instance, during the time she frequented the beach, when we talked about her bathrobe. Or, rather, her shower robe. I never asked her why she blushed then, perhaps because everyone knew that the showers in the bathhouse were visited by certain ladies and girls—Léa's two young friends, for example, who desired something more than the caress of water. And I would swear she also reddened in that long-ago summer when I, so ingenuous, told her of my aversion to the sophisms of sapphism. But she could also adopt an angelic air (was the seraphic pose easier for her than the sapphic?) and tell lies with impunity. She could stare into space, not blinking, and finally admit she had been wrong to hide from me a three-week trip she had taken with Léa. And that same morning she had told me she did not even know Léa! Léa and many others of similar leanings . . . Jealousy makes me read over and over again the report sent to me by Aimé, my private investigator and spy, in which he details the activities of *"Mlle. A,"* as he called her, or rather (*Mlle. A*), which was his own peculiar version of cursive and quotation marks. Beginning with the showers: who was the tall lady in gray with whom *Mlle. A* spent hours at a time, locked in the stall? The woman in charge of the showers did not know the name of the lady, but she had often seen her on the prowl, looking for young girls in flower. And when she left she always gave her a ten-franc tip. Though *Mlle. A* also came on occasion with a swarthy, nearsighted woman, she generally came with younger girls, above all one with red hair. And from the showers she moved to baths on the banks of the Loire with the little laundress. How I would like to have *Mlle. A* here before me and let her know that I know all about the girl from the laundry, know that you said in your excitement: "Ah! tu me mets aux anges . . . ," and that I saw your bite marks on her arm. Oh mordant amour . . . You went in the mornings to bathe in the river, and there on the bank, hidden by heavy foliage, you met with the girl from the laundry and all her friends, you dried one another, rubbed one another, tickled one another, and the little laundress glided her tongue over your neck and arms, even licked the sole of your foot as you stretched it toward her in lubricious, languorous equilibrium . . . You frolicked naked in the water, ducking and pushing one another. And I can reconstruct the scene with the bathers of Renoir, who turn everything black, and if I keep my eyes closed I hear your husky voice, Ah! tu me mets . . . , and with your mouth you searched out and sucked at her mouth. You see, I know everything. And if *Mlle. A* were at my side she would swear it was not true, she would assure me that Aimé was not a lover of truth, and simply to prove he had earned the money I gave him, he made too much of the laundress's tongue, and reported countless exaggerations, and I must be aware that the woman who runs the showers had a reputation in town as a mythomaniac and a confirmed liar, and I must recall that even my own grandmother had told me so many years earlier.

Which card or carte should I keep? Our visions of reality are so often fictions, formless or uninformed visions, fractions and refractions that deceive us, as when we see a stick apparently fractured in the water, and all these fragments we must complete with other fragments that are, in essence, as deceptive and illusory as the earlier ones. And *Mlle. A*, as Aimé called her, is also for me a series of fractions dissolving into new fractions and factions, a series as discontinuous as my own jealousy, she is several people, various masks, a series of moments, of fleeting silhouettes, visions, divisions . . . I saw the one who was corrupt, of course, but I also saw the one who had been good, serious, intelligent, full of affection, the one who read so many books to me, talked about them with me, played checkers with me, played music for me like an angel (her gold slippers still gleam on the pedals . . .), played sports, pedaled again along the quays toward the sky-blue sea.

As inconstant as the moon, her body also changed its form, and occasionally I was deceived when I attempted to fix certain specific details. And so I recalled a roguish birthmark on her chin that was really on her cheek. Her almond-shaped eyes, blue, brilliant, laughing, darkened at times into a black look.

Her round sensual cheeks seemed at first to be of wax, only to grow pink, red at times, a violet hue at others. Her robust, athletic constitution grew subtle when she was my prisoner in Paris, and for me alone she would put on the dark blue cape adorned with Kufic characters and arabesques that gave her so majestic an air as she walked around my room, followed by my adoring eyes.

The healthy, rosy girl could be transformed through the magic of a black satin dress into a pale Parisienne, refined and rather fanée by the vitiated city air and by her secret vice. At times she resembled a maja of Goya with her high comb, or an infanta of Velázquez with that heart-shaped knot of black hair over her ear, and at other times a madonna glowing pink amid white lace. And also pink in the light of the lamp in my room was her dark, full, strong throat that I so loved to bare with feverish hands. I would partially open her chemise and her two apples, high and perfectly round, became harder and yet ripe enough for me to touch them, tempt them, before I succumbed to the temptation of biting them. I also sank my teeth into her plump cheeks, as I did that time in the darkness of the car, and then I pulled back her hair so I could examine them, smooth and gleaming, in the moonlight.

That summer, outside of town, she often asked me to stop the car and buy cider, which always foamed out of the bottle and drenched us. We were in no danger, no, of being pressed for cider. After our cider shower she pressed her legs against mine, her warm red cheek against mine. And her voice changed as rapidly as her personality, it became husky, openly provocative, when she caressed me. I see her still, in her blouse with blue dots, bounding with so much agility into the car. If we did not stroll at night through the woods, a bottle of champagne under my arm, we took shelter at the foot of the dunes, her body against mine beneath the blanket, claire de lune on the dunes and the unmoving sea . . .

The moon shed its light at other times on our romance, and it was not totally edifying, for example, once, as we were returning from Versailles and she tried in vain to attract the eye of a robust pastry cook, a girl who had other tastes. From time to time our headlights illuminated couples lying together in ditches along the road. And then, when we had passed the Maillot gate, Paris loomed before us like a painting. In the light of the moon the monuments were lines, mere drawings without depth. And I remember the moon, as full as the one tonight, when we were returning from the Bois, and our car approached the Arc de Triomphe, and suddenly we saw the moon suspended over Paris like the dial of an illuminated clock.

And by the light of the moon how many nights did I spend watching her sleep. I could spend my whole life watching her sleep. On the whiteness of the pillow the jet diadem of her hair gleamed at night.

First I sat on the chair next to the bed, and when I had made certain that she was sleeping soundly, I would sit on the edge of the bed and finally move entirely onto the bed, leaning over to hear her slumber that flowed with the murmur of her breath.

When I touched her gently her breathing would change tones as if she were playing a musical instrument.

Asleep like this, she seemed more mine than when she was awake. At times she touched her hair, rested her hand on her breast, or moved her head slightly, producing the kind of unexpected change we experience when we touch the cylinder of a kaleidoscope, offering at each touch a new woman who yielded herself up to me, a transfiguration in dreams with each new gesture.

When her breathing grew deeper, I too descended into the

abyss and embarked on her sleep, lying cautiously at her side. Her slightly open mouth breathed next to mine, her life pulsating against my yearning tongue.

At times I allowed my entire body to brush against hers, in a rhythmic oscillation that was like a gentle shudder, a shivering to and fro, a quivering into sleep, and the sound of her breathing became heavier, creating the illusion of a gasp of profound pleasure when mine reached its climax.

While she slept I would always, eventually, take careful note of her kimono, thrown carelessly on the arm of the chair, for I knew that one of the inner pockets held all the revelatory letters that could resolve my doubts. I approached the chair, as wary as a cat, stood looking at the kimono for almost as long a time as I had spent admiring her in ecstasy; but I could never lower my hand into that pocket, I never even touched the kimono. I would turn and return to watch her as she slept. At times she spoke in her sleep, in tongues and nocturnal dialects, just as you do (I could have called her what I called you, Babelle au Bois Dormant!), incomprehensible murmurings that I attempted to decipher, listening with great care. I would have given anything to capture their sense, or their nonsense. At times as she slept she clearly pronounced a name that inflamed my jealousy. One night when she was half-awake, or just falling asleep with closed eyes, she said to me tenderly: "Andrée." I tried to conceal my consternation by laughing: "I'm not Andrée, not even in your dreams." "Of course not," she said with a smile. "I wanted to ask what you said to Andrée before on the phone." I was certain, and told her so, that she and Andrée had once lain together in this way. "Of course not, never," but before replying she had hidden her face in her hands.

I watched her sleep, and I could see her dead, the sheets, like a shroud, enveloping her body, petrifying her into a marble funerary statue, her backward tilting head seeming to emerge from a tomb.

That tense, powerful neck when she threw back her head, the throat I will never bite again. (Mordant, Mordre, Morder.) On the way here, as I walked through Sloane Square, the marquee at the Royal Court Theatre announced TOOTH OF CRIME, and it made me smile when I recalled the item in today's *Times:* a boy suffering the effects of LSD broke into the bedroom of an eighty-year-old woman in Farnborough, Hampshire, threw her out of bed and onto the floor, and bit her neck because he thought he was a vampire. The effects of LSD heightened, perhaps, by the full moon. As I used to tell you in English, more or less: In July you lie if you lie down . . . July is a month crueler than April. (Will you really make me wait an entire month while you decide whether or not you're coming back to me?) If you are not in London now, I hope you aren't in Lahore, where last night's hurricane—this is another news item from the *Times*—carried away eleven people and seriously injured another sixty-five.

The moon burns bright tonight.

But I should talk of the sun, not the moon, for today Earth is at its aphelion—don't worry, I'll explain: the point in its orbit farthest from the sun. I hope that I, at least, am not 150 million kilometers from you.

As I walked here along King's Road, the full moon, mounted like a jewel between two heavy clouds like the black wings of an eagle, reminded me that when *Mlle. A* went away she left behind two rings with the same eagle setting (who gave them to her really?) that pierced my heart. One was a gift from her aunt for her twentieth birthday. Is that true, or, as she would say, c'est vrai? C'est bien vrai? And the other, the one with the ruby? The roar of an airplane filled me with doubt and nostalgia (did you too take wing? where? another flight of jealousy?) and that was when I decided to tell you, in alphabetical order (for, after all, I might also consider myself a man of letters), about the women in my life before I met you.

I had to begin, of course, with this initial Fugitive.

Did she leave because my jealousy made her life impossible? Or to find a new life, with other women? Or because her aunt obliged her to look for a better, more secure match? Or to turn to the kind of a libertine life that in your language is called *bon temps*?

When I received the telegram from her aunt with the fateful news (how often I had foreseen this, and begged her to be prudent in Paris, and pleaded with her to keep in mind that if she had an accident I would never be consoled), I knew that now I would never overtake the Fugitive.

Though I often tried to deceive myself, for example when I heard the elevator stop at my floor, and my heart pounded as I told myself that she was going to ring the bell, that she had come back.

Her horse threw her against a tree.

A fortuitous accident? Or did she cause it, as Andrée finally suggested?

My jealousy resurrects her, restores her, revives her beneath the caresses of the little laundress, resuscitates her to seduce some other girl in the sand on the beach or perhaps in an abandoned cabin at the foot of the cliff.

Or was everything merely my imaginings?

I would be capable of turning to spiritualism, to the levitating table, the Ouija board, anything, if I could communicate with her. I would ask her again about a certain little laundress from Tours. But most terrible of all was that dead, she was no longer my prisoner. She escaped at full gallop, or by driving my car recklessly.

But she will return to free me and not free me from doubt, from this hell, to reveal and reveil her life and mysteries. Those seven lost hours at Versailles and what she really did from eleven in the morning until six at night. What she did and with whom when she hid for three days in Auteuil and disguised herself as a man so that no one would recognize her.

She has to come as she once did, every night, to offer me the communion of her tongue.

She parts my lips. I close my eyes and then her tongue glides along my neck, my chest, my belly.

The Amazon lady and the swarthy girl in the blouse with the dots (in this light they aren't blue now, they're violet) have stood up, and as they pass the bar they stop, drawn by the penny wheel of fortune. I remember you almost grew jealous that time when my fortune read *An important encounter.* But I don't encounter you today. The pub is packed on this first Friday in July. And now, at eleven, the groups of patrons saying good night at the door and calling out their good-byes bring back to me her final words, the last time I saw her, as I was taking my leave at the door of my room, "Adieu, petit, adieu, petit," she called me little one, can you imagine? and with this parting that tore my heart in two, I too say good-bye to you for today in the same words being repeated at the door at closing time: bye-bye.

eautiful
Samaritan with an angelic expression on her face leaning over
me to assist the taxi driver as he lifted me off the sidewalk. At
once maternal and majestic. I saw in a golden halo, in the light of
a streetlamp, the true face of my good protective goddess. In the
taxi that took me home through the deserted narrow streets in
the center of Vienna, I doubted for a few moments whether I
had as yet come to my senses following my brawl with three ruf-
fians, perhaps thieves (and my wallet? could I have dropped it?),
but all confusion vanished when I sensed in the perfumed darkness the sensual presence of that elegant beauty—thirty years
of age, I estimated—sitting so solicitous beside me. I recovered
quickly and our conversation, growing more and more lively,
revolved around boxing, which I eventually compared to theol-
ogy, and to love. She expressed astonishment that, after what
had happened, I would defend so brutal a sport. The body-to-
body contact of love, I counterattacked, can also be filled with
brutality . . . The conversation continued triumphant along the
various routes of Eros, and she, breathing faster, cautiously
moved a little farther away into her corner, and I would swear
that the light blush on her cheeks deepened. But the cab stopped
beside the black wrought-iron fence and I abandoned all hope as
I entered the house. My beautiful benefactress would not give
me her name or address, and drove off in the taxi.

The following morning she came unannounced to my house inquiring after my health, and we soon found ourselves in one another's arms. In this way the beautiful stranger became, overnight, my mistress. Although to honor the truth, or the complexity of feminine nature, I must acknowledge that in many respects she continued to be a stranger to me, and that in many others it took me some time to gradually come to know her. Of course, she often presented facts and events in so distorted a manner, or through so subjective a prism, that she made it difficult to form an exact idea of reality. For example, at first, when she referred to her husband, a well-known lawyer and judge considerably older than herself, she described him as a callous monster. In reality, as I later discovered, he was a good-hearted and jovial man, a great lover of the hunt and an able jurist, who had made the mistake of marrying a physically overexcitable woman with whom he maintained only sporadic relations. For her it was a marriage of convenience—"convenient," in fact, was one of her favorite words—and she believed she deceived him in order to escape from him, but she deceived herself as well, for she talked about her husband or the two children she had given him—the oldest, how the years fly by, was twelve—at the most unsuitable moments, even when she had thrown her arms about my neck, renewing or reknotting the matrimonial ties she claimed she wished to cut, or at least loosen, with each new adventure. An innate sense of respectability—even stronger than her sense of responsibility—forced her to lead a double life, and at times of crisis and remorse, generally in the empty times or emptiness that looms between two lovers, she suffered from self-contempt because of the many lies and degradations to which she had exposed herself, and her weakness, her inability to resist her "inclinations," as she called them, which made her fall lower and lower; but her weeping would eventually wash away her guilt or sweep it toward her solidly stolid husband, guilty of neglect and lack of proper feeling, she said, forcing her into the arms of another man. I was this other man for a period of time that was occasionally difficult, not free of ups and downs, tears, ruptures, and reconciliations. I said that she appeared as my good goddess, my Bona Dea, and I continued to call her that, not without a touch of mythological irony, which allowed me to appreciate her majestic, serene beauty and her natural sensuality without myself becoming totally bedazzled. Sensuality formed part of her nature, it emanated from her in the way that other people have other troubles, such as sweating of the hands or giving off certain odors.

I still see her lying half-naked or half-dressed on the divan of reflections—and effusions—her tender maternal belly rising and falling gently through white folds of batiste. In sweet abandon, looking at the ceiling, she let herself be carried away by her illusions.

We had agreed on a secret signal—our little ugly duckling: a wooden duck, its paint fading away, on the windowsill—to show her that I was alone. She, in fact, expected me to always be alone, for she was both possessive and jealous. The attacks of jealousy made her even more beautiful. The torments of jealousy tended to lead to a storm in bed followed by a calm, and I never failed to marvel at the prodigious transformation coming after her earlier agitation and frenzy. That serenity never seemed to leave her, though at times she struck me as sluggish, for example when she dressed lazily, unhurriedly, and in the end I felt a vague impatience, above all if the time was approaching for another appointment. I see her, through the half-open door, still half-dressed, sitting and looking so calmly at the pictures in a history of art that she held on her knees—they were dimpled, too. One might say she had emerged from one of those illustrations of classical antiquity. Moreover, at the time, her hairdo was almost Greek. A solid goddess with white shoulders gleaming like pearl. Though other, less classical forms sprang immediately into view. Especially her breasts, heavy and round, which she gently pressed between her arms as if rocking them to sleep.

And I could recall another scene, after a period of separation when she had suffered a great deal, cried a great deal, had many adventures and many disappointments, only to return, desiring a reconciliation with me. She was charming, melancholy, and beautiful as she sat before me, though she now had something of a stomach.

Suddenly rising, she took my dangling hand and kissed it. Overcome by emotion, she was about to fall on her knees when I pushed her gently back into the chair. I brought whiskey and then lit—a diversionary tactic—a cigarette. Her sense of respectability led her to maintain, against all odds, that a lady does not drink whiskey in the morning. Whiskey and Sodom, if she wished.

Sometimes I watched her as she dressed, and I always admired her steady painter's hand as she emphasized the fine arch of her eyebrows, the light dusting of powder on her cheeks applied with precision, the almost floral arrangement of ringlets on her not unclouded brow, dark little buds, faded or upright, depending on the vagaries of fashion.

I knew her predilection for quotations and clichés, and she would agree with me that love is blind. How differently we view the woman we love and the one we have stopped loving, the one we desire and the one who has satisfied our desires. Again I see her face in close-up after making love: her exhausted eyes, dulled, her dark nose with its two red hollows from which, I observed with repugnance, several hairs were growing . . .

When our relations had cooled she turned to fairly ingenuous devices to achieve her desires. The shoe she lost so that her foot, with its warm, rounded toes, would come to rest in my hand . . . Cinderella found just what she was looking for . . . Her faint shriek when suddenly she felt a sharp sting. And I had to help her find the flea, had to undress her, examine her carefully from head to toe. Beginning with her blouse, which had to be unbuttoned in front, baring her deep cleavage, and ending with her stocking and shoe. A flea favors the same areas as a lover. Did I forget one? It was probably a false sensation, I ventured, when I discovered that the flea was not to be found and had left no traces. I can't imagine what it could have been, she said, and my smile was truly, unexpectedly kind. Then she began to cry like a little girl who has just been caught red-handed.

Following fashion was her one fidelity, and her preferred way to be fickle. The hunt for a dress or an ornament could be a most exciting adventure. And so I was not too surprised to find her today in Harrods. Even though the first day of a sale might not have been the most favorable moment. In the silvered mirror I saw my good goddess of Vienna. The trembling veil on the little hat that she was trying to pull down firmly on her head. But the mirage in the mirror lasted only a few moments, until the black widow took off the toque complete with web and fly, and gave way to another: I could have sworn that in its depths you were trying on an enormous cabbage or Brussels sprout. Was I in a hall of illusory mirrors? In the mad shop of the Mad Hatter? Or were you emerging from the top hat of that uncle of yours, the magician in Los Angeles? The Great Karman! You've told me so much about him that I must actually believe he exists. Mandrake and Houdini in one. And a ventriloquist as well. Not in Armenian, I hope . . . I crossed the gallery, crashing through the crowd to catch you, but you escaped by a hair, I saw only your dark mane flying through the doors of the elevator. I ran down the stairs but arrived too late. I went down to the Palace of Food, "le Palais du Palais," do you remember? I crossed into the kingdoms of King Salmon and the Queen of Sea Bass, passed among salamonic columns of salami. I even bought some slices for the neighbor's cat. Poor Miss Rose, "La Rousse," doesn't know I baptized the cat Why. Better than the ridiculous Chinese name she had given him. What better name for a cat who always meows *guay* and raises his tail in a question mark? Here he is again now with his mournful guay because there's no more sausage from Harrods, he finished it and didn't let me read today's *Times* to you, I mustn't forget to pile it with the others so that when Miss Rose returns from Greece she'll find them all in order in the kitchen. And I don't feed the cat at regular times, either. Though he doesn't stop meowing if I take too long to come over and feed him. I haven't changed the sand in the litter box yet. I wonder if you're on vacation with Miss Rose on the beaches of Ulysses. I hope, at least, that if you weren't in Harrods, you weren't traveling yesterday on the bus that crashed into a truck north of Jyväskylä, in central Finland. Twelve tourists died, but Miss Rose's *Times* doesn't say what nationality they were. Primum vivere, the price of provisions: beginning on Monday prices are going up for cheese, chocolate, and beer. Two pence more for a pound of Irish cheddar, seventeen pence more for a pound of Cadbury's, a penny more for a pint of beer. It costs so much to live!

You'll see when you come back . . . I also wonder if you haven't gone with our mentor Reis on a Hugoesque vacation or evocation to Guernsey. The workers of the sea . . . The day before yesterday I received one of his postcards from Hauteville House. His Hugolatry knows no bounds . . . It's as if it were August. Everyone is leaving. Rimbaudelaire is resting in Liège, composing ethilyrical haikus . . . Reynaldo has gone a little farther, has left to be a Spanish instructor at a summer colony in Cologne. Albert Alter makes gargoyles and paints Mona Lisas in Paris. And you? Have you gone as an interpreter to some congress in the third world or the fifth circle of hell? Or to Los Angeles? Where are you? A question mark as large as the strand of hair you once left in my sink: ?

And now, stretching out on the almost Freudian couch of Miss Rose to watch Brazil vs. Poland, I suddenly recalled another scene on a divan with my good diva of Vienna, or, to be more exact, with a vestige of her passage through my life. I had not seen her for some time, and another woman occupied my heart and, for the moment, lay next to me on the divan, from whose depths she withdrew a hairpin (one of those my good goddess used for her Grecian hairdos) that she held aloft, red with jealousy. Ah, calamitous coiffeur.

Cometshaped
kites floating in the skyblue sky above the Round Pond (it always seemed more like a square to us) on this true summer's afternoon. A crimson hexagon had attracted my attention, at the risk of a stiff neck, when I was distracted by the froufrou and sphericities in motion that a wide black shawl could not conceal. "I said it as a joke," a bald mustachioed man said in Italian to the dark homely girl with Moskouri glasses and a friendless face, the two of them behind the monumental screen of the shawl. At the edge of the Round Pond I ponder, calculate, speculate, seek out analogies, try to imagine in Italian the joke hovering above the ponderous vastness of the veiled girl not quite so overpowering there in front of plump Queen Victoria grasping her scepter and sitting on her throne. From here her real royal flaking face is difficult to discern. Many tourists today in Kensington Gardens; but those two Italians, most probably immigrants. Like the dark young man on the next bench who takes refuge behind a fortified wall of strange characters. His Pakistani or Indian paper must surely recount, as does my *Sunday Times,* that yesterday a typhoon swept along the west coast of Japan and carried away sixty-two people. I assume you have not gone so far away. And no doubt his front page also speaks of the final match between West Germany and Holland that I will watch

this afternoon in the house of Miss Rose. I do not imagine you in Munich. Now an albino runner passes and a sausage dog standing at the edge watches him, shaking its head. Nelly! called a woman's voice, spectral or thinned by distance. A pretty Dickensian name. From this bench on the banks I follow the entire multicolored, multiracial parade, children and dogs racing, this other old man with wild white hair who looks ready to breathe his last, the zigzagging kites (where is the crimson one?), the little boats navigating past tempestuous gulls on the pond (now, kneeling in front of me, a fiftyish man in short pants keeps watch over his clipper ship), the splashdowns and takeoffs of gulls and ducks, more of a wingflap here between the long legs of two girls in miniskirts, and it's clear they get on famously, they and their crumbs, with the pigeons on the other bench nearby. "If there are too many people we'll leave," the tall slim blonde has just said in French as she pushes the old man in the wheelchair who wears a yachting cap and clutches in gloved hands on his lap a kite as black as a coffin. A gust of wind blows the skirt tight against her well-sculpted buttocks, and this vision in high relief turned me back nostalgic in time and space to a midsummer night in Chelsea, to another blonde with a sculpted ass, an Irish girl of the streets whom I ran into or who ran into me at the intersection of Cremorne Road and Stadium Street. As if I were still on that street corner, I can see her small round yellow head, green eyes, deadwhite skin, well-proportioned figure, height 5′ 4″, weight 123 lbs. I have kept the other measurements I made (bust 34″, hips 35″), thinking that in her idle hours she might stop walking the streets and start sitting for some photographer. At the heart of everything is one's figure. Show off your good figure, I told her, no one cares about your good heart. She was four when she left Ireland and all she could recall of the land of her birth was a bright sky. But she maintained her

connection to it through her only relative, her paternal grandfather, who lived not far away, and more recently—and for this
we might blame her future with no future—an impassive
Dubliner some thirty years of age with the cold and unwavering
eyes of a gull, who killed time in his soporific rocking chair
seeking nirvana in his barren back-and-forthing but not seeking
work or attempting to retire her from harlotry to the hearth, a
sweet little hearth, her great goal in life. She left him soon after
they met and stood her ground until he at last found work as a
nurse-of-all-trades in a madhouse on the outskirts of London,
which did nothing to improve his mental equilibrium, equilibri-
ating still in his bleak teak rocking chair, and would have dire
consequences for their affair. The truth of the matter is that of
late her stars had been unlucky. Two years earlier her parents
perished in a shipwreck, and she, their only offspring, leaped
into the gutterlife. Though more than once she was on the verge
of leaping off Battersea Bridge. And Albert Bridge. Water was
a great temptation, perhaps the ultimate solution. The girl-for-
hire, should she expire or retire? But meanwhile she attempted
to be tempting. Leading a life in London was not easy. Her
grandfather held his hands to the delicate bulb of his head,
which he still had despite his almost ninety years, and predicted
that she would get ahead. Indeed, he was her confidant, a shoulder for her to cry on, her hydraulic adviser: Better to leap into
the gutter than the Thames. But she did not heed his urging to
"chuck him," to get rid of that ne'er-do-well sweetheart. A
short while after their first breakup, not long after they met, she
agreed to go back to him at his insistence but imposed her con-
ditions. She would leave the streets and he would pound the
pavements for work. In the meantime they would live on her
scant savings and the monthly remittance sent to him by a
Dutch uncle, and rent a room: she wanted to change not only

her ways but her whereabouts. From the west they moved north, to Islington. In Brewery Road, near Pentonville Prison, they found an enormous ramshackle haven where her sweetheart's rocker looked like a toy next to two massive upright unupholstered armchairs, similar to those killed under him by Balzac. The high walls were a Vermeer yellow that matched the vivid lemon of her sweetheart's tie. And the blue, gray, and brown linoleum matched that Cubist bric-a-brac. There, she thought, their life would change. Above them lived a retired butler who paced as incessantly as a caged lion. The muffled sound of the old boy's shuffling slippers resounded overhead. Perhaps he found repose at last when he cut his throat with a cutthroat barber's razor. A barbaric tragedy with great outpourings of blood on the Braque-colored linoleum, throwing the whole house into an uproar. Plucking up her courage, and in order to survive on her limited means, she moved into the butler's room, smaller than hers but also cheaper. That happened when her Dublin sweetheart had already left, taking his rocking chair with him and going to the suburban sanatorium, though she still hoped he would rock at her side once more. Her sweetheart, custodian of lunatics, seemed happy at Mercyseat caring for his peers and playing chess. Endgame. She found him when he had no job and lost him when he found one. And his job was his doom. His escape came to an end with another escape. Of gas. And the ensuing explosion of a radiator (shoddily installed in that asylum) as he rocked in his perpetual rocking chair.

She went back to the gutter. To walk the streets of Chelsea. Her familiar silhouette in a waterproof of pale blush buff along Lots Road. Don't look back? All these misfortunes she told to me in a West Brompton pub while having a sandwich of prawn and tomato and a dock glass of white port off the zinc. She received the news with fortitude and went to the mortuary to identify the body. Unidentifiable. The wood of this bench is too cold now. It's time to get up, to go and watch the game. Identifying marks? She remembered a huge pink nevus on one buttock of her beloved. There was no quid pro quo. The birthmark was still on the pinnacle of the (right?) buttock of the deceased.

D

erry

& Tom's, I believe, the old name of these large stores recently made into a Babylon of bibelots and multicolored bagatelles, which, one might say, meant revisiting better days, the mad twenties, with the disjointed Charlestonant of this thé dansant thundering across to me here in the Babylonian terrace of Biba. I thought this hanging garden was the ideal setting for plucking the petals of the day's daisy and telling, perhaps, the tale of the enchanting fay who was turned into fate. Seriously: I decided to come to this tea for two thousand as I passed the Empire this afternoon, I even looked for you in the line of Robert Redford fans, and I told myself you too would probably fall by here. (If you are not in London, I trust you are not inopportunely trysting in Oporto or Lisbon, where, according to the *Times,* new cases of cholera have been reported.)

Pleasant to a high degree (73°) today on this roof garden of delights. You marveled when we discovered it this winter: under thick sooty clouds, among chimneys and dark roofs, a luxuriant Eden, complete with apple trees, for the fruitful enjoyment of forbidden fruit. Now a garden of despearate waiting, though I am not too hopeful. Not a soul on that icy afternoon, but one would think you feared the eye of the great Voyeur. Golden or wax? You did not want me to bite the apple of discord, or your lips like blackberries. Darkly mordant, amor. And I feel as if I were in Bedlam, not Biba, when I recall that lost kiss. It was so hard to get you to part your lips. Until, at last, to prove your experience, you decided that the shrub wrapped in plastic was a wild pear tree. Oui, duchesse! I made so many wily wordplays with apples and pears in pearadise, remember? that you had to plant your feet firmly and protest. Enough! Another pearouette, no . . .

The wail of the aphonic saxophone, blues for a blue Monday, at gray teatime, made me realize: I came to this art deco bazaar to decorate my nostalgia, to find you perhaps as I told the story of love damned in New York.

I would tell you this story *ab ovo:* Once there was a summer in West Egg and East Egg, the shape we give to the prominent capes of Great Neck and Glen Cove, those two Long Island promontories. There I could see how the rich lived and played—in mansions with parks, marble pools, and private beaches—so different from we poor mortals. That summer burned away in princely parties, and a woman was the incandescent center—and cause—of the blinding blaze.

All these mannequins in white dresses who flit past and pose and flutter now in the garden remind me of her. In particular the beauty in the mauve hat with a lock of hair like a dark brushstroke on her cheek, who allows herself to be carried like a queen, lighthearted and haughty, on the crossed hands of two beaux in white flannel suits who laugh, She has twisted her ankle . . . , and set her delicately on the divan-swing at the far end of the garden. She is the queen of the garden, of this summer-afternoon tea, and from time to time beauties and beaux come to pay homage and swing beside her. I thought of the Queen of the Fairies in a Victorian painting of *A Midsummer Night's Dream* we once saw at the Tate. The magic of pale

cheeks and cheekbones like rose petals. Poor thing, she's paralyzed, I thought for a moment before I heard the laughter of her
wellborn bearers, and I remembered the first words I heard
from the lips of my Louisville beauty the first time I saw her, on
a hot, windy summer twilight when I came for supper to her
East Egg mansion in the company of a distant cousin of hers, a
college friend of her husband's: "I'm p-paralyzed with happiness," she laughed and greeted her cousin after attempting to
rise from an enormous couch where she lay next to another girl,
who was slimmer and looked athletic and also wore white, and
was the one who truly seemed paralyzed, though not with happiness, lying in precarious balance. I remembered her first
words, but in fact at first it was her voice, that voice so typical of
her, caressing or disturbing, thrilling with a tremor of a thrill,
soft or husky, modulating so, that all of us who have fallen in
love with her can never forget. Hushed at times with emotion,
suddenly bright and warm like a flame at the climax, languid
and dreamy in repose, with a bitter touch of indolence or boredom, silvery and instantly bubbling, breaking into laughter and
almost childish stammering in happy situations, at other times
insinuating in sinuous murmurs, as if to make us lean toward
her. A rich voice, and (was that her secret?) a rich girl's voice.
As her new rich lover saw and heard very well: Her voice is full
of silver . . . jingling, tingling, singing, full of splendid music.

The subdued sob, very low, of a banjo. Am I blue? This
blues can't be trusted, it goes right to my head, as you would say.

Though it is only a dull teatime, I would like you to bring me
bourbon, ice, sugar, crushed mint leaves, and fix a julep. The
cool sweetness of a sweltering New York August. And it
wouldn't be bad either if you showed up now in a short beaded
skirt and pearls looped three times around your neck, shimmy-
ing over with a glass of Scotch in one hand and a gin fizz in the

other, to coax me out on the dance floor. And raise a glass first to our drinker. Drink, dance, and be merry, our essential watchword. Save me the last waltz, please, though it's three o'clock in the morning, before the embalming begins. Another danse macabre?

Don't tell me "The Prisoner of Zelda" doesn't appeal to the poor boy from the midwest, prisoner and prey of that mad wife, his chastising Zelda, though she was the one confined, I told you in my mind a few hours ago in Leicester Square as I passed the posters outside the Empire advertising the film. I imagined how miffed you would be, accusing me again of macho mockery.

Leaning now against the wall of this hanging garden, enveloped in aromas of cool jazzmine, orchids and orchestra, surrounded by swains and maidens in white who think of themselves as doubles of Robert Redford and Mia Farrow, I think again of the unfortunate Scotch "Gin" Fitz, as we alcoholized him once in defiance of the dry law, still lost in thought one hundred feet above the centipedal scurry of the crowd along Kensington High Street. And in fact I see her again: her sad, seductive face, eyes filled with light, passionate mouth blood red, the gleam of her dark hair that I kissed beside the fire that cold afternoon the day before I left for Europe, when she spent a fleeting eternity in my arms. Her face was a changing mask that could assume a bored expression, and then her lips would form a scornful fold. A shallow person at the edge of an abyss? Again I caviled as I looked around me. I could guess at her figure on the divan-swing as I watched her shapely slender legs sheathed in white silk stockings.

Thanks to her cousin Nick, I began to know what she was like though I never really got to know her (did anyone?), I learned about certain episodes of her past, her origins as the daughter of a well-off family in Louisville. Although I was never in Louisville, Kentucky, I can recall the streets where her footsteps echoed alongside the military ones of a lover in uniform one November night when leaves were falling, I can relive in a vicarious way certain critical moments: I am the lieutenant who kissed her for the first time, standing fast on a white sidewalk in the moonlight, under the stars; I, the lieutenant-come-lately who had her on another quiet October night, the same one who two nights later kissed her again on a wicker love seat on the posh porch of her house. She was chilled and her rather husky voice sounded especially seductive. That month of love could not last forever. After some failed attempt at rebellion, she yielded to the wishes of her affluent family and left the soldier with no future for a better future and greater profit: a wealthy heir from Chicago who would give her everything she deserved.

I didn't doubt it when I found myself in her gorgeous Georgian colonial mansion, but I also understood immediately that her large, athletic husband—"hulking," as she called him, driving him mad—could not provide the sophisticated emotion she sometimes needed. (Sophisticated, yes, she considered herself sophisticated though she was only twenty-three.) Luxe and calme, with no volupté. Perhaps she sensed that, five years earlier, in a moment of lucidity—or was it remorse?—the night before her wedding, when she drank a bottle of Sauternes, became drunk for the first—and last—time, and threw the gift from her future husband into the wastebasket: a pearl necklace worth, if my calculations are correct, $350,000. (But she needed to be free, freed from her possessive family.) After a cold bath and a few sniffs of spirits of ammonia, she recovered her senses and the necklace, which she displayed at the marriage supper. The wedding was lavish and they lived happily ever . . . until five years later, when her former impoverished lover made his appearance, transformed into a magnetic magnate endowed with great powers of attraction. Money is a powerful magnet. The mysterious magnate bought a huge gloomy mansion in West Egg—the less fashionable of the two Eggs—an almost exact, extravagant replica of some medieval Hôtel de Ville in Normandy with a tower on one side, all of it right across the bay from the cheerful East Egg red and white mansion of the woman he loved. On some summer nights he would walk out on the terrace of his mansion to contemplate the polestar that polarized his attention: the green light at the end of the dock of her house. I began to attend the multitude of parties given almost every night by the magnate with the dark past and even shadowier present; powerless, I witnessed his maneuvers to approach, surround, and recapture his lost love. But it did not take me long to understand that he would not attain his desire.

He had elegance and a roughneck's air, and was painstakingly careful in his speech. Thirty-one or thirty-two years old, of the same generation as his rival. Though not of the same class. He no longer lacked money, as he had in Louisville, but he did lack, I believe, the lack of scruples, and the brutality, of her husband. And immediately I can see how he broke his lover's nose (yes, the husband also had his lover, a married woman with whom he rendezvoused in New York) with one punch when she insisted on repeating his wife's name. The lack of scruples, or perhaps it would be more exact to call it conscience, would be displayed once again when he attempted to get rid of his wife's lover.

The rivalry between husband and lover came to a head one stifling August afternoon when we rented a suite—there were five of us, I think—at the Plaza Hotel, with the absurd idea of having mint juleps. In reality she instigated it when she suggested we rent five bathrooms at the Plaza and take cold baths.

Loves That Bind

We opened all the windows, hoping for a breeze, and I looked out over the trees in Central Park, losing my way along paths that led to the past. She turned her back on us and began to comb her hair in front of the mirror. (I saw her long ago, in her lover's bedroom, brushing her hair in delight with a golden hairbrush.)

The suite became the ring for a long boxing match that lasted from four in the afternoon to seven in the evening, and she was the beautiful trophy. And the referee. She finally chose security. And I don't believe she did it only for Pammy, her three-year-old daughter. She finally chose the security of a husband with as few scruples as she had.

They exchanged no more than words (she acknowledged in front of everyone, after some preliminary hesitations and retreats, that in reality she did not love the lover who had emerged from the shadows of the past and who, as her husband had just revealed, might end in shadow because he surely was involved in shady dealings), but those words were so bruising they put her lover hors de combat, as dead as he would be two days later when he was killed by bullets in a series of circumstances and misunderstandings so rocambolesque they belonged in a novel. He was not really killed by the cunning of his lover's husband (who convinced the husband of his own lover, who had been hit a little while before by the car of his wife's lover, that he had been responsible for her death, when in reality it had been his lover, that is, his own wife, who had been driving the car at the moment of the accident), he was killed by her indifference. The pistol shots were merely the coup de grâce. And she, what did she do? She went on a trip with her husband when she heard about his death, and didn't send a single flower.

At the beginning of that summer of love and death she recognized that recently she had become too cynical. Perhaps she was right. Just recently? I've saved this image of the beginning of our idyll for last.

We are sitting at either end of a long couch, staring at one another, and tears have left their wake on her pale white face.

It is time for me to leave, and I too go to pay my homage to the immobile beauty on the divan-swing. A perfect, impassive show-window mannequin, as well dressed and soulless as she ever was. Ever.

ENTER

A DIFFERENT WORLD, in gold letters along the side of the new double-decker bus driving across Hammersmith Bridge. This repeated advertisement, Harrods' golden legend, makes me think that on Saturday I may have entered a different world, a maze of reflecting mirrors and multiplying hats, where I thought I saw you, caught a glimpse of you at least in that tumultuous rise-and-fall of lowered prices. Were you the willowy brunette, her hair hanging loose, wearing a black jacket and slacks, who was trying on a ((hallucinogenic?)) mushroom-shaped hat, or was it merely a mirage? I still have my doubts, in this overcast twilight, as I move against the current of the crowd along one of our favorite walks, Lower Mall, and watch the rapid passing of the Thames. It reveals its treasures now along the bank. A basketball sneaker half-buried in the mud displays its toe cap sprinkled with stardust.

The suspension bridge at Hammersmith, which always reminds me vaguely of the Brooklyn Bridge, makes me realize that Emil was still in New York (:Don't be childish!—I know, it bothers you when I talk about myself in the third person), though not with the same girl as yesterday. Today's beauty had hair the color of copper, long coppery lashes, large gray eyes, and she was as slender as a ballerina (I imagine her finally transformed into a little porcelain figure under a bell glass), with a figure (I see her again in room 108 of the Brevoort Hotel when she undressed and caught sight of herself in the mirror, stood naked looking at herself with her hands on her tiny breasts as firm as apples—other fruits, ah, so fruitfully tasted . . . I wish your body were an edible fruit, her mordacious amour would say to her) and a sensuality calculated to drive any man crazy, as one of her frustrated suitors acknowledged, and even capable of making the mature attorney who would become her third husband lose his reason.

Low tide leaves behind oily pools. A sluggish looking glass that captures clouds, passing shadows. Three gulls wheel above the broken boxes, empty bottles, orangerinds, wrappers, spoiled cabbage heads, cigarette butts that heave between the splintered planks of the wooden wharf just a few steps away, facing the terrace of The Blue Anchor, where I made my first stop to begin writing to you.

(The older woman with red hair at the next table, with her Lauren Bacall air and a TWA flight bag, must have thought I was a tourist, too, when she saw me open my satchel and take out the tablet of airmail stationery, *Belles Lettres*—registered trademark! Brassy-looking in that Nile-green nylon blouse. And she watches me out of the corner of her eye as I write to you.) At the very top of the pilings on the pier a gull stands guard and stares at the bouquet of rusty roses deposited there in the mud. Is he wondering if the floral offering is edible? A faded bouquet withering here on the wasteland of the shore (where are the roses of yesteryear?) turned my thoughts back to her and New York, to her room on 105th Street, east of Broadway: her pink silk step-ins and a stocking and her brassiere and the other stocking tossed on chairs that I will bump against as I grope my way in the dark, and again I breathed in the stuffy smell of the room softened by the fading freshness of yellow roses on the bureau. Aren't there any without thorns? The bouquet of roses she brought to her father on that stormy Sunday when she told him she was going to divorce her first husband. "They're red roses like your mother used to like," the old man recalled. He surely knew the reason (as well as the gossip about her reckless lover), but he was too old-fashioned and she could not explain anything in detail. Could not tell him that Jojo was homosexual, and that she in fact had married this actor/ess to further her career in the theater. For two years before she met him, she had lifted her voice and legs once too often in sad cafés and tiny theaters off-off-off Broadway. She leaned over to breathe deep of the roses she had just put into a vase, and was distracted as she watched a little green measuring worm cross a bronzed leaf. The fragrance helped to freshen the dust-heavy air. Certain furniture from the house where she grew up, on 100th Street, made her father's new apartment in Passaic, New Jersey, seem familiar. She dropped onto a sofa, and if she stared long enough at the faded red roses on the carpet she would be transported, as if on a magic flying carpet, to one of her earliest memories: it is another Sunday afternoon and her father plays the piano and she dances, stepping carefully among the red roses on the sunny field of the carpet, stepping faster and faster until her feet become entangled in the Sunday paper that has just fallen from the table, faster and faster, tearing the sheets under her tiny nimble feet.

She married and divorced to have a career—a curriculum vitae that she summarized at the time as: married at eighteen, divorced at twenty-two. To be continued.

A rose is a rose is a—don't play it again, it's the rose in "Secondhand Rose" that the man who would become her second husband listened to as he lay on his back on top of the sheet on that sultry night, imagining perhaps how she was making love in the next room to Stan, the hard-drinking student. Her friend Stan had asked him to lend him a room for the night, let him find refuge there because her husband the actor/ess had begun to take too seriously the role of deceived husband. And then suddenly, when it was terribly late, the Punch-and-Judy show began: she burst into Jimmy's room draped in a sheet and asked him to talk to Jojo and make him go away to sleep it off, for he insisted on sneaking in by the fire escape and shouting incendiary proclamations through the window, while her lover shook with laughter, hiding naked behind the two couches made up together into a vast adulterous bed. And she had hidden in the closet in the room of the man who, years later, would be her second husband. (Yes, one must keep the numbers straight . . .)

At last her husband went back into the great night, and she to the arms of her lover, and he to the solitude of his room where there were still traces—I can smell it—of the cedarwood scent of her heavy-coiled hair.

I buried my nose in her hair, drinking in/thirsting for her perfumes in that rose-tinged light, while we danced and I felt the tips of her breasts, the smoothness of her belly, her firm thighs meshing tight, an intricate machine of sawtooth steel. In her arms I understood how erotic an ice-cold artifact by Duchamp or Picabia can be.

The coolness and softness and smoothness of her recently bathed pink-flushed body.

Two crimson rose petals on her handkerchief, after the kiss.

Hardly breathing during the kiss. She had taken my hand as we walked down the stairs, and at the door, in front of the letter boxes in the shabby hallway, she let me press her head back and kiss her. Hardly breathing as we floated down 105th Street toward Broadway.

The rose on her cheeks that she contemplates in the moon glass of a store window, shortly after leaving the office of Dr. Abrahams. Would she also have named him Stanwood? She decided not to keep the child of a dead father. (Her reckless lover, in one of his alcoholic deliriums, had burned himself alive, a suicide for the love of death, a horrible death by fire.) I think it was necessary for the father and child to be dead, because she recognized that she could give lasting love only to the dead. She had just had an abortion, but the glass reflected an impeccable mask: scarlet lips, well-powdered cheeks . . .

(Dr. Abrahams . . . The seed of the unborn is as countless as grains of sand in the desert . . . The knife of Dr. Abrahams in that clinic in King's Cross that you could mark with an ×.)

Miss Rose's *Times* here on the table awakens the curiosity of the solitary tourist, a Yankee no doubt, who casts steely looks at the photograph of Mr. Kissinger shaking the hands of children in St. James's Park. I suppose you won't be running the San Fermín at Pamplona: yesterday there were four serious injuries. I suppose that yesterday you weren't in a five-story building that burned down in Montmartre: five people died (four of them jumped out the windows) and thirteen were injured . . . If the tourist continues to look at me this way, I'll have to tell her what I've written to you. I am still arranging the bouquet of love.

Her life was not precisely a rose-strewn path, but a few more petals could place us at another culminating moment of her career.

(When I raise my eyes toward the Woolworth Building I also see her with the eyes of her dead lover: at the top of the skyscraper, in an apartment made of cut glass and cherry blossoms.)

Some time ago she abandoned a promising career in the theater, but she still plays to perfection her part as clinging vine.

She is going to divorce her second husband, the out-of-work reporter Jimmy, with whom she had a child; she edits a fashion magazine. But it's clear she aims higher. She has just come to the Seaside Inn accompanied by the lawyer who took care of her two divorces and will become the district attorney and her third husband. She imagines that we are at a nearby table eating steamed clams. As she lays her gloves on the edge of the table, her hand brushes against the vase of rusty red and yellow roses and a shower of faded petals flutters onto her hand, her gloves, the tablecloth. Her wish was his command: "Do have him take away these wretched roses, George . . ." Her explanation suited her exquisite beauty: "I hate faded flowers." And as it turned out, in that restaurant on Long Island not even the lobster was fresh.

For dating this letter I would gladly use the date of her anniversaries, although—let me count—there are still exactly twenty-four days to go. She was born on August 4—in Stamford, Connecticut: I know, another Yankee . . . —and be it fate or chance, the most important events of her life arrived punctually on that canicular date. On the day she came of age her Uncle John, a recently retired button manufacturer who supposedly had a "heart," took her on a tour round the world in the company of a sort of gentleman traveling companion, an amateur dauber called Jimmy. The following August 4, almost at the end of the long initiatory journey, Jimmy made a woman of her. That birthday gift was presented to her in an English manor house near Ledbury, which had shamelessly been turned into a house for refined guests, just one day before she found herself obliged to hurry back to the United States with her uncle. Another John would take her to Europe again, and her Jimmy, remaining in Paris thanks to her generosity and her uncle's, pretended to study painting at the Julien Academy. And the following year, also on August 4, she made a hasty marriage at dawn to a wealthy property owner from Philadelphia, and that same day, in the afternoon—a honeymoon sea voyage best suited their plans—they boarded the "Pocahontas" in New York, bound for

Europe. They set sail in a storm that was the cause, her husband was convinced, of her weakened heart. (A graduate of Vassar in Poughkeepsie, New York, she had a propensity for displaying her culture, pret-a-reporter, learned to the nines, and I can picture her during the crossing, between two heart attacks, or two attacks of seasickness, relaying to her husband the history of the princess Pocahontas. The unfortunate Indian had also married a John she did not love. Or perhaps she talked and talked, poor chatterbox, of Captain John Smith and the early colonists in Virginia.) When they disembarked in Le Havre, a dark fleshy man was waiting for them, his hands deep in the pockets of his jacket. Voilà Jimmy. It must have been hard for her to recognize him, because the Jimmy she'd left in Europe a year before had been slim and attractive. After a year of the good life in Paris, and its restaurants, the fellow had grown fat. Paris held no more secrets for him, and they decided it would be very useful to give him lodging in the spacious Parisian flat that awaited them. The marriage, unconsummated on account of her serious ailment, had turned the husband into a mere nurse. The excitement of travel was not good for her, and they settled in Paris. Fortunately, Jimmy was there (for almost three years . . .) to lend a hand, to amuse the wife who needs serenity. Did she also lecture him, that Monet manqué, on the difference between a Hals and a Woovermans? as, on picturesque outings, she would tutor her English lover? But that was later, in the German city of Nauheim, where she was drawn, attracted no doubt by the curative powers of the ferrous waters of the baths, recommended for the circulatory and cardiac problems afflicting people of her class.

The Hessian spas would offer positions as bath attendants to students during July and August, and I literally made hay while the August sun shone in Nauheim. That was where I met her.

From a bull's-eye window in the building that housed the

baths, its stone looking as if it too had rusted in the heat, I see her walking lightly along the gravel path, in animated conversation with her husband, an elegant little man. Small and pretty, wearing a white dress, its full skirt figured in a Chinese pattern as blue as her eyes, she seems to walk on tiptoe in pointed blue and white shoes with exceedingly high heels. The gleam of her copper-colored hair, very nicely done, in the warm morning sunlight. And the blood-red drops of coral beads on the perfect whiteness of her soft throat. When the door of the bathing place was opened to receive her, she would look back at her husband with a little coquettish smile, so that her cheek appeared to be caressing her shoulder. For whose benefit did she really flirt? The bath attendant's? her husband hazarded a guess without giving it too much importance. And the truth is I also believed that her equivocal smile, when she looked at us over her shoulder, was an unequivocal invitation: Here I am, so white, so docile, venturing into those vapors, and you're a man . . .

In fact I became her husband's confidant. Perhaps my white uniform, with its medical air, inspired confidence. For almost two weeks I listened to her husband. Is a deceived husband to be believed? I still ask myself that question.

The baths, and new friendships made at the spa, seemed to have been beneficial for his wife's heart, because for nine summers, until her thirty-ninth birthday, she came punctually with her husband to Nauheim.

On her thirtieth birthday, in the presence of a Lutheran relic, she annexed the handsome English Captain and landowner who was three years older than she, and who, before the week was out, would become her lover. That happened under the very noses of her husband, and the Captain's wife, who were powerless witnesses to that annexation. At the Hotel Excelsior in Nauheim they had met the English couple (typically English:

she so tall, so blond, with blue eyes, in a tailored blue suit; he just as tall and blond, with very blue eyes, Apollonian, in a dark suit, and a complexion the color of brick) and immediately became intimates. The Captain was an inveterate sentimentalist, and his wife must have foreseen that before long he would be up to his old tricks with the attractive and coquettish American. It was she, intending to begin the education of the unenlightened Captain, who organized the excursion to the castle at Marburg. She delighted in organizing and guiding visits to ruins, museums, and monuments. She prepared for the occasion with Baedekers and manuals consulted at the last minute.

If she were sitting here now at this solitary table on the terrace of The Queen's Head (the pub won't open for another two hours), she would surely inform me that the two-story brick house on the other side of the tennis court, there at 90 Brook Green, was the childhood home of the distinguished author of the best French novel in English, although no blue plaque commemorates that fact. Or indicates that on occasion, in the garden of this pub, Dick Turpin would hide his mare Black Bess.

On that particularly hot August 4 the two couples took the 2:40 train in Nauheim and in fifty minutes arrived in Marburg. They lost their way in the maze of streets in the old city, visited cool double-spired churches, looked out over the broad green valley of the Lahn, and went up to the castle of Saint Elizabeth of Hungary. Her husband did not say so specifically, but it does not seem improbable to me that during the ascent she told them about the life and miracles of the saint. They went up and down winding corkscrew staircases, crossed chambers in shadow, and finally reached the top of the tower, the castle museum, the archive room, where she wanted to see and show them the draft of the Letter of Protest drawn up by Luther during his stay there. The Captain leaned his palms on the glass case that held the relic. And now a silence fell around her explanations: This is the Protest that makes us Protestants, this unpapal paper makes us sober, honest, industrious, clean, different from the Italians, the Poles, the Spaniards, or the Irish, especially the Irish . . . And now, another pause, to find the metaphor or the comparison that can explain what followed. We touch our finger to a switch and there is light. We press our finger to a button and create an explosion. Find, I entreat you, other, more powerful images. The finger of God touching Adam's finger? Or the finger of the devil?

And then she laid one finger—I would guess it was the third, the finger of the heart—on the Captain's wrist. Did she feel at her fingertip how his pulse was pounding? It was a moment of queer, electrifying intensity, and the panic on the Captain's face reflected that of his wife, and that of the husband, for the three of them understood immediately that an irresistible attraction had just been unleashed. The Captain's wife finally dissimulated, thereby wiping away the initial suspicion of the unwary American husband, who attributed her disquiet to a simple faux pas, since it turned out that she, who looked so English, was in reality an Irish Catholic . . .

On that 4th of August, her thirtieth birthday, the American Protestant also rid herself of her rival, a dark, very young English girl with a very weak heart, with whom the Captain had possibly platonic relations in Nauheim. The "poor little mouse," as the Captain called her, heard through an indiscreet screen in the hotel lobby everything he said about her, about her meaning nothing in his life, to the American lady. It was too much for her fragile heart, which broke as she, in a passion, was packing her bags. So thin and weak, like a crumpled marionette in the jaws of a portmanteau. That's how they found her. She was, in fact, the one who really had a bad heart, for the American lady, an excellent actress, had deceived her husband and the doctors with an imaginary ailment that she had planned with Jimmy so they could continue to be together. When the English lover came on the scene, and perhaps even before that, Jimmy lost his power, and she would see him, to her own humiliation, for what he was: a fat pimp lacking all charm, a crass mistake . . .

In December of that same year the Captain came to Paris to visit the American couple, and above all to violently expel from his free paradise the parasite who was now de trop.

They would spend nine years in a perfectly managed ménage à quatre, or rather à trois—since the American husband, it seems, continued to be, as he put it, the unseeing cuckold—in which the two couples met every summer in Nauheim, saw each other occasionally in Paris, and spent almost six weeks together in Menton. The Captain's wife, accustomed to the sentimental roving and rambling of her husband, more a sentimentalist than a libertine, was confident, perhaps, that this new adventure would be his last, that he would return to his senses and the virtuous path of the perfect husband. In any case, she preferred her husband to do what he did under her nose and not deceive her in form or in substance, not lie to her, as he had on other occasions, when he could not control his excesses and the risks he took and his imprudent expenditures of money.

It was a tranquil adultery, one might say, until the American wife and mistress had her thirty-ninth birthday. The husband never suspected, but the specter of the "poor little mouse" haunted, perhaps vengefully, the leafy tree-lined walks of Nauheim on the ninth anniversary of her death. She had been displaced by the American lady in the heart of the Captain, and now, exactly nine years later, another dark young girl, twenty-one years old, though very tall and slender, would, in similar circumstances, take the place of the adulteress who was close to forty.

She was an odd girl, with an elastic mouth that at times seemed grotesque, and at other times really beautiful. They remind me of her, there on the tennis court, those two awkward adolescents who may be twins, with their thick shocks of really identical black hair and identical white minidresses, who are striking a feathered ball with their rackets.

Badminton shuttlecocks . . .

The Captain's wife tutored the girl, the daughter of her only friend, and she did not have the prescience to see that a new feminine presence, no matter how innocent, must not be put in the way of so sentimental a husband. Was she not aware, after eight years, that the girl would become a woman?

The fatal denouement, as the cuckolded American would confirm, was to occur once again on the 4th of August.

Like the "poor little mouse," the American lady would hear lethal words from the Captain's own lips. That night the Captain was to escort the girl to a concert at the Casino and the American lady followed the pair, intending to join them. The Captain, instead of taking the avenue to the Casino, led the girl under the heavy foliage in the park. They sat on a bench, surrounded by night, by muffled music. The American spy hid behind a tree and heard the Captain's words of love. And she could see by the light of the moon the girl's radiant expression. Was she reading those expressive features correctly? The Casino orchestra attacked the Rákóczy March.

The American lover's robust heart raced at full tilt, faster than she could. Her husband, from the lobby of the hotel, saw her hurrying along the lamplit gravel path, whiter than a sheet of paper, clutching at her chest with one hand. She dashed through the revolving door into the lobby, and to her great misfortune almost ran into the talkative stranger who had been attempting, to no avail, to start a conversation with the American—her husband—in the armchair next to his, more monosyllabic or yesnosyllabic than an Englishman, and who turned out to be not such a stranger after all, because he was the owner of the manor house near Ledbury, and he wasted no time in telling the American that the woman was the very same one he had seen coming out of Jimmy's bedroom at five in the morning. She covered her face with her hands when she saw the English parrot, and hurried up to her room. Her husband found her dead, lying on the bed in an almost studied pose, holding in her right hand an empty small brown bottle that must have contained amyl nitrate. The husband still believed his wife was an invalid, and he did not realize at the time that she had killed herself. Vanity killed her, according to him, not so much the loss of the Captain's love as her own humiliation at the discovery of her relations with someone as base and vulgar as Jimmy, which would also lose her the respect of her attendant husband.

On more than one occasion I doubted the husband, doubted the veracity and impartiality of what he told me. What if the deceived was in turn a deceiver? What if he was the one who substituted poison for medicine in the small brown bottle? He even confessed to me that he hated her. Wasn't this a way to avenge so long a deception? Life itself took its revenge with another death: the Captain wanted to renounce the girl's love, to cut off at the root a relationship that was not yet intimate, and he cut his throat instead. With a penknife. My God, how could he do it?

Tragedy means carrying over to the next column until one comes up with the sum in which love and hate are consumed. The girl went mad when she heard of his death, and the American widower married her in order to continue in the custodial nursing role to which he had grown accustomed. The Captain's widow also remarried. The landowner is dead, long live the landowner.

The American told me several times that his was the saddest story. And at first I thought he was saying, in English, a sadist's story. His wife's story? because she made her poor husband suffer so. He talked and talked to combat loneliness, of that I have no doubt.

Like him, all I know is that I am alone . . .

Last night I saw from my dovecote window the couples cooing kissing coming on the grass of Brook Green. A hippie in a tunic, with long dark hair and a red band around her forehead, lay sprawled alone on her back next to the well-lit wire fence around the tennis court. I was about to descend from my self-control tower, as you call it. I could have asked her to come up, even offered her Miss Rose's empty bed. But I told myself she probably preferred sleeping in the night air. I hope you're not wandering the world with a knapsack on your back. If you're sunning yourself in Corsica, be careful, because according to the *Times*, the partisans of independence are still setting bombs. The hippie on the grass made me think of the Indian Pocahontas. Do you remember her solemn portrait with the ruff at her neck and the tall felt hat and the feathered fan in her right hand? Do you remember when we made our pilgrimage to Gravesend?

The grave is our only end?

And now I am alone. Holding not too bad a hand, because you don't know yet that the card game of commercial letters in French and Spanish has ended. Mr. James left his business of adulteration—excuse me, importation—of wines to declare himself as the Conservative candidate for Aldridge-Brownhill in the next election. By the way, today at Christie's there was an auction of 400,000 bottles of Bordeaux, Burgundy, Rhine, and Moselle.

Now I remember she liked Rhine wine mixed with water. How bitter that final swallow must have been.

And I forgot to mention that posed in the repose of death, faceup on the bed, one would almost say she was looking in perplexity at the light that hung from the ceiling. Was she hoping, before death, for the arrival of grace?

knot. I keep a memory so intricate and intriguing of my last weekend at Newmarch—the last and final one, for my expeditions as a bon snob into the jungle of high English society came to an end—that I have returned to my point of departure in an effort to disentangle it. From this same platform in Paddington Station I departed on that pleasant summer afternoon for a new frontier—Land of the Angles as terra incognita?—whose uncertain borders may be those of my own progress through the labyrinth (drawing rooms, corridors, galleries, circular staircases, terraces, dining rooms, promenades: hypotheses, speculations, presumptions, doubts . . .) of Newmarch. In that mansion surrounded by a park of forking paths, a scant hour from London, I thought I glimpsed a new, unsettling dimension in which strange mutations were perhaps produced.

As if to prepare me for the changes that awaited me, on the platform I saw the striking, tightly curled, handsome but stupid head of Gilbert the Stolid. I so little expected him to recognize me that I stopped short, turned, and looked for another carriage. I had met him at Newmarch only, and one did not need to be Sherlock Holmes—the great sleuth, of course, frequently departed from this station for his adventures—to deduce not only that he was not traveling to Birmingham but that he was one of the guests invited to our country retreat.

Just a moment ago I was reading the great black panel of destinations (I would like some day to travel to Land's End) and I told myself that just as all these trains will depart, hastening toward Birmingham, Cardiff, Reading, Penzance . . . , so my memories may also depart in various directions from Paddington Station. If I retreat to the rear of this nave of iron and glass, regress a few years to the morning of the first Saturday in February when I climbed to the elevated platform of the Metropolitan line, I will find myself there alone, stamping my feet on the ground—the ice, one might say—waiting for the train that would carry me to Ladbroke Grove; but in reality I was waiting without realizing it for the slender traveler with the black hair and black eyes, well protected in a fur-lined jacket, rather worn, it must be said, who after a few minutes would resolutely come forward to ask me in English if I had been waiting a long time.

All my life, should have been my reply to you then, and you would have laughed, shaking your head in disapproval, as you would do now, if you read me, wiping away my words with your hair.

But now I retrace my steps in order not to keep Gilbert waiting, for he was no longer stolid and came down to me as if for a greeting, and struck up a conversation with me and even proposed, showing signs of good sense, to move to my compartment.

He came back with an attractive stranger who was, quite simply, unrecognizable, because she had grown so much younger, this woman of forty or fifty—I was never certain of her age—who had married, some five years earlier, a man of thirty who had the face of a baby and whom I—and she—would call "poor Guy."

Guy would take the next train to Newmarch, escorting the brilliant Lady John (these changes of partner are very fashionable at Newmarch), while his wife traveled in our good company. What a lucky thing, then, I said with a laugh to Gilbert, that with the husband so out of it and relegated to the timetable's obscure hereafter, it should be you and I who enjoy her. What I said then in jest hid in truth, I know it now, my deepest desire.

Hours later, at Newmarch, in one of the corridors, I came across a gentleman unknown to me who looked quite sixty and who was in reality, or in unreality, because I could not credit my eyes, poor Guy. His smooth polished baby's face was now a pale parchment mask. I was able, at dinner, to examine him more closely, and he looked more lackluster, more withered and sad next to the splendid girl of about twenty, resplendent in cloth-of-silver and diamonds, who was his wife. Her large blue eyes, her décolleté gown displaying a beautiful bosom and smooth shoulders, her entire appearance radiated youth and vitality triumphant.

I estimated twenty, but if she had dressed or masqueraded in proper fashion she could just as easily have looked fifteen.

We change every seven years, she once said to me, but I change every seven minutes.

La donna è mobile . . .

Really, she laughed, I'm ninety-three.

And I even asked myself, at the end of my stay at Newmarch, if she might not be telling the truth.

Was it possible to retrace the course of one's life back to its secret fount?

Youth, beauty, intelligence . . . were these actually vital fluids that could be transferred from one being to another? How? Through some amorous alchemy? What osmosis existed between Guy and his wife?

She herself encouraged my initial conjectures and perhaps even sowed them, from the time of our meeting at Paddington

Station. She explained that the transformation undergone by Gilbert was because of late an extremely intelligent woman had come into his life . . . : Lady John.

But shortly afterward, at the start of that weekend, I was able to determine that the brilliance of the vain Lady John was merely mundane and superficial, lacking the necessary weight to transform a congenital fool into a clever man. On the other hand, her vivacity and flashing wit showed no signs of being extinguished, or even of dimming, so that Gilbert's intellect might shine.

Giving youth, beauty, or intelligence to another—and there before me were poor Guy and his wife—inevitably meant losing them oneself. Without the sacrifice, voluntary or involuntary, the miracle could not occur.

Poor Guy's wife seemed to agree with my inferences, although she appeared (was it a precaution?) not to understand the full extent of my theory.

The morning following my arrival at Newmarch, as I was strolling with her on the terrace, she suddenly discovered in a rapture of intuition, or pretended to suddenly discover, Gilbert's secret victim. (Victim, according to my theory; benefactress was her euphemism.) Beautiful, spiritual, and enigmatic, with innocent light eyes, Mrs. Server (what's in a name, good Lord: she is the servant, the gentleman's handmaiden) radiated abnegation and even a certain craving to be sacrificed. Her timidity perhaps dissimulated (did she go from one guest to another in search of one who might decipher in her increasingly sad gaze and increasingly thin smile her need for help?) the inner torment, the terror, the tempestuous trials (and vilifications?) to which she was subject. I had the impression that, more than the other guests, she wore a mask.

I remember her especially in the great portrait salon with

Gilbert and the painter Obert, standing before the man with the mask in his hand. The figure represented is a young man in a black greatcoat with a whitened face and a stare, from eyes without eyebrows, like that of a sinister clown, who holds in his right hand a beautiful mask in some substance not human, perhaps wax.

The Mask of Death, was the dramatic interpretation of Mrs. Server.

Or of Life, I ventured, which is going to mask the dreadful face of Death.

Or of Art, which is going to embellish the grimacing livid face of Life.

Was the young man about to put on the mask, or had he just taken it off?

Was his whitened face in reality another mask? And was there yet another mask beneath that one? What did these superimposed masks finally and definitively hide?

The painter Obert opportunely observed that the charming wax face in his hand looked remarkably like Mrs. Server.

And Gilbert remarked with some reserve that the Man with the Mask resembled poor Guy.

A double divertissement of superimposed masks, of Life and Death . . .

Long afterward I would develop an oniontological theory, let us call it, in order to peel away being or nonbeing and nothingness, to reach the heart of the problem. We remove masks, faces, successive layers, and in the end there is nothing, there is no secret.

But I was convinced, at Newmarch, as if I were a new Ponce de León, that I would discover the secret fount that secretes life.

I do not know if I was actually in a Cretan labyrinth or the cretinous maze of a ridiculous obsession, following the increasingly tangled threads of my conjectures, or deliriums, which I discarded and replaced to excess, thanks to the assistance of poor Guy's wife. I was the bloodhound that she conveniently unleashed, serving her own convenience, no doubt. I observed, or rather I spied on, the guests, their movements, gestures, looks, proposing various possibilities that would allow me to establish the relations they maintained with one another, surmising hypothetical ties that unraveled in the light of some new clue that would weave new ties perhaps no less illusory.

I knew perfectly well the who's who in that high society but not the *whose* who.

Did poor Guy belong exclusively to his wife, or did he perhaps have or aspire to have relations with Lady John, or Mrs. Server? Or with all of them?

According to Mrs. Server, Guy cared not for her but for Lady John, who cared only for Obert. And Obert, if I saw at all clearly, was interested in Mrs. Server.

Poor Guy's wife went so far as to accuse me of seeing too much. I am not certain. What were her relations with Gilbert? And his with Lady John, with Mrs. Server? Did he use the striking Lady John as a screen to hide his relations—perhaps unconfessable—with Mrs. Server? Or did he attempt to hide with manifest lack of skill his feigned relations with Mrs. Server in order to better mask his real relations with Lady John?

On the eve of my departure, in the small hours of the morning, Guy's wife came to see me alone (at Gilbert's request?) and our encounter turned into a contest.

She conquered but did not convince.

A short while ago, on one of the central platforms, I saw a whirlwind in uniform slamming all the doors to all the carriages on the train that was about to leave for Bristol. A bearded Indian in a blue turban, alone in his compartment, was imperturbably reading the *Times,* which certainly reports today on the deaths by fire and water in India.

I presume it did not occur to you to go so far, much less to travel to some appointment in Multan. Twenty-four persons were burned alive yesterday when two buses crashed near Multan, two hundred miles south of Lahore. And twelve persons drowned yesterday when their boat sank in the Indus, also near Multan.

The doors to the carriages were being closed violently and I thought that in similar fashion Guy's wife had closed off my escape routes, one after the other, demolishing the defenses of my castle of hypotheses, my palace of thought. I had gone too far, she said, I was an egotist imprisoned behind the walls of my own obsession, and she even thought I was crazy.

Everything she had suggested at the beginning, even our associated speculation, she flatly denied.

Was it all my invention, a projection of my own phantoms?

Did I vicariously experience the relations I had not had the courage to establish? Did I judge others for actions that I myself wished to engage in?

And yet . . .

A real fact, a verifiable one: I never saw poor Guy smile.

Perhaps he was ill and his wife only feared that I would reveal to him his ailing appearance, his premature aging. Why, then, did she at first encourage my inquiries?

Too late I offer this hypothesis: she gave me feet and wings, from the very first moment, thinking that my mad theory of secret osmosis and the fountain of youth (a young man's fancy?) was a way of making us accomplices who would begin a "new march" at Newmarch, perhaps one that was nuptial, and—why not?—initiate an idyll, which ended in a duel really when she realized I was an incorrigibly eccentric egotist interested only in resolving an enigma (there is no greater adventure than the intellectual), in solving the crossword before his eyes, failing to see the admirable person sitting at his side.

To conclude my recollections of Newmarch, or to create a contrast to them, when night fell I left Paddington Station for the Wimpy's across the way, in Praed Street. I read the neon sign backwards, OPEN ALL NIGHT, and fold Miss Rose's *Times*. I may even begin to work the crossword.

Here I will not find the fountain of youth. Perhaps only the Lethe of watery tea for the elderly. The old man with the clouded eye looks at me lethargically. I read to you, from this sheet of letters, about other disasters: Generalissimo Franco has phlebitis in his right leg, the Pope has arthrosis in his right knee. At least now we know where they stand.

The taxis drive rapidly down the ramp to the station.

Screech, shout, crash.

Right here, next to the newsstand.

Poor Guy, crushed under the wheels of the taxi, and I could barely move away his wife, who embraced his body. As I held her in my arms for the first time, her face began to acquire the parchment-like mask of her ninety-three years.

It was a vision that vanished rapidly, long before the ambulance from St. Mary's Hospital came to take away the wild-haired victim. Sitting on the ground for some time with a partially displayed placard that read NUT. Master, no doubt. How I hope it is slight, the master's lesion.

I drink my tea, and my theory, down to the dregs.

No, I believe that if Guy dies she will preserve for a good long while the quintessence of her infused youth, that she will continue to mask the passage of the years, the days, the hours.

omicide,
after all, or suicide?

(I never spoke to you—or did I?—of my suicidal Swiss period . . . Appropriately enough, I am in Swiss Cottage, the terrace is deserted, and now I see myself again in Zurich—the self is unreal?—walking like a somnambulist in the small hours at the edge of luxuriant water along the Schanzengraben. And now—behind the cloud, a sliver of waning moon—this image of my real noctambulations through that unreal city: an icy aura of fine mist that the wind scatters around the streetlights.

I wandered at night along Finchley Road and confirmed once again that there was no light in your observatory, your glass-enclosed dovecote. No pleasure dome now . . . I believe. And the fact is that not an hour ago I thought I saw you at the entrance to the Swiss Cottage station. I returned to the café across from your house and watched, camouflaged behind the newspaper like a bad detective, until I was convinced, with not too much conviction, that you could not be in London. Are you on holiday, or have you gone on one of your Babelic assignments? At times I think you became an interpreter because you could not be an actress . . . I hope you haven't gone to Baltimore, where last night's rioting and looting left one dead and two hundred injured.

I went down to The Golden Cage—Friday's noisy crush in the cage of cheap glitter and chattering crowds: an Arab-Israeli brawl at the entrance—but I did not dare venture into the discotheque of discord, and I came to Swiss Cottage, closed for almost an hour, to talk to you of other Swiss taverns and the nocturnal prowling of wolves.

Alone at a table in my favorite tavern, my steel helmet of Mambrino, Stahlhelm, and in front of me a jug of Alsatian wine. Pity the man whose soul is not assuaged by a glass of Alsatian and a piece of good bread. Above all when he has tasted no food since the night before. On other occasions I had decided not to go out into the fog and had stayed, drinking alone, in my garret, my lion's den or wolf's lair. Raising on high the plump-bellied bottle in its straw wrapping, or a thicker bottle of kirsch. I was waiting then for the arrival of my next birthday in order to close—with a single stroke—the perverse parenthesis of my life. A suicide separate from all of society—a misanthrope and lycanthrope: a lone wolf for himself alone, feeding on himself, far from the flocks—for those nine months. Until an easy woman came into my difficult life. We were the poles that attract, the extremes that eventually touch.

She, who never lacked for company, bad company, would come to recognize that in the midst of the multitude she was as alone as I, so fierce and solitary, and that, like me, she could neither love truly nor take life, or other people, or herself, seriously.)

Or had I killed my soul's twin?

But it was on her body lying naked at my feet, a knife thrust in below her left breast, where I had just seen the telltale marks of a recent love bite.

Her lips red as her blood.

And white as a corpse.

And still rebellious, the boyish lock of hair falling over her forehead.

Her platinum hair, bobbed à la garçon, revealed the mother-of-pearl of her exquisite ear.

My sorella, my sister, my hermaphroditic hermana . . .

Hermana Herman, I could have called her that, too, for she reminded me so of my boyhood friend Herman; and she, the sinner who knew the lives of so many saints, especially Saint Francis, might have called me Hermano Lobo, Brother Wolf, above all when we were in The Old Franciscan restaurant.

A harmed Aphrodite, infertile . . . for our relations never brought forth the desired fruit. Or perhaps they did.

She'd had her way, finally; the prediction came true that she had made barely three weeks before, in the Alten Franziskaner, two days after we met: you will obey my orders, though you won't find it easy, and you will kill me . . .

Was she a hysteric in search of a histrionic actor for her rehearsal of buffa death, or a calculating woman who had surmised my thanatotic tendencies and was attempting to make me her slave?

One Sunday night, after tireless prowling through the outskirts of the town, my lost steps brought me to the clamor of The Black Eagle, Zum schwarzen Adler, as I read on the old signboard over the entrance. Through the smoke and the smell of wine and the crowd one could see, in a room at the back, figures dancing to a frenzy of music. I remained in the rowdy noise and smog of the nearer room. Crushed and pushed by the crowd, in a saving surge I found myself wedged against the demoiselle of the camellia, alone on the settee near the bar. She wore a filmy minidress cut very low, and with a smile moved to one side to make room for me.

Good-naturedly, with a touch of mockery or teasing, she

began to take the poor helpless devil in hand (what shall we
drink?) and even wiped my glasses for me. That was when I
could see her clearly, beginning with the faded camellia in her
hair shingled à la garçon. And her attractive, slim, rather
epicene figure; her face too was thin and very pale, with well-
defined features, and there was a contrast between her blood-
red lips and ice-gray eyes. She ordered wine and a sandwich,
clinked glasses with me, and obliged me to eat something. She
liked my docility. The fox-trot tames the fiercest wolf . . . (Soon
she would call me her little wolf: her Wolfchen.)

She wanted to dance with me and was scandalized (she
firmly shook her waved and shingled head and a rebellious lock
of hair fell across her brow) when I told her I didn't know how.

I implored her not to go when she got up to dance in the
other room, and she told me to sleep for a little and that she
would be back in a while. Despite the uproar at the bar, I leaned
back on the settee and dreamed of a smiling old man, who may
have been Goethe, until she came back and placed her hand on
my shoulder. I wanted her to spend the night with me, but she
had an engagement at the Odeon Bar. She agreed to have supper
on Tuesday, at The Old Franciscan. I was there punctually, her
humble servant more servile than the waiter also named Emil. I
was able to admire her more carefully than at The Black Eagle.
Her laughter, her series of serious gestures, jokes and gravity
without transition, the fire of her red lips and the ice of her light
eyes. How beautiful she was!

In her gray eyes lay the sadness and solitude of an iceberg
moving away in the night.

That night she also said she wanted to make me fall in love
with her, though she was never going to fall in love with me. I
needed her to teach me to dance, to laugh, to live. She needed
me, I suppose, to help her to die. It was there she announced that

I would kill her. But she immediately regained her good humor and her appetite, she sliced into her duck leg and—Open your mouth!—she had me taste a choice morsel.

The following afternoon her dancing lessons began.

She began with a fox-trot, my silver fox, she showed me the first steps—See?—then she raised my left hand, put my other arm around her waist, and I followed her, as conscientious as I was clumsy, colliding into chairs at every step. Oh! how stiff you are! You're like a stick! But I only seemed that way, for I noticed the swaying of her belly, her thighs pushing me so firmly whenever I took a false step.

The balance of these beginning lessons—and what balancing acts they were—took place at a dance in the Balance Hotel, where I lost my balance once again and my teacher pushed me into the arms of another dancer, a friend of hers with short, luxuriant blond hair, who would make me feel her willowy waist, the cadence of her taut hips, the rhythm of her quick and pliant knees, the flex-ability of her legs. Her name was Maria and she would soon make me her lover, one of her lovers, or should I say clients.

One night I returned home more despondent and solitary than usual, and as I began to undress in the darkness of my room, a very special scent—not the customary acrid aroma of tobacco—of perfume and woman made me look around, and there I saw the lovely Maria lying in my bed, smiling at me, her large blue eyes a little startled.

My dancing teacher, my pandering dancing partner, had given Maria the key to my room because, it seemed obvious to her, I needed other kinds of physical exercise. In fact she was preparing me for the Fancy Dress Ball that would take place in three weeks in the ballrooms of the Globe.

She had also introduced me, at the time I met Maria, to a

dark-skinned Orpheus, a handsome young South American named Pablo who played the saxophone, or, I should say, two saxophones, at the dance in the Balance Hotel. I felt something like jealousy, how prescient of me, when we met. And yet I had no problem accepting the fact that he was one of Maria's lovers, I knew how to share her with him. What I could not accept, one night when Maria and I were smoking and drinking in his garret, was sharing her at the same time in a love orgy for three.

My dancing teacher also went to bed, or had once gone to bed, with Maria, I supposed, because she was well acquainted with her most intimate caresses, a peculiar play of the tongue in kissing.

My relations with the handsome Pablo were ambivalent, a mixture of fascination and repugnance. He was, as well, the secret wizard of drugs, an alchemist of arcane mixtures who had remedies for all the ills of the world. I frequented the notably low dives where he played, and drugged dawns often found me listening to him at the City Bar.

And the great night arrived, the Fancy Dress Ball in the Globe Rooms, or Globus Rooms. Would my dancing teacher finally grant me the other dance? The dance of life? Ah, global deceiver, for she would not tell me how she would be dressed. I won't tell you, because you know as well as I do what it's like— an uproarious clamorous cyclone of masks and music, a swirling whirlwind that spins us around and makes us lose our head. I went upstairs and drank, I went downstairs and was embraced, I went to another room and came flying out only to meet more kisses. Pablo, playing with enthusiasm on his silver serpent, blared out a saxophonic salutation when he saw me. But I still had not come to hell, the final room in that pandemonium.

On the pitch-black walls wicked garish lights shone, and at the far end, voltaic Orcus, an electrifying orchestra of contorting devils played furiously. I went to the bar and asked for a whiskey. As I drank I looked at the handsome youth, unmasked and in evening dress, who sat on the stool beside me. Despite his makeup, I recognized the beautiful profile of the friend of my youth.

She smiled. Have you found me? And I did not know that soon I would lose her.

We sat on our stools and drank, we strolled through the other rooms, we paid court for a while to the same girl . . . Then my dancing teacher asked a great beauty, who appeared tragic and forlorn, to dance; she brought joy to her spirit and body and later told me she had made the conquest with the spell of Lesbos.

We lost ourselves in the labyrinth of bodies, and I lost all sense of time. People had begun to leave, and in one of the half-deserted rooms I saw a charming black Pierrette with face painted white. We danced, and as I bent down to kiss her mouth she smiled, equivocal and superior, and I recognized her unequivocally. We kissed, an intense moment. When the music stopped we were still in an embrace, and then the ashen light of day behind the curtains began to flood the room. We all danced again, frenzied couples pressing close, soon to be dispersed by day, and in that final dance my teacher abandoned her triumphant air because she knew she no longer needed it, for I was hers.

The dance ended, the dancers drifted away, and what I recall is as fragmentary as the rest of that night. She and I were the last in the hall, alone until Pablo the saxophonist appeared in a gorgeous silk smoking jacket and offered us one of his potions; he filled three glasses with the mixture and took three long thin yellow cigarettes from a small box of painted wood. A dizzying kaleidoscope—myriads of iridescent images—with each sip and each inhalation. I saw and heard visions that could be recounted only by one who had a thousand tongues (O dass ich tausend Zungen hatte!), a thousand eyes, a thousand ears. I know that I had a thousand selves, and to name them I would need a thousand names and a thousand aliases.

When I was myself again, neither my teacher and mystic soror nor Pablo was with me. I walked through the empty rooms again, and when I opened the last door I found them side by side, naked, lying on rugs on the floor, she and Pablo in a sleep of deep exhaustion after love's play. I saw the teeth marks of the Latin lover beneath her delicate breast. I took out my knife and plunged it in to the hilt. Pablo smiled and folded a corner of the rug to hide the wounded breast. Get thee behind me, audacious musician, I had fulfilled her wish. Everything was unreal. Nothing was true because everything was permitted. Permutated. The knife was an illusion, but the stab wound of my jealousy was real. With it I had not killed the real woman—a poor little whore in the arms of her pimp—but my ideal.

I inhale Courvoisier, the elixir of love in Kyoto, and that elicits the intoxicating female fragrance of my inebriated Japanese, an unserene siren in the bath where she would invariably take refuge before losing consciousness.

I look at the bottle (it was difficult for me to convince the barmaid to leave it on my table, here in Le Routier, and she does not take her eyes off it as she wipes glasses behind the bar): a black idol with a long phallic neck, I realize now, and the golden laurel-wreathed Napoleon on the label is transformed into a great-bellied Nipponese, Hotei, the laughing god of happiness whose image I saw everywhere in Shimabara, the old pleasure district of Kyoto.

Camden Lock is not that locus amenus, if you'll permit me the Latinism, but the curved bridge in the background, spanning the lock, always seemed to give a Japanese air to this corner of northeast London.

The little gold key resting on the ample white décolleté of the brunette barmaid (a while ago she spoke Italian on the telephone) gleams and titillates in her deep cleavage at each turn of the glass she is wiping.

I recalled a Kyoto key that opened a small Japanese box holding the most intimate secrets. And a tricolored face superimposed on the image.

The hair black, the face white, the lips scarlet—that is how I saw her floating in a dream last night, and when she opened her mouth her teeth were painted black.

Mechanically I take out a cigarette (you like it when I mimic the dense smoke on the pack) but don't light it, I sought out her scent again, and again secretly raise the glass of cognac to my nose, swirling it, filling myself with her fragrance, remembering her, brandy and randy, cognac and cunt, kissing and sucking oh succulentcubus, seeking her bouquet, inhaling her in the mists of the bath and of alcohol, her hair hanging loose as I tried to dry her limbs, the sheer cotton chemise saturated still with cognac and clinging to her wet body on that night in March when I followed the example of her husband, my master, and courted her with Courvoisier, the shortest route to rutting: from cognac to consummation.

It was her husband, a francophile professor at the university, who fomented her fondness for cognac—always the fine champagne Courvoisier—an almost therapeutic remedy, he believed, to help his wife lose herself, lose the inhibitions imposed by a strict Confucian upbringing. The treatment had become especially intense when I began to frequent his house, a dinner guest invited by their daughter, a student at the University of Doshisha. She was the key that opened the door for me into the home of this mature Japanese couple (he was fifty-five, and she ten years younger) who opened their hearts to me from the very first meal. Sushi and Courvoisier, in memory I breathe in the marine bouquet.

They supposed I was courting the daughter, though she never displayed excessive interest in me; but it was in reality the mother who pleasured my eye and maddened my heart. Though twenty-five years older than her daughter, she was far more attractive, an incredibly youthful woman with her slender figure and elegant movements, above all in a kimono. But she seemed more seductive in Western dress, when she displayed her slightly bowed legs. And I have not yet mentioned her innate lasciviousness, the insatiability that eventually knew no restraint and that she—as her spent husband would discover in his own flesh—could prolong with extreme artfulness. It was in no way remarkable that the mother was the one who captivated me, and even her husband openly acknowledged that in my place, he too would have found her more attractive.

After paying his conjugal debt (every ten days, the tithe he found least taxing), the husband found himself drained of both strength and ideas, in a simple state of exhaustion. Prematurely aged, and suffering from a cerebral arteriosclerosis that was manifested in his altered vision, balance, and memory, the husband, fearful he would fail to satisfy his wife's growing appetites, sought the assistance on the sly of a monthly injection of testosterone, and every two to three days, without the knowledge of his physician, he injected himself with five hundred units of gonadotropic hormones. But the true stimulant to his sexuality would be the jealousy occasioned by his youthful rival (I play this heartwarming role) and cognac, that helping hand always at hand on the shelf, the *tokonoma,* which raised his spirits and brought his wife low until she fell unconscious or, her sixth sense exacerbated and completely complaisant, sank into the role of docile marionette who surrendered to his nocturnal manipulations.

The first time she swooned in her bath, on a night when the three of us had a great deal to drink (it was a Saturday late in January, the twenty-eighth, I believe), the husband lifted her out of the water and asked me to help him dry her and put on her chemise and carry her to bed. Later I understood that he was aroused by the thought of thrusting her into my arms.

When he was alone with her he could, at last, contemplate

her nakedness for as long as he wished in the light of a fluorescent lamp he brought from his study. She, whose puritanical obscurantism obliged him to turn out the light when they made love, now allowed him to explore even her darkest recesses. In the harsh light, I see hovering over her the metallic brilliance of his face as smooth as illuminated aluminum, his thick steel-rimmed glasses. That night he never knew if she slept like a log or played at being a sleeping beauty (but she always had a half-wakeful, half-drowsing air, a certain languid, seductive reserve) so that he might give free rein to his most obsessive desires.

A fervent foot fetishist—a *feetishist,* to say it once and for all (I observed in the bathroom the care and devotion with which he dried the spaces between the toes of his senseless wife), yet she had never even permitted him to kiss her instep. That's a filthy thing. And how pretty her timid little feet were; no one would ever say they were the feet of a woman in her forties. She generally wore, even in summer, those socks that leave only the great toe free. I too liked to feel it slide in my hand, liked to hold it to my nostrils, uttering obscenities in a nasal voice, before baring her foot. Skin like snow.

On that first night of license the husband could lick her toes to his heart's content, then move on to kiss her sex, an exquisite, exceptional moment when the clumsy myopic let his cold glasses fall on her warm belly and almost woke her. He quickly turned out the light, and after giving her a Luminal liquefied in a communicant's kiss, again enlightened his life with his newly illuminated wife.

From her sex he moved on to her armpits, one of her erogenous zones. He kissed them salaciously. I too tasted their saline savor.

She touched his chest, his limbs, caressed him as she had never done before, and in full hallucination pronounced the name of her future lover. On another inebriated night, in March, she bit her husband's tongue and called to her lover in her passion, nibbled at his ear, where she murmurs his name, shouts it in the mortal spasm of orgasm. Her little death foretelling the greater one. Mourra bien qui mourra le dernier . . .

One day later, on the twenty-fifth of March to be precise, she at last made love directly to her lover without the husband as intermediary.

A few hours ago, a little after noon, as I emerged from the tube at Camden Town, a group of hairless boys and girls chanted their hara-kyries. (I remembered that in one of your dreams or recollections of incarnations, you disguised yourself as a Buddhist monk and hid in Himalayan temples, running from a husband or a jealous lover. If you have taken a notion to make a pilgrimage to Katmandu, I hope you have had all your shots, because today's *Times* reports that in the past three months two hundred people have died in Nepal of smallpox.)

And in the overcast sky I saw a snowy cloud with a rounded bottom, and that made me recollect the landscape of moons, no, of dunes, yes and no, of exceedingly white and tremulous buttocks emerging from their bath as the pornophotographer husband developed in my darkroom (my bathroom) the photographs he had treacherously taken in the dark of night.

I told him about my Polaroid and even lent him the camera, but the results could not satisfy his hyperrealistic appetites, his meticulous fondness for the foreground, and he turned to his Zeiss-Ikon. The fine points of iconology (sex-icon . . .), and with the greatest naturalness he asked me to develop the almost gynecological views of his wife. All those poses that he, possessed, had her assume without her realizing it. And he made me an accomplice to his voyeurism.

Her pristine ass, her belly and breasts and underarms, her

most secret recesses . . . The lusting husband was right: not the tiniest mole, not a speck on her white body, as I would soon verify for myself in that rented room in Osaka.

It excited the husband to imagine that we made love there in a Western bed (jealousy aroused him, permitted him to impersonate her lover on nights of lubricity with his wife, who closed her eyes, surrendered to the game, and prolonged in the increasingly weak arms of her husband the vigorous encounters of a few hours before), a bed or futon, nous foutons, as the French say, et nous nous en foutons, we made love, and the rest did not matter, we reinvented a Kamasutra on the floor and fell even lower and she gave herself over, with the perfect immodesty of her photographic poses, to acrobatics and sexual flexions and exercises, to Asian and even Swedish gymnastics . . .

Her body was slim but strong, and in shape. In her youth she had been a tennis and swimming champion.

So gentle the small curves of her breasts, her belly, her thighs (her loins a perfect carved O joining her sex), her succulent cleft.

The husband, as his arteriosclerosis worsened and his hypertension rose dangerously, imprudently redoubled his amatory efforts, spurred on by jealousy and the elusive lewdness of his wife, and he began to think of only one thing: making love to her, and in particular taking the part for the whole in that entity or enigma he called his wife's exceptional organ.

The truth was that any part of his wife's body, suddenly revealed, could arouse him. Even without the stimulus of alcohol, as on the night of the thirty-first of March, when she was imprudent enough, or impudent enough, to let the tips of the toes on her left foot peek out from the blanket and he, glimpsing the gleam of the nails, moved to her bed and immediately and with uncommon vigor penetrated his astounded wife.

The gleam of her earlobe, of an unimaginable whiteness, also had the power to work miracles. Even the luster of pearls in her earrings . . . As on that day early in April, the eve of the festival of Inasi, at four-thirty in the afternoon, when the husband caught sight of his wife and followed her as she strolled along the Kawaramachi; he was attracted by the pearls in her ears, earrings she had not put on when she was with him, which she took off before returning home. But she would put them on especially for him, and to spectacular effect, nine days later, on the night of Sunday the seventeenth of April, after her supper and her bath, when the husband had already gone to bed. She decided to wear the earrings as she slept, or as she awakened his passion; she turned her back, and the sight of her lobes from the rear, the splendor of her ears, seemed to him like a pearl beyond price, and he left his bed to enter hers, nestling and nuzzling into her back, and kissing her ear. How clumsy are his kisses, she said to herself, drawing an invidious comparison, but she did not find the darting of his tongue disgusting, her initial iciness was melting (she always seemed cold at first) and she burned with a double flame, repeating with her husband what she'd done a little earlier with her lover in a room in Osaka. She displayed or replayed, one by one, every one of our games. But she betrayed him. She knew how ill he was and took no pity on his torpidity; she aroused him, provoked him to a frenzy, enlivened him to death. In his supreme passion he collapsed on her like a stuffed toy, his mortal embrace growing faint. It was one-thirty in the morning, and his left side was paralyzed. His wife would acknowledge that the flame of his jealousy was not extinguished in the days that followed. The master died of a second cerebral hemorrhage on the second of May, an ill-starred Monday, at three in the morning. It may be that on an earlier night he had heard my furtive footsteps in the jardin japonais.

Je regardais seulement . . . , unless she actually said: I was only looking. I thought, perhaps too hastily, that she wanted to emulate the unknown drowned woman of the Seine, looking down from the Pont Neuf, on tiptoe, and for that reason I approached her.

Across the bridge the gold letters were brightly lit: LA SAMARITAINE. And the good Samaritan had just gone into action (good works?).

I had seen her alone, with lowered head and bent shoulders, on one of the curved stone seats on the bridge (it was already dark and beginning to turn cold) a little while before she leaned over the balustrade. Small, even with her high heels, and recklessly bending toward the river. Her dark, rather short coat revealed the backs of her knees, polished and fine, like her legs.

She hadn't the slightest intention of committing suicide, she said, and her breath smelled of alcohol. (Yes, she also drank, and not just brandy . . .)

A few nights earlier almost the same thing had happened when she leaned over the parapet of the Quai des Grands-Augustins, and a young policeman, as uneasy as he was unwary, walked toward her. The Seine, in fact, fascinated her. Above all at night, and after she had been drinking, when it seemed secretively (sealike Seine, secret sea . . .) to hide mysterious reflections in its bosom.

Two leads to three, and I became the third stranger to have approached her in the street recently. The fourth, really, if one counted the tourist from South Africa who tried to pick her up in the tube, in London, some twenty days earlier, as I would learn when she retraced her steps and we sat in the small café on the Rue Dauphine where she had drunk two Pernods barely half an hour before. There a former lover, an Englishman, had said good-bye to her forever—and given her in parting the last money he would ever give her. She asked for her third Pernod, and lit a cigarette before telling me about Mr. Mackenzie.

A sad, almost doglike expression crossed her beautiful dark eyes—the eyes of a beaten dog—that were made to seem even larger by the deep black shadow painted beyond the corners. Other times, as she spoke, they shone with an almost childish innocence that with barely a transition would turn into cunning or suspicion. A small blue vein throbbed for an instant just below her right eye when she pronounced the name of Mr. Mackenzie. Or perhaps it was Mr. Horsfield. Her mouth frozen with fatigue or bitterness. Blackness when she lowered her eyelids. Her eyebrows, very thin and arched, indicated that she was still careful about her makeup. She was probably thirty-five or thirty-six years old, though the dark shadows under her eyes and the faint wrinkles at their corners made her seem older. The short dark hair framed a round face, quite pale. A few locks trembled on her forehead as did her slender, long-fingered hands, like those of an Oriental. Her thick black hair had reddish highlights, natural, as I would later learn, when I could caress her head, feel the downy softness of her hair.

Indeed, the breakup with Mr. Mackenzie had occurred some seven months before they happened to meet again on the Rue

Dauphine. And the final parting a little over a month ago, on the night she stood across from Mr. Mackenzie's house near the Boulevard Saint-Michel and followed him to an Alsatian restaurant on the Boulevard Montparnasse. Mr. Mackenzie was an Englishman of the middle class, of middling height, middle-aged, forty-eight years old precisely. He had retired from the family business, spent long periods of time in Paris, and could be categorized as an "anglais moyen sensuel"—his "liaison" with her certified him as such—and had even committed a youthful sin: he had published a small book of poems. His affair in Paris with this compatriot whose nationality seemed as uncertain as her class perhaps had its origin in his repressed poetic impulse, which drew him from time to time to the anomalous and strange, and to the dangers of sentimentality.

But it was not a poem she received that day when she dared to follow him, her legs growing weak, but a massive blow from Maître Legros, Mr. Mackenzie's solicitor, who notified her with the enclosed check—for fifteen hundred francs—that his client was discontinuing his weekly allowance to her.

The check was a good deal less than her humiliation, and in a café she began to write to Mr. Mackenzie—emboldened by a Pernod—but her attempt at a letter was decorated with little flags. (At other times, when no letter would come, she doodled more and more faces, round faces of a childish simplicity.) She had begun to doubt that Mr. Mackenzie was in Paris and decided to find out in situ. When he saw her walk into the restaurant, pale as a ghost, Mr. Mackenzie must have thought she had come to make a final scene, or at least ruin his supper. But he started very calmly to eat his veau Clamart, he had to establish normalcy, and she accepted only a glass of wine that she poured for herself from the carafe. She was not prepared to accept more humiliations, and his bullying lawyer had demanded the return of letters that she had torn up. No doubt he feared some vague sort of blackmail, feared she would disclose a sentence like this: I would like to put my throat under your feet . . . Nor was she prepared to accept that humiliating check, but she walked out of the restaurant—after lightly hitting or perhaps caressing his face with her gloves, in a démodé beau geste—without returning it to him. And when she saw Mr. Mackenzie again, in the small café on the Rue Dauphine, bygones were bygones and she went so far as to ask him to lend her a hundred francs. When you think you've lost everything, you can still lose your dignity. But on the night of the scene with her glove, George Horsfield, a dark young Englishman who would become her next lover, walked into that restaurant on the Boulevard Montparnasse. Three quarters of an hour later he walked out to search for her in the bars of Montparnasse, and his instinct was correct because he soon found her (at La Coupole?) drowning her sorrows. And sinking even further into her cups as she consoled herself at his hotel, consuming the bottle of whiskey he kept in his room. He guessed she was stuck for money: she opened her bag, took out a few francs, and told him she had said she would return the check for fifteen hundred francs. She took without protest the bills folded in four—exactly fifteen hundred francs—that he put in her hand; but he would not become her lover until she returned to London.

Her sister lived there, and there her mother was dying. But she was hardly in touch with her family. In fact she had married, some ten years before, to escape London and a mediocre past. She had wandered with her husband all over Europe—except for Spain and Italy, she said—and their marriage had ended when the money gave out and their little boy died in Hamburg. They were able to bury him thanks to a loan from the prostitute with a heart of gold who lived downstairs. Then she had worked as a mannequin and an artist's model in Paris. And when she had passed out of fashion and could find no one to pose for, she managed to live on the money given to her by various men. The last time she had gone back to London, three years before, she could bear no more than two weeks. London had seemed drab and depressing. But her next English lover, Mr. Horsfield, urged her to return, and he gave her his address in London before putting her into a taxi. In any event, when she woke from her drunken stupor the next morning in her hotel room on the Quai des Grands-Augustins, she decided to leave her decision to chance: she would go back to London if she heard a car horn hooting before she counted to three. Perhaps it was the sound of an English horn, an Anglo-claxon . . .

From the time she left Victoria Station, London began to defeat her again. She had asked the taxi driver to take her to an inexpensive, quiet hotel in Bloomsbury, and found herself in a small, cold room with filthy curtains, similar to the one she'd had in the same district ten years before, when she first left home. Her life had moved in a vicious circle—vicious in the sense the word has in English: cruel.

She sent letters to her sister Norah and to Neil, her first lover and, she believed, her friend forever, telling them she was in London. Her sister came straight to her hotel, perhaps to gauge what new problems her prodigal sister was bringing back with her. She was awfully sorry she could not put her up at her flat in Acton, where she cared for her mother, because a friend of hers, a nurse, was in the only spare room. Norah was thirty and seemed older—looking at her face was like looking into a mirror—but actually she was the same as always. She suffered new humiliations and insults, from Norah and from Uncle Griffiths, for since her divorce she had become the black sheep of the family. Norah had always been jealous of her and showed it again when she came to see her mother. Norah could not accept the fact that the beautiful senile lady with her white hair in plaits had really recognized the daughter who returned so casually, after years of silence, while the daughter who nursed her with so much devotion had not received the slightest sign of recognition. Perhaps she had returned to London to say good-bye to her mother and accompany her to the cemetery on a pleasant spring morning. She recalled how close she had been to her mother, until Norah was born and demanded all her attention. Then, when she was six, her father died. How easily we lose what we love best. Or even kill it. One of her childhood memories: she was happy when she heard the beating of wings against the tobacco tin where she had put the butterfly she had caught in her hand just a little while before. But when she opened the tin, the butterfly with battered wings could no longer fly. She was not cruel, though they said she was, she only wanted to keep those colors that flashed in the air. She was convinced that you are truly yourself only in childhood. Later we become what others want or expect us to be.

Mr. James, that is, Neil, had been her first lover, when she was nineteen, and their affair had ended Britishly, without scenes. He promised her he would be her friend for life, and on various occasions had lent her money that she planned to return one day. Mr. James was a rich collector, much older than she, who really cared only for his paintings; but he received her kindly, gave her three quarters of an hour of his valuable time, offered her a glass of whiskey, and promised to send her some money. He kept his promise, days later, but let her know in a note that these pounds were the last.

She still had Mr. Horsfield, George, who would soon be her lover.

She had moved to a boardinghouse in Notting Hill and liked to walk the surrounding streets. To remember her, and hopefully to find you, I too have wandered the gray and red labyrinth, the identical deserted streets on this Sunday afternoon, Chepstow Crescent, Pembridge Villas . . . I moved on to Moscow Road to have coffee in Maison Bouquillon, where the aroma of croissants had so often filled you with Parisian nostalgia.

I hope nostalgia has not taken you to Portugal, because there are more cases of cholera and fourteen people have died, according to my *Sunday Times*. Lisbon and Oporto are the cities most affected, but cases have also been reported in the Algarve.

At a table next to mine a lady in a large yellow tulip-shaped toque attacks her brioche with brio, and with no need for a madeleine I am transported in memory back to the small café-tabac on the Rue Dauphine at the corner of the Rue du Pont-de-Lodi.

She had telephoned George soon after arriving in London, and on the second night they went out, not long after the death of her mother, as he was saying good night in the taxi at the door of her boardinghouse in Notting Hill, she asked him not to leave her alone. He went up with her to her fifth-floor room, enormous and sparsely furnished, that looked out on the common garden at the back. They made love listening to the throb of a distant train (I suspect she also said to him in French, slowly, slowly: *doucement, doucement*) and he wanted to leave soon afterward, as if he had already reached his destination, but she reminded him that he had promised to stay the night.

In any event, she had no illusions: when she decided to go back to Paris and he said he would see her there, she did not believe him, or did not care.

And she told him she did not care whether he sent her money or not, whether he came or not, because she could always get somebody.

After ten days she was back in Paris, first in a hotel on the Ile de la Cité, and shortly after that in the one on the Quai des Grands-Augustins.

The night before she left for London, as she was walking back to her hotel, a man followed her along the darkened quai. She left him indignantly at the door to the hotel, but later, when she was alone in her room, she was not entirely displeased to think that she—a woman with no money—in fact might be worth money.

One night soon after her return, when she had drunk two brandies in a café on the Place Saint-Michel where she had tried to write to Mr. Horsfield, and was walking toward the Place du Châtelet, another stranger followed her. The man drew level with her, and she was waiting until they passed the next lamppost to tell him to leave her alone. She did not have to because the man was young and saw that she was not, Oh, la la! he exclaimed with eloquence as he turned away. She began to laugh, accepting the affront with amusement, but it mortified her to acknowledge that in the end, time does us all a bad turn.

Whatever happened to her? Mr. Mackenzie maintained that she lacked an instinct for survival, the most basic instinct for self-preservation, and he was certain she would not get by.

What was there left for her to do: drown her sorrows or drown herself? Perhaps she went to the river because she liked to feel the damp caress of the night mist on her face.

And though the landlady at the hotel on the Quai des Grands-Augustins might have preferred it otherwise, it was easier for her to take a bottle to her room than a man. Lying on the large bed, she would look again at a small unframed oil painting hanging in a corner, which she had come to hate: a half empty—or half full—bottle of red wine, a knife, and a piece of Gruyère cheese.

And yet, in that same soft bed covered with an imitation satin quilt of faded pink, she could lose herself gently, with pleasure, and not simply to please . . .

Sometimes I wonder if she hasn't returned to London in order to feel definitively defeated, or to recall a happier past, like her mother, who had lived in South America as a girl and missed the heat and the light in this cold, gray country.

Today the sky is a rare, hazy, and tender blue she would have liked—the blue of the London sky in spring—and I've decided to look for you, as I did last Sunday, in the Gardens of Kensington.

.O.,

or almost a knockout—almost out the window with a right to the chest—my featherweight American panther è mobile . . . an agile pugilist as lithe as a cat in a skintight minidress the tawny color of a lion. Her lynx's eyes flared in the darkness. It was a clear night, but the leafy top of an old elm tree outside the window let no moonlight in.

She cared not at all for what might happen and with great strength pushed me again toward the window. She locked me in a well-applied wrestling hold. Pertinaciously pinning me down.

And to think that she had seemed so sweet and affable a mere two hours earlier, when, at a rather late hour, I arrived at her country house just outside New York. At night a leopard has no spots . . .

Her father, Mr. Pollunder, who was a friend of my uncle's in America, had brought me from New York in his motorcar to meet her. Would she be as I had imagined her?

Only the ground floor of the enormous mansion was lit, and despite the full moon I could barely make out the form moving rapidly along the avenue of chestnut trees, coming out to meet us. I heard her before I saw her: she greeted us in a cool, clear voice. And also announced, to her father and to me, that just a short while before, an unannounced, self-invited guest had also arrived: Mr. Green. Her father did not seem very pleased at the news. He was a banker, and he had bought this huge house out-side New York in order to place a wall between Wall Street and himself, to move some distance—apparently not far enough—from the closest disturbances.

As we climbed the steps to the front door, we had the chance to study each other in the light, she and I. I hadn't imagined her to be so pretty. What red, beautifully shaped lips. Fortunately she hadn't inherited her father's sagging lower lip . . .

Mr. Pollunder was as imposing as Mr. Green (both had the solid bulk of respectable-looking businessmen, both were good friends of my uncle's), and in view of their respective corpu-lences one could predict that this would be no light supper . . . It was weighted down with boredom for me, for I took no part in the dull conversation about business which Mr. Green had with Mr. Pollunder, and I did not see an appropriate moment when we could leave them to their after-dinner talk and she and I could withdraw to her room, as she had promised, though only to play the piano for her, as I had so imprudently promised. Nor could I take part in Mr. Green's base games with her, a pat on the cheek here, a pinch of the chin there, a squeeze of the hand and another bit of fondling somewhere else, taking advantage of any occasion to touch her, the rambunctious old roué, right in front of her father. I saw quite clearly how she closed her eyes when the lecher laid a lewd hand on her earlobe.

(Or was I a finicky, foul-minded fellow?)

I was uncomfortable, I found his tasteless teasing tedious, and even the golden soup that I barely, or unwillingly, sipped seemed soporific to me.

My lack of appetite was amply compensated for by Mr. Green, who sat between Mr. Pollunder and his daughter and, without haste or hiatus, chewed steadily on everything that was served (roast meat, pigeon . . .) and was prepared to make a meticulous trek through the menu down to the most minute trifles. I rose impatiently from the table, thinking we had finally finished, but my hostess signaled surreptitiously that I should resume my seat, and said in a low voice that soon the two of us would be alone in her room.

Appetites are not small, either, here in Daquise. Five o'clock tea and cakes. Especially for the half dozen doddering old coots calling across the tables, telling stories in Polish. They eat and are never quiet. Watched over by the stout cashier. In the pictures on the wall the light brigade charges to the rhythm of their chewing. An Apollonian Polonius with four white hairs, wearing a white suit, unfurls a plethora of platitudinous bromides and apophlegms—in English—for the benefit of the harridan in the straw hat the color of grapefruit who nods her agreement while sinking her teeth—of gold—into a resistant piece of pastry. Old age whets the appetite . . . If you were here now beside me (and each time the door opens, I think you're going to walk in), you'd make me explain what I meant by "apophlegms." I would tell you they are phlegmatic apothegms, or sluggish sayings.

I took refuge in Daquise when it began to rain. I have, in fact, been looking for you for some time in South Kensington. Last night I dreamed I would find you in the Victoria and Albert Museum, next to the painting of the enormous monkey who opens his chest to display two lovers enthroned in his heart. Dreams are mere dreams, or are they desires?

Miss Rose's cat got me out of the museum with his meowed why. O guay! O woe! I forgot to give him his supper. I'll bring him a cheese pastry to make up for it. A French *mouse*, all right? Beata hasn't worked here for a long while, Beata my eternally virgin Polish waitress. And the clairvoyante polonaise Madame

Starzinsky isn't here anymore either to read your palm: A journey. Danger . . . Though you won't believe it, I read your horoscope—an accidental voyeur in a women's magazine, I don't
remember which one, on the display rack at Smith & Son, High
Street, Kensington—and it said that you should take precau-
tions if you traveled because you were in serious danger. Seriously. That's why I read the news every day. The Russian
newspaper raised high like a curtain at the table across from me
hides the face of the woman reading it. Lecteureadora? In
golden tights almost like a bullfighter's, tight around her calves.
Slim golden ankles, with a gold chain around the left one.
Golden slippers. What is she reading? A depraved *Pravda?* I
trust more in the truth of Miss Rose's *Times:* last night bombs
exploded in the downtown districts of Manchester and Birmingham. Though I don't suppose you're in places that are so
industrialized. But who knows . . .

I haven't forgotten that I was still locked in a hold by my
judo-playing Yankee. And that I wrested myself free with a
twist of the hips. And caught hold of her instead. She shouted
that I was hurting her, but I did not loosen my grip as she
strained against me in her skintight dress. She asked me to let
her go, still gasping for breath in my arms. I wondered why she
had so much difficulty breathing when I was no longer squeez-
ing her very tightly and could not hurt her very much. I must
confess that at the age of sixteen—it was my first trip to America—I was fairly innocent. And yet I had been initiated with no
small craft into the art or artisanry of love by a maidservant
almost twenty years my senior.

Perhaps I loosened my hold even more because I again felt
the strength of her athletic body straining against mine until she
broke away. She thrust me before her, moving with her feet
wide apart in a judo stance, and, holding me by the lapels,

pushed me to the wall. She threw me down on the sofa and with feline suppleness immobilized me by arching against me.

Cat! Wild cat! I tried to shout, in a confusion of rage and shame. You must be crazy, you wild cat!

She slipped one hand to my throat and began to press so forcefully that I could only gasp for breath, while she swung her other fist against my cheek, again and again, threatening blows that hurt me more than if she had really buffeted me.

The fight began because she liked to be obeyed on the spot. When supper had ended and she was leading me to her room, she showed me in passing the door to mine, located in the same corridor. The enormous villa was under reconstruction—both restoration and modernization—and the electrical wiring had so far been laid on only in the dining room. It was a shadowy maze in which it was easy to lose one's way. She seemed impatient for us to reach her room, but I first wanted to look at mine, though it was sunk in darkness, and I sat down on the window ledge and stared out at the night.

Are you coming with me or are you not? and she struck me so hard I almost fell out the window.

After the pretense of boxing my ears, she ordered me to get up from the sofa, but I did not move. She lit a candle, and with my eyes I followed, as I lay on the sofa, the gigantic zigzag pattern that appeared on the ceiling. I was still diminished, even by her shadow. All I wanted to do then was sleep. And in reality, what happened to me next might well have been a bad dream.

She spoke to me again in a sweet voice, as she had at first, and said she was going to her own room and that if I felt like coming to see her later, her room was the fourth door from mine. Twice she told me the number of doors between my room and hers. She would not exactly be expecting me, but if I wanted to come . . . It was up to me.

I made up my mind to stay no longer in that dark house, and after she left I ventured carefully, candle in hand, down a series of corridors that I supposed would lead me to the dining room, where I would rejoin Mr. Pollunder and Mr. Green, for I planned to ask my host to instruct his chauffeur to drive me back to New York.

I was not at all sure that I was going in the right direction: could I be walking in circles in the dark? I was about to call for help, ah, when I saw the saving light, there in the distance, coming toward me. He appeared, like a ghost or an arcane card from the Tarot deck—an old man with a white beard, holding a lantern. This servant was my guide, and also the bearer of surprising news: my pugilistic judo player was engaged to Mack. How disappointing! Mack was the first New York friend my uncle had introduced me to: a skinny kid, son of a millionaire, and a great lover of riding. And probably, who knows, of scuffling with his fiancée.

The servant led me straight to the dining room. Despite his kindness, and though he expressed no annoyance at my impetuous request, Mr. Pollunder could not take me back to New York until seven the next morning because his chauffeur did not sleep at the villa, and the car was in a garage a good distance away, at least until they finished building new carriage houses. And work had been halted for some time because of a strike by the construction workers.

We agreed, thanks to my insistence, that the servant would accompany me to the station, which was not very far away, and that there I would board the next train to New York. I would have to leave the house shortly before midnight. I had barely half an hour to spare, but Mr. Green insisted that I say good-bye to my hostess, and the old servant easily helped me retrace my steps.

I was late, she declared (she was already in her nightdress), and she seemed annoyed again. Fortunately she was different from what she had been before, she was smiling, and she asked me (how incandescent her eyes in the light of the candelabra) to play the piano.

Time did not seem to pass at all, but it was already a quarter to twelve and the servant said I had to go back. Why did I let him go without me?

Despite the late hour, I made a martial assault on the piano (De la marche, de la marche, avant toute chose . . .), a march before I marched away.

The sound of loud applause in the next room.

Who could it be?!?

Mack, she whispered.

I leaped up from the piano stool and opened the door: half reclining in a huge double bed with a canopy, the blankets loosely flung over his legs, was the slender lover whom she could put hors de combat with a single blow of her fist. And I saw that she, leaning against one of the bedposts, had eyes only for him.

Many years later, in an enormous bed at the Gramercy Park Hotel in New York, though not as big as the Ware bed that awakens our fantasies in the Victoria and Albert Museum, I allowed my arms to be pinned down again, beneath the whirling arms of the ceiling fan, by another young American feline in a yellow leotard, whom I had picked up earlier in a drugstore near the hotel because she reminded me of my wrestler from my first trip to America. I lost track of her. I wonder what became of her?

The reader (who may have been a man) lowered the Russian newspaper. Indefinite age, between thirty and forty. A sharply angled face, with Slavic cheekbones, and very short, very dark hair that may have been dyed. Dark eyes, deep-set, and outlined in black. I have seen that face before. The reader thinks I recognize him, or recognize her, and he or she looks at me. And pats a golden pack of cigarettes. I'm going to close before he or she asks me for a light.

When I left that strange country house and walked in the bright moonlight listening to the barking and leaping of dogs that had been let loose in the grass, I was not quite certain where I was going or where New York really was. Everything in that house seemed oppressive to me, and I had to go out into the free night, the free air of America. I was far from suspecting that I would remember without rancor, and with nostalgia, my bare-fisted tussle (I don't know why, but I think now of Jacob's battle with the angel) with my freestyle American wrestler. But struggle, after all, is what defines life.

L_{o!}

Lovely! No, how terrible: she has returned. The living image. In her majorette or is it minorette pink miniskirt, closing and opening-closing-opening her knees. She's stopped, for the moment. She's here, alone, at the table across from me in the Rendezvous Café, savoring a little dome of ice cream awash in red syrup as I write to you. From time to time licking the corners of her mouth as if laminating them. Brusque, now, as she leafs through a notebook covered in iridescent stick-ons and scrawls. She has worked her foot out of her sandal, and with her bare heel rubs again and again against her right ankle. Don't stop, don't stop now, please. Did I say that aloud? She looked into my eyes, then looked away toward the curled vistas of the port of Corfu behind the counter doggedly defended by the black-clad harpy dedicated to her knitting. Fate is fate. The ghostly memory came back to me: that distant Annabel who died of typhus in Corfu: *un esprit de Corfou* . . . Devil in the flesh? But in a caprine association I capered now to Capri since she, genuinely capricious, was a Capricorn. Born on January 1. New year, vita nuova . . .

Can she be the same age as the other? Five thousand three hundred days. Or is it years? I thought the other day while contemplating a prenubile Nubian Venus de Nile in the British Museum.

And this newest avatar looked at me now with a curious gleam in her eye. Did she recognize me? I saw her, noticed her for the first time almost a week ago, in a telephone booth in Brook Green: the freckled Saint Paul schoolgirl in shorts and white socks who made me wait with laughter and whispers, whispering and laughing on the telephone as she balanced a tennis racket with her right hand and from time to time coquettishly touched it to her calves. She looked at me, as if it meant nothing, and burst into giggles again. With whom was she laughing? It began to drizzle.

Once more her vacant tittering, gently softening, but her voice turned shrill again when she became irritated, and I can still hear the echo of her hoarse murmur when she breathed into my ear everything she was forced to do by her step-papa the pied pedophile of beautiful young attendants and infantas terribles. And I did the same, and more, when she fell into my hands unattended during that week of passion.

And still she goes on reading, licking, laminating her lips. And then nibbles at her nails—or nail enamel? Dear God, and now, as if that were not enough, the fly on the rim of her dish. I close my eyes (phosphenating?), and the fly nudges one nipple, then the other, nestles on her rosy aureolas, while she demurely devotes herself to reading her miserable movie magazine. FRED ASTAIRE IS BACK, but she had never heard of Austerlitz. Leave your history lessons for another day, okay? And she gave a little skip and began to dance all alone. Glamour that moves only the other stars . . . Rhapsodomy in blue stardoom: stardustiny. Your destiny is written in the stars of Hollywood, I said, but the apprentice starlette did not hear me or pretended not to hear me as she continued to consult her horoscope in *Screen Land,* sprawling again on the bed just recently unmade by our wallowing. Did I say destiny or doom?

In reality her destiny is a gray star—cinders to cinderellas—
that no longer shines.

And faster and faster she chews her gum. Mmm, clicking
away at clichés, this was my madeleine. Now I would have to
speak of the dolorous, the odorous, smelling again on her
breath the fragrance of strawberry gum, or the bittersweet scent
of currants and green apples. And the unmistakable aroma of
amore reeking in the recesses of our love-nest bed, that unruly
redolence of chestnuts, withered roses, mint, algae, and a certain faux-French perfume (Eau de Roches Roses), a gift to her
from her step-papa the *père fumiste.*

And that smell of damp powder, of gunpowder, during a
tempestuous orgasm. The *petite* terrified at our (our?) little
death. Was she afraid she would be struck by divine lightning?
Ray of rays, King of Kings . . . An El Greco sky (heaven in *The
Burial of Count Orgaʒ?*) over that small Kansas town. When we
get to Kansas descansas—you can rest—I had promised her in
vain. There were other heavens—and hells . . . *Ad astra per
aspera . . .* Just wait, step-père, and you'll see. But she was interested only in film stars though I tried to teach her to recognize
the stars in the sky ("Are you serious?" and she laughed) on
those starry nights of drive-in movies plus driving moves in our
baby-blue convertible Melmoth.

Quasi-Cassiopeia:

.
.   .
.
.

Five freckles on her upturned nose. A constellation still
twinkling on nostalgic nights. Freckles, freckles, ever more
freckles peccantly speckling the rise of her Florentine breasts
in flower . . . More suspension points. On her rosy cheeks,

beneath her eyes, peccadillos of her misty gray glance. And the most piquant of her peccancies. How she licked, laminated, in a gesture of pleasure, the edge of her upper lip, the plumper lip. More identifying marks?

Let me reveal her with veils and dales. The soft blond down rising to the caress sliding along the valley of her rump. The peach fuzz on her slim, honey-colored legs. The light strands on her silken temples. The tenuous shadow on her mound of Venus. And the scar like a tiny trident or the Hebrew letter *sin* below her right knee, the mark left by a skater's blades when she was a blatantly precocious child in her native Pisky. That scar (yes, sí, *sin*) at the elastic top of her white socks. Let me put them on for you—and she, not raising her eyes from her Hollywoodesque review, condescended from the red easy chair to extend one leg (how delicate her ankle, how well polished the back of her knee) and then, impatiently, the other. Oof.

Like an arrow piercing: when her eyes fixed on mine. From the first day her visage came into view. *Il suo viso . . .* And now once more I see her, tanned, in the sun again, as she was the first time. Once more I read her in the shadow of memory. She is as she was and forever will be, she is not a phantom. Kneeling, stereoscopic, on a mat checkered with reflected light, she spies me over her dark glasses, raises her eyebrows, partially opens her just-licked crimson candy lips, raises her hands to her neck as graceful as a heron's, to the knot of the red-dotted indigo scarf as Spanish as her name, Carmen of my Karma, that serves as her bra, then runs her slender hands through chestnut waves of hair, ruffles the ringlets at the nape of her neck, abruptly leans backward, tensing her spine, as agile as a contortionist monkey, to at last peel a plaster from the nail the color of peeled cherry on the first toe of her left foot.

She had a facility for adopting difficult postures, even those forced poses of minimodels and Balthus's *petites danseuses* who stretch and stretch and feel so comfortable on Procrustean couches and beds. But I also see her in more classic poses, like a cozy Venus more or less veiled against a cloud-streaked background. Or a rosy Venus on the half shell. *Beautyshelli. Beauté par Botticelli*. But more picaresque, a little sluttish and cheap. She even would have thought it cute, despite the choler of her classic rapist step-papa, to paint a mustache on that Venus by Botticelli and scrawl on her cuntish conch (she adored the rupestrine hieroglyphs in gas-station rest rooms, my Duchampollion of pornograffiti . . .) in great black letters: *L.H.O.O.Q.* What initials these are! Look for the Q . . . Cherchez la flamme!

At times I called her Carmen, other times I wrote only the first letter of her name.

Elle! you might have exclaimed in French, and I, an L is an L, would mentally say oui, nodding as I elected that first letter of my shooting starlette pliant as elastic, pealing in the labyrinth of my ear.

Elle: read in reverse: ever the rêve of dear elle.

L elevated so elegantly on the tip of the tongue to begin to preannounce her name.

Would I remember it all, from Motel Alice in Carroll, Iowa, to Virginia Hotel in Virginia Beach? Hotel Virginia, was that before the struggling siesta tussle in Lacework Cabins? Memory also makes its own filigree . . .

With so many pleasure jaunts and educational tours (all-inclusive) through so many states, from August to August, memories merge and intertwine. Last night I attempted to recapitulate.

Lovingly I would bring her breakfast in bed after her morning exercises. I always tried to keep her in trim. And along with the obligatory daily exercise, I would take her to pools and tennis courts in the towns we passed through.

Her smooth stippled armpit as she raised the racket for the serve—I discovered that erogenous zone in southern Arizona. Needles, California: needles quivering at the tips of her long smoky lashes moments before she plunges back into trembling blue light.

We frolicked, too, on lonely beaches. The mist rising from the sea like a ghostly sheet and she, dipped like a croquette in damp, sticky sand, had gooseflesh, pouting, ready to cry . . .

She, in the snow, with a red pom-pomed hat, slides and shrieks.

All climes were good for reaching climaxes . . .

On another distant horizon of memory: Claude Lorrain clouds threatening rain.

Did I really ask for the town fountain when we were having breakfast in Soda? In any case she didn't care for mineral water with gags, or simply no longer liked my aqueous humor because I recall very clearly her sarcasm when she quipped: "Your humor is Sodasplitting" . . . only to burst into laughter, a dam breaking, one might say.

Rolling Soda water gathers no moss?

What about tears?

Last night I attempted to amass memories.

A light fog veiled my eyes.

Or did the pages of a novelette close over the face of this hypocrite voyeur no longer keeping his vigil?

I heard her weeping in the dark, into a pillow, and woke again from that wet dream: one summer afternoon after we had made love on a blanket spread on the ground at the edge of a thicket, she fetchingly cried salt tears in my arms. Ellechery (*sic*) cannot deny ellipsis . . .

And to this corraptor of minors there remains nothing now but words, brilliant words, strings of words to toy with, child of my desire, to keep my tongue twisting as if it could part your gorged engorged lips, ah yes the *vermeillette fente* (oh lo lo! how our unfailing French annotations drove her to a frenzy), that succulent red cleft where my desire never dies, or my torments of a Tantalus enthralled, forever in thrall to labia (oh, my nymphess, where are the nymphs of yesteryear . . .), my mouth devouring and diluting the delicious name of my sweet candied loca who still makes my mouth water, water you will never sip again (mythic Soda . . . *Romance à l'eau d'Eros* . . .) that sweeps me away with words, *mots* and mottos for my continuing travels along dusty railways highways byways mindways until I find *le motel juste* just like the one farther down memory lane: there at the entrance an almost extinguished neon PARADISE where in the center only AD burned red. A heaven in darkened letters or a red hell in ad hoc Russian? Ye who enter abandon all ho . . .

Lost at long last. She abandoned us, her damned step-papa and me, for a debased dramatist named Cue and ended melodramatically with a certain Schiller. Her unlucky star. Mrs. Schiller died in Gray Star giving birth to a stillborn child. But the girl in my memory did not die. In my camera obscura a red neon heaven and hell flash again in retrospect. Ah oui, da, oh yes, *le mot juste,* ad infinitum, just there behind that linden tree (a North American basswood? *Tilia tilo* I would baiser my Lo) or white poplar (may an asp envenom me if it wasn't a quaking aspen) and velvet lawn, desire under the lindens and in the shade of the poplars or whatever they're called, in that cabin of gilded logs, there behind the venetian blinds, in striped darkness where the apple of my ear, languidly lounging, coiled between my arms and legs, murmurs in her bittersweet husky voice that I should keep on doing what I want to her, go on doing whatever I want to her after she whispers all the filth (awful filth, unlawful filth . . . ?) done to her by that slavering baboon her perverse beau-père, satyr enslaved to the grape and to rape, my coviolator and accomplexed accomplice, who shuddered and stuttered at the coquette's first touch and drenched her at the second, leaving behind his slimy trail ("Don't drool on me," stop your slobbering . . .) on golden-downed smooth thighs (her name spewed out around the mound of Venus) and behind along the succulent split peach, ay, tender durazno endures . . . And the bright morning star trail still gleams on her belly, I glimpsed it at dawn, my pawn (*Corps fou & Gray Starets*), I fawn, my face over the fountain of pleasure that cannot slake my dry debaucher's mouth, sedulous seducer who had already touched stardust, *ad astra per aspera*, as they say in Kansas, raised up by a gray glance (*Gray Stare* . . .) verging on blue, let her be? but I was beginning to crawl again without saying a word: . . . *And the stars, and the scars . . . ,* cicatress and (*sic*) actress, at the sight of the scar like a viper or the Hebrew letter *lamed* (belle lettre!) laminated above the upper lip of the minorette across from me who closes-opens her knees again because perhaps I am making her nervous with my indiscreet glances.

I dissimulate, unfolding the paper: I hope you haven't been unlucky enough to seek out the sun in Cyprus. It's not at all clear how the coup will turn out, and there is still shooting in the streets of Nicosia. I suppose it's even more unlikely that you're in Birmingham or Manchester, where new bombs exploded yesterday. Ira belli . . .

Now I would swear she is soliciting, clouding my gaze. I opened my eyes even wider and remembered. Madly we made our way. Has she returned? I licked, laminated her lips, her eyes. My lingering tongue in her eye. First the one with the mote, then the other. Ay. *Lamed.* The lingual letter that begins the recitation of her name, its resuscitation in memory.

bien gracias y usted, she tried to practice her small Spanish and abundant charms, my lush Andalusian prima donna with those great dark eyes and that mop of dark hair and that toothsome body as ripely piquant as her mother's, olé la Laredo!, pretending we were in the Spain of operettas and she brought my breakfast to bed, *dos huevos estrellados, señor,* and burst into laughter when she mounted me in the old rickety bed that began to creak again beneath our kiss jingling those loose brass knobs on the rails at the head of the bed, tarantaran and rintintin at each lubricious lunge of her belly and rump, rotund and sumptuous, though to keep down the noise she knew the old trick of tossing the eiderdown down on the floor and putting a pillow down under her opulent bottom, ugh, offering up fine orifices as open and dark as the mouth of a wolf, ugh, to clutch me tighter and implore for the sake of God and Gounod's Virgin Mary to make my thrusts slow poke her pian pianto, 1 and 2 and 2 and 1, behind like canines and as the canons command that's what Señora Mastiff something-or-other taught her (and she learned the lesson, her husband left her *embarazada*—another Spanish word she still remembered—good and pregnant the first time right after watching at the window how two dogs coupled and uncoupled in the street) after that fevered shoving all in front

avante like her fervent lover from Playboylandia baptized Hugh
in the holy land of Hibernia though never did he let her hiber-
nate but had to fornicate when it was almost time for the bullfight, *bravo toro,* at exactly four in the afternoon by the
Greenwich meridian and did it 3 or 4 times at least (and an inter-
lude in bed, an intermezzo, an interpasto of canned wild boar
and some opportune swallows of port to fortify himself) or 4 or
5 in her room, if not 7 at siesta time, this was the tenor of her
murmured calculations and with it all they had time enough to
rehearse for their next concert in Belfast, *Lacci d'harem,* and
even to wrap legs around each other again, for there are loves
that bind, before her husband came home, Mr. De la Flora the
unstinting cuckold who even with his numerous nocturnal
omissions had more sap in his heart and more sense in his head
than the huger Hugh, as per her measure, but glimmers of
memory grind no grain and her husband no longer gave her
pleasure in conjugal congress and she had done her fair share of
feigning oohing and cooing until he came, par derrière and par
décevant where he didn't fill her up either and there, engorged,
like a diamond in the rough and ready, ho! where there's a way
there's a will! and he had his way with her with his uncommon
member shared by many in common and that was common
knowledge (bigger and redder it was than the one on that
feeble-minded flasher with red hair who pretended to pee behind a tree, a cherry tree? and suddenly showed it, shaking it
at her when she passed pretending she didn't see) him with his
prick the size of a rutting stallion's or that tauromantic raper
of Europa stripping and sticking her like a beast (when she had
prinked and primped and perfumed herself so carefully for
hours . . .) or rushing when she undressed behind the curtains
to ride her and goad her and with one thrust of his sword (her
hair disheveled, her tongue hanging out, gasping for air on all

fours) drive home like that bullfight in Línea de la Concepción that she still recalled with alarm when the fierce bull charged and gouged out the guts of those poor horses rooting in their entrails like Hugh in her, he almost tore her in two with his thing so deep and dirty he was too slapping the plump cheeks of her bottom, Hugh! and the great savage almost ripped off her nipple (his teeth marks still on the round whiteness of her right breast), naturally those breasts full and firm and white as milk or marble finely veined in lapis lazuli on the soft undercurve would drive the most torpid man mad which is why Mr. De la Flora in his day had sucked them firm for hours like a great suckling Solomon at her maternal breast, a wise man who knows that his lips, his life, are sweetened by mother's milk and hers so hard and swollen like a nanny goat's, he drained the via lactea with delight and even wanted to milk her teats into his tea, well, with everything I've said you could write a whole book, she was sure, and what she crooned in bed with no commas or periods I translate for you now with no breaks either in our pub on Hammersmith Broadway, another song from *The Swan* while tuneless and hoarse those four sons of Erin here next to the Charrington mirror raise their glasses on high, *The Swan Way*, in their own way and with bad manners and worse modes as they always do near closing time, and then a sudden backfire in the street (from an exhaust pipe?) brought back with a start my uneasy fear that you are back in France because yesterday, according to the *Times*, Spanish anarchists placed several plastique bombs in your sweet land to sabotage the "Tour," though my alarm is no doubt exaggerated, or I exaggerate to make you think I hang by a thread on your return but I take up the thread again of that woman bursting at the seams with talk: we had reached the point where with everything she had told me I could write a whole book, she was sure, like one of those books about coquettes by Leopold de Kock that her husband brought her, borrowed or bought secondhand, to provoke her most perturbing fantasies, getting things into you, wasn't that the way? though she only tried with a banana and was disturbed when she enjoyed it thinking it might break off inside and you could find all kinds of lost objects in those vaults in a woman but what also moved her in days gone by were the love letters from her beloved, all those lovely things about a thing of beauty is a joy forever, yes, yes, and she had them at her fingertips, all those lyrical lines, for sometimes she stroked herself 4 and 5 times a day she was so ardent, so artful, and would remember too the first ones mouth-to-mouth, a long twisting kiss that would make your head spin, and the first little touches on the banks of the canal where your back loses its chaste name and that drove her straight to confession and she also had bad thoughts in bed when the sheets stuck to her, voluptuousness leads to vice, my child, she'd like one of them to embrace her looking so splendid in his cassock and that perfume of incense and candle wax, or some little curate led astray, but in her bovaryish ravings from 1001 nights night after night she also saw herself at nightfall or dusk behind the Custom House and along the docks searching for a Sinbad just come ashore to do it anywhere, standing in a doorway, or going to meet one of those Gypsies on the green dunes of Rathfarn with his blackguard's face and Spanish eyes who attacks her in the dark and rides her up against the wall deaf to her cries and not saying a word, like her Hugh, or she was the victim in an alley or cul-de-sac of an elegant Jack the Ripper who split her in two without even taking off his hat, what was she thinking of, my God, and she kneaded her lustrous beer-drinker's belly that fortunately had not swollen to the size of her friend Ben's, the bass "barreltone" as she called him, or she imagined the door forced by a ferocious vagabond when she

was alone at home (a time to kill . . . :Ecclesiastes 7?) though
she consoled herself with sweeter thoughts, new sweets of sin,
of how and where she would seduce an innocent boy showing
him her new garters, and she raised her close-fitting dress to
show them, violet, to me, and then she would begin to stroke his
cheeks when he was already red as a tomato, and she was even
prepared to pay a handsome lad, another boy from Playboylandia, or a gigolo from Paris and she would show him her *embon-
point* in *déshabillé,* all for him, for Raoul!, or one of those little
naked gods in the sun on the beach at Margate, and she would
kiss him everywhere, there's real beauty for you, eh, all those
little riddles she'd say to excite her husband ten years back (the
last conjugal debt was paid on November 27 when she already
had an eight-month belly and that rowdy little fetus kicking
inside), or slowly she took off her stockings close to the fire,
lying on the rug, or put on muddy boots, if her fine foot or last
pair of smeared drawers were not enough, to testify to her
fetishism, and certainly she was ready to do it with a coal miner
and with a bishop of Rome and even with an uncircumcised
wandering Jew, another parenthesis, she needed at least one new
man a year, she exaggerated and recalled the organ of that Italian organ-grinder, *La ci darem,* and she wanted to try a black
man's, another tenor's alto sax, maybe to see if his was as dark
and long as her Hugh's with that flaming iron bar, like a dog up
to his old tricks, and the second time conquered and incomplete
almost and he made her pant fuck or lickshit, shout fuck up,
love! fuck up, love! felicitations, giving pleasure in her hungry
hole for five internal minutes, ticktock tactile, touching her
behind with his finger rooting, thumbing sweet thumb and ring
finger in the dark eye until she could bear no more, confounded
or ready to faint, O Lord, and she surrendered and put her arms
around him O Lord, and remembering him inflamed her again,

as red as a hot coal, and it tickled her with joy just to think about him, Sir Hugh the Great Rooter, who would not be back till next Monday, she assured me, and led me on, I'll bet you're one of those who likes to cross the red sea, and went on rambling in the night as if having recourse at home to verse 7 of Ecclesiastes, and the sea is not full, a time to love another time, look how white and smooth, my sun, you've never seen such lustrous thighs, yes, open your legs and close your eyes and the flowers on the wallpaper in her room shining like stars in steaming splendor and she would recall for me alone that she got up from bed half-asleep, just as she was, and standing right there next to the lamp she could see her husband and a much younger drink-ing mate (ten or twelve years younger than she) taking a long piss outside her window, yes, this is good, could he be the young man of her life promised by the cards? be patient and deal tomorrow's another day and she went back to bed to dream of the rock rising like a giant when the Levantine wind arrived black as night bringing back her nostalgia for the south, for another night in Ronda and the posadas and castanets, and the first one who put his tongue in her mouth kissing her slowly under the Moorish wall and she waved good-bye with her drenched handkerchief, full of emotion the day before her departure on a day in May flowering and beautiful at the cliffs covered with Spanish firs and once again she would put the rose in her hair like the Andalusian girls and hum deep in bed her night tune, olé! o lay! in the mouth of another dark Mary Morena, a singer too but Irish by birth and ten years younger and twenty kilos lighter at least though with a body as well developed as her voice who sang ballads in a Kilburn pub when I met her on another June night and from night to morning she would repeat in my bed *cómo está usted* and undress standing next to the vamp-lamp screened by a wig found in the Islington market and let her hair black as night tumble down her eyes shining and open and blue, bluer than the aquamarine that her Hugh was going to give her, go to blazes! and repleting strings of obscenities in that unperformable play that would never be staged, my scenic version or perversion of a summer night's dream in a Dublin tender as the night but she roundly refused to rehearse the original scene of the chamber pot when she spoke in streams, the streams of gold of Erin, that coursing current, and had to say in her Irish accent L'odore, L'eau d'or, je suis ravie, content in the shower of gold, the waters of Lahore pouring now, those of the Orinoco rushing now, go to hell! and she said no I won't No.

eurotic,
or perhaps Neuroptic—Optic Nerve—that's what was said or
read in accented (Slavic?) French by the "queen of hearts"—so
called because of her brazen black sweater with the flaming red
hearts—a slender blonde with disheveled ashen curls and a long
face with great somber shadows under equally somber eyes,
alone at the table on the left in the Mardi Gras, though this is no
carnival Tuesday but a Thursday, the eighteenth of July (a
national holiday, with the matador still lame, still unable to pre-
side over the parade . . .), and she is sitting in front of an open
book with a blue cloth cover, and an empty coffee cup, and an
ashtray with a cigarette that burns, the smoke coiling in the air.
Almost like the red neon cobra across the way at that Indian
shop on Bute Street, shining more and more brightly as night
falls.

Naja naja. Burning bright . . .

Rapid blinking.

She has been reading, head down, for some time, her arms
intertwined, taut as a straitjacket across her chest, and occasionally she murmurs something incomprehensible.

Optic nerve?

Once again I looked, engrossed, straight ahead, through the
gray windows at the razed house on Queensberry Place, not

even the sign is left, DEMOLITION IN PROGRESS, almost nothing is left standing of that house where we lived in less intemperate times, and tempering nostalgia I contemplate a segment of wall with the tattered remains of blue lily wallpaper and vestiges of the fireplace like a pink and black picture frame, the colors of delirium in the cozy light of gas as you sit naked on the floor, drying your hair with a towel, pink-black-white, in another picture not yet blurred in my memory, no, no, you do not fade, I do not forget, the outlines of much older memories form and dissolve, a bolt of lightning traced by a hand in the night, a maniacal movement of the forefinger toward the flashing shattering bolts in the livid sky, l'amour foudre on the Rue de Seine, and she mocked and derided again my wretched tormented r's, "Ton erre" . . . , yes, my ill-humored air at times, for I could not comprehend her madwoman's humor.

For example, in other verbalistic verbiage, that afternoon of unbridled appetites when we wandered the Boulevard de la Chapelle and the Faubourg Saint-Denis and she stopped before each restaurant to construe and misconstrue the minutiae of each menu:

—Haddock cru aux peines perdues.

Ad hoc cod to chew the cud.

—Maquereau aux orages amers.

Red herring for pimps.

—Gigolo rôti aux flageolets.

Ditto.

—Canard de Barbarie à la Presse.

Humbugged duck with fresh scoops . . .

—Confiteor de porc aux hommes confondants.

Auricular confusion.

—Espoir Belle Haleine.

Hallelujah we've come to dessert.

—Phare breton.

Let there be light (éclair au café) . . .

You'd say I'm têtu comme un breton, as headstrong as a man from Aragon, but I can't get it out of my head that you, wherever you may be, are in danger. Wouldn't you even heed your horoscope?

This morning when I opened Miss Rose's *Times* I saw you again in your camouflage T-shirt, splotches of green and black, waiting for me at the door of the WC at the Tower of London. It never would have occurred to me to visit the spot, and I acknowledge you did a good job as guide at that histouristic Tour. You insisted on my passing through the Traitor's Gate, announcing or denouncing me to the hordes of tourists: Avanti, Signore Traduttore . . . But the man who warns is no traitor. You are in serious danger. Where? You might have been the woman killed by the bomb at the Tower of London, yesterday at two, or one of the thirty-seven people injured. Or I myself, you might have said, if I'd had the feeling I would find you at the Tower. Better to castle elsewhere. Recalcitrant rook.

Returning to my electrified lector or lectoress who seems to hurl lightning bolts from her staring eyes, as if she were about to X-ray the page in the dark of night, just as it is reflected in the black glass of the window, and I wonder if I ever spoke to you about the wanderer who thought she was an errant soul, about her lives and miracles in the Paris of marvels.

"Do you see it, there, that window?" and more with her glance than with her finger she pointed across the Place Dauphine: at a window, as dark at that hour as all the others that were facing us.

We had just eaten supper under the awning that covered the small terrace of our bistro on the square, and she, her red and black dress too thin for autumn, shivered like the leaves of the plane trees gleaming silver in the light of the streetlamp, or like the rest of the flan breton that she touched nervously with her spoon.

"Do you see it?" and now she pointed with her spoon.

I saw it, black, the shutters open.

"Well, in a minute the light will go on, a red light."

The faithful drunk circled our table again, babbling his stream of verbiage:

"Un vers blanc comme un verre luisant . . ."

(A blank verse white as a brilliant vase or glass? Nightjars or chamber pots communicating . . .)

And the window lit up, right on time, with a red light, its draperies red.

She barely smiled a mysterious smile and the drunk—shhhh!—raised a finger to his lips.

"Tu viens, Jules?" beneath the trees she called to him again, the pale white wanderer.

At last Jules paid attention to her.

Had he become fearful, as I had, or had he foreseen something, in spite or because of his drunkenness, something that still escaped me?

But there was also a flash of alarm or anguish in her bewitched eyes, reddened, encircled by a black mask of makeup.

It was better for us to leave that unsettling triangle, that's right, and as we hurried along the Quai de l'Horloge, she shivered with cold beside me, her wild dark hair windblown; but suddenly, like another bolt out of the blue, she wanted to retrace her steps to the Palais de Justice.

She stopped, filled with horror, at the wall of the Palais prison, la Conciergerie with its sinister past.

There were brilliant tears in her eyes the color of fern as she clung, distracted, to the bars over the window of a condemned prisoner's cell, next to the chapel.

"Poor thing, poor thing . . ."

She barely answered my questions, as if she were remembering all alone.

"Who."

"She puts her black shawl over my shoulders."

"Who."

"A lady in black, very pale. She resembles Marie Antoinette. She passes her hand along my head, brushing away some straw and arranging my bonnet."

"Who are you? Where are you?"

"I am one of her ladies-in-waiting, and she is consoling me in a dark room with damp stone walls. She has just tied the ribbons of my bonnet and says to me, smiling: Madame L'Etiquette would never approve."

"Who is Madame L'Etiquette?"

She does not know or does not answer, but now she is weeping, whispering something incomprehensible, or praying.

The gleam of her perfect white teeth.

Finally I pulled her out of that discomfiting past and position with a passionate kiss, and we continued walking, in the direction of the Louvre, until she stopped without warning and leaned over the stone ramp to show me the hand of fire burning in the waters of the Seine. Useless to try to make her see that lights winked capriciously on the inky current. At midnight we made another stop at the Tuilleries, this time to contemplate a fairly phallic fountain that seemed to fascinate her almost as much as the man who passed back and forth so brazenly before our bench.

He was her night-blooming beau from the Tuilleries whom she had met on some other midnight, and he might have been a good father to her little girl. Sometimes I wondered if her daughter existed only in her overheated imagination, but on that cold night early in October she dissolved all my doubts with a detail that endowed the child with definitive existence: her little girl was so curious, what a child, that she always pulled out the eyes of her dolls to see what *was there* behind them.

The optic nerve? A vague resemblance to the maga, the sorceress of Paris (who was really from Lille), grown older, though her age is indeterminate. Between thirty and forty. Or perhaps she looks older than she is.

Her fragile figure is reflected in this dark window and she goes on with her reading, absorbed (now she rubs her forearms, is she cold?) as we walked along the Rue Saint-Honoré toward a bar that still had its lights on: Le Dauphin.

And she, after treading again the lost steps of the past, asserts with good black humor that we've gone from the Place Dauphine to the Dauphin. From the dolphin's fin to finality, the last of the line. But a red trapezium of mosaic tiles extending from the bar to the floor brings back a flood of blood-soaked memories, "Monsieur, couvrez-moi," her eyes wide with horror, gesturing as if she were wrapping herself in a shawl, Cover me, and we have to escape before the time machine starts running and the guillotine drops again.

On an excursion to Versailles she spoke again of the old long-gone days, the days of Marie Antoinette and even of Madame Elisabeth, the days of cheers and applause when heads rolled, and in a kind of trance she remembered with so much certainty that I struggled not to lose mine, or my way in the night fog, while I drove back to Paris. As we crossed the forest of Fausse Repose she kissed me, impulsively, covered my eyes with her hands, and with her foot pressed my foot down on the accelerator. And we accelerated with celerity until I reasserted control. Accelerate love or make death. I couldn't, I didn't have the courage, to follow her. She had other lives. All of mine are in this one.

And I could not follow her in all her madnesses and deliriums and oblivions, more and more each day and night, as we waited for hours or centuries while all the clocks melted, tick-tock tacky, yes, time is the Giant Joker, on so many adventures and misadventures and random meandering processions along the narrow streets of Paris, though her slender silhouette would reappear on the Pont des Arts in another final avatar, and I could not hopscotch across that line either (all the way to The Hague, where she tried to deal cocaine . . .) or follow her into the insane asylum at Vaucluse.

There were no dark words at the entrance, not even an andante Abandon all hope . . .

What's in a name?

Nothing, niente, nada?

Espoir Belle Haleine . . .

Again I kiss her teeth and once more they chatter with cold in the night.

And yet again I see as if in last night's dream a great brightly lit sign for the lightbulb MAZDA in which the z turned like a wheel of flame, MAZDA, MAZDA, burning bright . . . and sometimes it was MAZDA and other times it was MANDA (it commands, it leads the way), the z spinning round into N.

A magic circle or a vicious mandala?

MANDA . . . te.

And my electric lectoress? She has slipped away, disappeared, like a spirit of air, a will-o'-the-wisp, unnoticed.

"She comes here often in the afternoon," the waitress told me, "and some mornings for breakfast. She's a doctor, I think."

The optic nerve. An ophthalmologist?

*O*ak *Tree*, in faded gilt letters on red cloth, the first word almost worn away, *The*. I could not help but notice the title of the slim red volume of verses as I ran to rescue it from the grass and return it to her, for she lay precisely at the foot of a great oak. It was a peaceful October afternoon in Hyde Park and I had knocked *The Oak Tree* out of her hands when I attempted to return a badly aimed ball to some stumbling soccer players— quatre Pelés de la pelouse—who waved their tattooed arms at me almost at the edge of the Serpentine.

But before I saw the squared little red book (Mao? I ventured to guess when I went to pick it up), I had admired the reader: the brunette of uncertain age (perhaps in her forties, forty years well carried and well worn) who had the graceful figure of a page with a short curly mop of hair and long legs, velvet breeches and a leather jacket of the same rusty color as the leaves upon which she lay. I thought I had seen her a few days earlier, in a jacket and trousers of black velvet, the solitary and mysterious and rather Hamletian dark lady strolling among the fountains in Kensington Gardens. A most distinctive demoiselle . . .

The ball had struck the book from her hands, but it brought back an old memory—almost four centuries old!—of the head of a Moor (or was it a Turk?), the color and shape of a football, hanging from the rafters in the attic of her manor house in Kent, at which she would slash with a sword still too heavy for her arms. This occurred around 1588, and she was, at the time, a charming boy of sixteen.

What attitude must one adopt when a perfect stranger (quite mad or simply loquacious?) calmly begins to recall in a hushed voice and in one's presence (which may well be absence, for she truly spoke in a most absent manner) the lives and metamorphoses of her life, her former avatars and earlier adventures.

But that, after all, is not really extraordinary. I remember that you too remember former lives, quite disturbing ones in disturbing dreams. The last time you woke me you were a witch named Babel, I believe, burning at a stake of the German Inquisition.

And be wary of the flames again if you are wandering through Greece, perhaps even in the company of Miss Rose, for today her *Times* reports that mysterious fires are devastating the forests of Attica. But I must return to the blaze of that sunset in Hyde Park, wreathing the autumn afternoon in orlands of gold and blood and making that mutable creature fall mute. She cast an uneasy glance at the crimson horizon. For almost two hours, before darkness fell, she expounded on her extraordinary lives. And so, at the foot of an equally centenarian oak, and as she lay decubitus prono, she pronounced the most ordinary names— Moll, Nell, Rosina Pepita . . . —that sounded as strange as others much more uncommon—Marusha Stanilovska Dagmar Natasha Iliana Romanovitch, Rattigan Glumphoboo . . . —and mentioned places in London—Blackfriars, Curzon Street, Greenwich . . . —that resounded as exotically as Constantinople and the Sea of Marmara . . . and said sentences in Turkish that seemed not so incomprehensible as others in plain English, for example, the reiterated "A toy boat on the Serpentine," followed by the exclamation "Ecstasy!" . . . I saw no toy boat, but there on the edge of the Serpentine I believed myself to be on the verge of understanding. "A toy boat, a toy boat, a toy boat" . . . , she returned to her unrestrained refrain, perhaps the trinitarian tercet of her salvation. I was about to propose a ramble to the Round Pond, in the Kensington Gardens close by, to watch the sailboats on the pool cutting through waves and fluttering wings. She had turned, and leaning on one elbow, she spoke, her gaze fixed in the direction of the Serpentine.

My posture was more uncomfortable, for I still vacillated between discreetly withdrawing and continuing to crouch as I lent an ear to her thousand lives and miracles. I was beside her on the grass. It was, after all, I who had approached her, as a result of my poor aim, I who had initiated the conversation that unleashed her singular soliloquy. Had I really asked her—without great perspicacity, apparently—if she was alone?

The first words to cross her lips ("I am alone"), I first read in her eyes like drenched violets.

She passed her hand over her broad brow, so pale and polished, toward the delicate medallion of her temple, and acknowledged with a smile (the lips themselves were short and slightly drawn back over teeth of an almond whiteness) that she had just emerged from the dream of a rest cure and found it difficult at times to remember, especially more recent events.

Was she an escapist? Had she escaped a madhouse or an asylum? It had occurred on other occasions: she would fall unexpectedly into a trance and waken after a week or even longer.

The first image to manifest itself in her memory, and it had come at the same time as the ball, was the head of a Moor which her father, or perhaps her grandfather, had cut off on the field of battle.

She saw herself at the age of sixteen sinking upon his knees—in future we must say "his" for "her," "he" for "she"—to offer a bowl of rose water to ancient Queen Elizabeth, who had just arrived at the vast manor house. He was so overcome with shyness, kneeling there in the banquet hall, that he saw no more than her royal ringed hand in the water: voracious, thin, depredating and debauching, made to command and control, a hand that before long would undress him at her pleasure, appreciating the charms of a docile lad, and soon after she would order him to attend her at Whitehall to name him her Treasurer and Chief Steward. His youth was the old queen's chief treasure, which she would have liked to keep for herself alone. In the winter of her life, one snowy afternoon when the crows called in Richmond Park, she would see in an indiscreet mirror a boy kissing a girl. Was it he? Perhaps it would have grieved her less to discover him a short while later in the arms of another white-bosomed noble youth sleeping among the treasure sacks of Spanish gold on a black ship lately anchored on the Thames. And then the dark lady spoke, like the open book of verses at her side or like the King James Bible, of how brief are our days and how long the impenetrable night that awaits each of us. All ends in death, she repeated in funereal melancholy.

The shadow of a bird in flight passed, fleeting, over the grass.

A starling, she said. And added with a sigh: Vita brevis . . .

Perhaps she glimpsed again, in the shadow of a rapid fluttering wing, her lives and loves. She accepted a cigarette and at her first exhalation looked up at the hazy blue of the sky. Tears spilled over the lower lids of her great violet eyes.

Hours later, in the trembling bed with the scarlet hangings in her house filled with antiquities, at the end of Curzon Street, she would ask me, as her naked body coiled and uncoiled—not to draw too fine an analogy in these annals—to make love to her in the fashion the Virgin Queen had commanded once long ago. And after the first act, rolling over like an agile Roland, she reversed roles, and with so much mounting went over the mountain, ultramontane . . . as if she had changed sex again and remembered her rapscallion gallops atop court ladies and serving maids lacking maidenheads in the taverns of Wapping Old Stairs.

The queen passed to the next world, a poorer world perhaps, in Richmond, on that twenty-second of March in the Year of Our Lord 1603, bringing to an extravagant golden end the Tudor dynasty, and at the court of her successor, King James, the former favorite would continue to be young, rich, and handsome, the darling of the ladies. He was about to wed one of the most noble and distinguished of them, a Britannically phlegmatic blonde of Irish descent who had an infinite number of family names beginning with O apostrophe like an unending string of exclamations, when the Great Frost put a chill on their engagement. In reality, frost was the fire in which their first passion burned and was consumed in flames.

The Great Frost was, historians tell us, something never seen before or since in these islands, a phenomenon of another Ice Age.

So intense was the cold that birds froze in midair and fell like stones to the ground, or turned to ice in variegated poses atop walls or at the roadsides. Above Blackfriars a cloud of rooks cawed a raucous congealed call and clattered down like black hail. The Thames was frozen, and the king, to celebrate his coronation, commanded that it be decorated and given all the semblance of a pleasure ground, with mirrored mazes of ice and the drinking booths and food stalls of a fair. The court was at Greenwich, and immediately opposite the palace gates he cor-

doned off a vast space reserved for courtiers and notable foreigners. While the rest of the country remained paralyzed by
cold, and many unfortunate wayfarers were solidified into land-
marks and signposts and milestones along highways and
byways, London blazed in frozen festivities.

It was during one of those soirees on ice, at exactly six in the
evening on the seventeenth of January, that his heart was stolen
by an equivocal skater in loose-fitting trousers, whoosh! who
was, unequivocally, a Russian princess. And soon afterward, in
the snow, he would take her in his arms and know for the first
time the ardor of true love. The passion of the lovers abated for
a moment as they lay on fur cloaks, and he recounted in French
his past loves, which now seemed to him mere simulacra. And
they fell to loving again wrapped in sable.

The Muscovite princess also had so many names, so larded
with so many h's and k's, that he called her Sasha for short, and
also because it was the name of a white Russian fox he'd had as
a boy, which bit him so savagely that his father had it killed. The
love bites of love?

Several hundred years of solitude later, confronting the
team of clients and clerks at Marshall & Snelgroves, he would
recall the first time he knew the glitter of ice and the bitter gall
of betrayal, during the Great Frost.

Othello on ice, that was how he first saw his own tragedy
staged on the frozen Thames. But she was no innocent, and he,
instead of strangling her, attempted to strangle the enormous
sailor who, he supposed, had held her in his arms in the dark
hold of the ship of the Muscovite embassy. And days later,
when the ice began to melt, but not his jealousy, he watched as
the vessel sailed away carrying the faithless woman out to the
tempestuous sea that was death.

When he doubted what his own eyes saw in the doubtful twilight, there on the Russian sailing ship, and perhaps in order to begin to put her out of his mind, he imagined for a moment the willowy Sasha transformed into a wide-hipped forty-year-old, the agile skater a somnolent matron . . .

More than three centuries later, in the time it takes the doors of the lift at Marshall & Snelgroves to open and close, she thought she saw Sasha as graceful as ever in furs and Russian trousers, but it turned out to be a stout bejeweled woman with gray hair stepping with ponderous tread from the past to the present. When she walked out into Oxford Street her eyes filled with tears, she had the sensation that time was fragmenting just as she had, that her visions were passing as rapidly as the flood of motorcars and passersby that appeared and disappeared all around her.

And through her memory there passed in rapid succession the years that followed the great disillusionment. He retired to the manor house of his fathers and alternated periods of solitude and society; there he turned thirty. At times he was satisfied with the company of his servants and dogs, his walks along the ferny path to the hill dominated by the centenarian oak that in a sense was his own family tree; on other occasions he sought out animation and companionship, received the poets and wits of the court, gave banquets almost every night, held fetes for the neighboring nobles, and for one month the three hundred sixty-five bedchambers of his vast house in the country were occupied every night. And when it seemed that love might come to wound him once again, he fled, having learned his lesson, and asked King Charles to send him as Ambassador Extraordinary to Constantinople.

The account of her life in Turkey was almost telegraphic, for she did not wish to go on at length about the soirees and ceremonies, the services rendered to the Crown; but she did not omit her mysterious marriage to the Gypsy dancer Rosina Pepita. The secret wedding certificate was discovered by his secretaries at the embassy while he was sunk in a profound slumber that lasted for a week and no doubt saved his life, for while he slept there was a rebellion against the sultan, and the insurrectionists who broke into the embassy thought he was dead. At the end of seven days, or, rather, nights, he awoke a woman. A ravishing woman of thirty.

His, or should we say her, marriage to a Gypsy also saved her life, for with the help of Rosina Pepita's tribe she managed to leave Constantinople and, after meeting with a variety of adventures, boarded a merchant ship that returned her to England, a young Englishwoman dressed in the height of fashion.

The ship on which she sailed, and which carried her back to the white cliffs of Dover, was called the *Enamoured Lady*, but many years and several English monarchs and generations would have to elapse before she, by sheerest accident, was to find herself truly transformed into a lady in love. This occurred in the reign of Queen Victoria and as a consequence of a fortuitous fall. Until that time it was a lover she had asked of life. Now, for this was the nature of the Victorian Age, a husband was what she needed. And he appeared at a gallop, tick-tock-tick-tock, and she with her heart beating against the earth, lying facedown on the ground after stumbling over some roots (of an oak tree?), and he went to help her, fearing she was hurt. "I'm dead, sir!" she replied, and a few minutes later they became engaged. And not long afterward they married . . . (On a Tuesday, the twentieth of March, at three o'clock in the morning, she gave birth to a healthy boy about whom she would say nothing . . . Was she a good mother? Was he a good son? How long did he live?) And her husband, who had shortened his long name and came to be called Mar, had sailed away briefly to voyage round Cape Horn. And there, facing the Serpentine, I at last understood that the little toy sailboat was the brig of her Mar, the maritime plaything of waves and tempests.

On that shrunken sea I was occasionally your gondolier, Sinbad the Sailor or the Moor of Venice (row on, Moor . . .), and we were on the verge of plunging into the water fully dressed along the netting that separated bathers from boats . . .

But I left Hyde Park to search for you in the far reaches of southwest London, perhaps where she once lost her way in the distant time of the Tudors. We were here before . . . No! Yes! We've passed this way . . . The excited voices repeating: There's no way out! This way!

You must have guessed by now, though once again I had no luck and have wasted tuppence: I am writing to you from the heart of the hedge maze at Hampton Court. Sitting on one of two benches next to the gnarled tree, and when I raise my head I can see the lion that crowns the great entrance.

Hours later I returned to the center of another maze, vast and intricate, in Curzon Street; in vain I tried to recall which was the façade of her Georgian house. Did she still live in Mayfair, or had she retired to her old house in the country?

I pictured her to myself lost once more in the tide of autos and automatons on Oxford Street, her personality fragmenting along with a constantly fragmenting present. Do we live only in the present? Does the past truly exist?

She might say, and rightly so, that she had a past, and one so long that perhaps the present had not yet had time to come into being. Or that each instant of the present, some trivial detail, the flight of a blue fly against the coffered ceiling or the gleam of a rosy sail or the gentle touch of the strap on an old traveling bag would carry her off, far into the past. Or perhaps in her there beat simultaneously the multiplicity of times and selves she carried within her.

Memories came more quickly than the motorcar she drove along Regent Street, I imagine she smiled as she passed the winged statue of Eros in Piccadilly, turned right into Pall Mall East, circled Trafalgar Square to proceed down Northumberland Avenue, continued right along Victoria Embankment to Westminster Bridge . . .

I would have been pleased to accompany her to her historic manor house, now a kind of museum open to the public at certain hours.

Together we would sip a glass of good Spanish wine, and perhaps tumble into the bed where Queen Elizabeth and King James had slept, removing first, as a precaution, the notice with its inevitable legend: PLEASE DO NOT TOUCH . . .

And she would be likely to lead me along the ferny path to the centenarian oak tree and we would stretch out on the grass as if we were still in Hyde Park and she were about to exclaim Ecstasy! as she contemplated the pool now darkened by nightfall.

In the light of the invisible moon, sitting in Berkeley Square and facing the ill-smelling gray plastic bags that lean against the railing, I became almost tragicosmic and wondered if they are really dead, those dead stars whose light we still perceive.

Patently red-skinned, she lies facedown in the canoe, stretching to her full height (six feet!) while I so care-ah-fully smear Nivea on her long long legs. Burning, like her bony sharp shoulders and the narrow red patch of her back. She turned her pointed Iroquois profile toward me and bit the thin line of her tightened lips. She was in the middle of an aah or an ooh. Even though she was so dark. Ah, rub it in well. Finishing up the jar. Don't poke . . . aha, earlier you smear her aquiline nose. More like an owl's. The mark of eyeglasses on the bridge. Two burning coals for eyes. And I too (after so much mutual solace) had my own overdose of old sol. It would be my turn next . . . I'll smear you, too—but there'd be no cream left. The red badge of heat on my knees. The scarlet leprosy of my thighs. Nivead Nereid aaah! . . . (Her cry in the water . . .)

Paludal pictography. A world of signs in the Dummersee. Le lac des signes: V, le vol des cygnes into the setting sun. Swans, or geese, or some other web-footed waterfowl? I did not share the ornithological passion of Erich's father—Erich was my holiday companion. We should have brought old man Kendziak's field glasses. Erich was far away by now, in the other canoe, with the friend of my redskin. Who rested her bony back against my chest while I persisted in perusing the lake scenery:

S, the silhouette of the diving loon almost like the S on our rented canoe: S5, black on white iiiiii . . . , the line of chicks coming out of the canebrake. And two geese paddling toward the canoe: 22. And three, a great swallow swoops and glances off the surface of the water: 3. Its extended claws (43!!) raised two large exclamation points at our bow.

Downstrokes of drumsticks in the marsh. Nice and slow, good lakeography: my shorthand typist standing next to the canoe, inscribing my name in the water with her slender asparagus-forefinger. And dotting the i with a little circle or watery cipher. A water nymph's writing. And on the spot I had to tell her the quaint aquatic tale of Ondine, l'amour fou de Fouqué, whose real name was Elizabeth von Breitenbach. Bess from the Big Brook. My God, what's in a water name? Or maybe, I'm not sure now, was it Breitenbauch? Big Belly?

Fine hair (black locks trickling over her right shoulder) on my belly. Black on blue. Would she notice? Rocked back and forth in the canoe. She closed her eyes and moved her head against the straining blue of my bathing suit. I'm getting you all wet! But I didn't care. Can she feel me hardening beneath her temple? Erecting? I caressed her arms, her humerus-cubitus-radius, I barely brushed her eyelids with my lips. Her warm temple, was it nodding its assent? She opened her eyes looking straight into the Prussian blue sky: there on the horizon the great winged V, feathers at full velocity. She too might have said in passing: a bird of paradise in hand is worth two of Emil exploding . . .

A paradise of passing moments. Let inane eternity evanesce in the ether . . . This swallow does the summer make. This July afternoon does not brown and wither. The back and forth of the waves. My undine undulating in the lake. What is fleeting does not lack in intensity. The burning sun still burns. The fly's sting on my forearm still stings. And that kiss that tastes of cherry plums, savor it. Carpe diem! tout court: the fishermen with their rods there on the shore and beneath them the girl with the slippery smooth belly leaps like a carp.

Rapid little nibbles, floating in the lake and holding on with both hands to the edge of the canoe while I placed in her mouth—one and one more and then one more—a kilo of cherry plums. A little Indian snack for a Tuesday afternoon.

Dejected thinkers: that late Tuesday afternoon in the hot gray mist. I laid the paddle across the canoe, slowly drifting. In front of me, withdrawn, who knows what my long and lanky redskin was thinking (the night before I had learned, from her friend, that she had a fiancé; but in the morning, the first time I saw her, I had already seen her engagement ring), with her bony knees against her temples and her chin pressing to her chest. Were we real or mere apparitions that would disappear again in the turbid air? The great swallows almost grazed us as if the canoe were empty.

Small details, of small significance? to remember her from beginning to end. Begin at the beginning. A resting place and restaurant. Pension Holkenbrink, in that almost lakeside village Dummerlohhausen, where I met her. That Monday late in July. After looking in vain for lodgings in Lembruch, we came to the other end of the lake, to tranquil Dummerlohhausen, the sun in our faces, a little before eight in the morning, and Erich the Red (more precisely, an almost bald redhead) stopped his motorcycle in front of a building that was new, spacious, and clean, with flowers at the windows and a garden: HOLKENBRINKS PEN-SIONHAUS. A truly complete pension. We arrived in time for breakfast (they had a room for us) and before dispatching the potato salad and selection of sausages (a string of them: Knack-Schlack-Blut-Leberwurst!), the bread and butter and real coffee, we had already divided between us the two early-rising guests: the one who was nothing but skin and bone and longer than a day without bread, for this Quixote; and for Erich the stout Sancho Panzer the plump allure of the fleshy girl who surely did not suffer from anemia though her name was Anne-mie. Mine (in a wasp-waisted dress belted in white and yellow) I estimated to be between twenty-five and twenty-nine years old, but she was actually twenty-three. As was her friend. Both of them stenotypists in nearby Osnabrück. And it seemed they too were going to swim in the lake that morning.

Too much sun. Where are the snowy Niveas of yesteryear? Ay, smear it on after making love. The second night, in my room. (Erich enjoying himself the whole night with Annemie at the other end of the lake—the charm of Lembruch by night! We had discovered that one passed easily from our room to theirs by a connecting eave.) Paludic and ludic when we touched. Trembling with fever when our hairs made contact, electric pubises. The harp of her ribs. The xylophone of her spine. Her breasts two small coppery cymbals. The tight tambourine of her belly. A musical scale of moans. And after supper, we lubricated one another again. Ah, yoking the beautybeast with two backs. Red hot. And her coral snake arms burned me. Laocoontented . . . in spite of the heat. But that night not everything was making love and setting each other on fire. In the middle of the night she woke feeling nauseated. She had eaten the two pork pies (I didn't have the courage to try mine) I bought for supper. And I played the solicitous nurse, holding her forehead as she threw up reddish yellow clots—of pork, I speculated, and verified it de visu, not turning up my nose at the vividly colored sight. Then I helped her to rinse her mouth and get back into bed, and I folded a pillow under her neck: Du biss gutt!—yes, I was a very good boy. And a little later, the violent convulsions of the nocturnal storm.

Eating her, that night, before supper. Man does not live by

bread and water alone. A brief struggle before overcoming her resistance. I slid my mouth along the smooth delight of her belly tasting of cherry plums though I, fainthearted, did not reach the anus mirabilis. Oh ma belle de nuit! Still she attempted to move away. Rocking her back and forth from right to left, like this, succulent cunnilingustation. Impaling her with my cunning tongue. I opened the red valves (that afternoon, on one of her dives into the lake, she had come up with two freshwater mussels in a handful of mud: one was dead; but the other resisted— the mollusk was pure muscle!—our opening it for our lesson in biology: mantle, byssus, beard . . .) and with the tip of my tongue I licked (we'll talk about palpi and palpation another day . . .) her small tuberous swelling. Licked and licked again, and sucked longingly. Another greedy lick and her voluptuous little scream, just one. And then, the powerful clamp of her knees moved me away from the marshy salt lick.

Perfumes of yesterday. The aroma of waffles (the cone crackling in her large teeth powdered white) and thin broth and damp earth, here on the bank of the Thames, brought her back into my arms, and all that's missing is the night and the grinding of the circular saw on the outskirts of the village. And for a moment I thought the red and white umbrellas at this pub at the end of Old Palace Lane leading steeply down to the river were those at the Beach Café Schomaker junior. (O! Maker!—in old Oldenburg they couldn't pronounce the initial sch . . .) And the little glass of liquor after the meal, as we watched a long white wake in the sky unravel, had sip by sip—Schnapsidee!— the sweet coolness of the clouded water of life we drank on the last night in the canoe that should have been a burning piragua. Tooth-to-tooth, and we could almost chew on the thick fog of the lake.

Poco a poco, little by little, on this, another July afternoon, the images—and sounds and smells and tastes—of that holiday on Lake Dummer return. Again, the bumblebee droning around the pints of beer (Hummelancholy! J'ai le bourdon . . .) brought back the memory of the other bee she rescued from the water on that first afternoon and set out to dry in the sun on the tip of the canoe. I'd be tempted to drink a shandy to its health. And three afternoons later she picked all those slugs, one by one, out of the ditch and carried them to safety. Moved to tears by one that was squashed. That was the afternoon she told me she had been deflowered at the age of fifteen by one of her professors. A prof proficient with prophylactics. Later came the driving rain. And it drove us to take refuge. There behind the poplar. Against the poplar. In the shelter of the poplar. Trembling poplar. In low-heeled shoes she was as tall as I. We made love standing up. How my knees shook afterward. We were soaked to the skin. The last time we made love outdoors. But before I come to the end, I want to refresh more recent recollections for you.

You and I made a pilgrimage to Gravesend—is it three years already, late March or early April?—to lay a daffodil recently picked at the Royal Terrace Pier (you would have preferred to find snowdrops, dogtooth violets, and snapdragons in the garden next to St. George's church) on the grave of the Indian princess transplanted from her native Virginia to the court of King James I, because you had been reading that garnet-colored novelized biography from which you would recite for me selected passages, such as the ending, almost sobbing: She smiled, was content, and sank gently into death . . . Or something like that. At the age of twenty-two. A brief imaginary life. I must have told you then, in that church as cold as a refrigerator or a whitened sepulcher, not about the real Indian princess buried there since 1617 but about the German redskin I baptized with her name, Don Juan the Baptist, both of us immersed in the waters of the Dummer. In reality her baptismal name didn't matter very much, Selma didn't suit her, just as few people recall that the Indian princess was baptized Rebecca. Even fewer know that her true name—her secret name—was Matoaka. Unless it was Matoata. Names to maintain anonymity. Selma Wientge. She too had a true name, Pultuke, which I gave her pretending to be a caveman. Me Uthutze, you Pultuque . . . Tarzan of the Apex! And we invented a crude neolithic language with words like weapons for hunting down wild prey, exes like axes of stone and kays as cutting as flint blades and arrs like harpoons, which she softened talking softly in bed as if she were murmuring at the muddy bottom of the lake, slithering eelingualanguage, languid . . . Those were our true names. Uthutzepultuqueing in our Stone Age, fishing for salmon and curing bearskins. A clean-living girl, her only concern was that we wouldn't know how to make soap. Nor did she forget to put o.b. tampons in her pouch (that brand never fails to intrigue me) which, she was certain, she would begin to use on the following Friday. And observing the fine embroidery around the smallpox vaccination mark on the arm of my redskin on the Dummer, it didn't occur to me then that the poor Indian princess in fact died of smallpox in Gravesend as she was preparing to return to her native Virginia.

Powwow: an assembly of redskins. I came to Richmond, that riche monde of signs, to remember them. And follow your trail. The old crank of a bookseller in Richmond Hill sent you his regards (the clock next to the shopwindow is still stopped at 4:30, Greenwich time), but first he turned red with rage and coughing (yes, he was hardly phlegmatic) because his current shop assistant had put *Amerika* in the travel section. Kafkaput! The other customer (a stout Teuton?), a rubicund man with four hairs to brush and eyeglasses like Truman's, seemed to seriously disapprove of my jokes. Still! We are not amused . . . And he continued dusting off newspapers from the pile.

Ducks in the water. The hoarse vibration of the plane (:You haven't gone to Cyprus? The Greek and Turkish fleets are steaming there full speed ahead for an all-out sea battle. I also wonder if Miss Rose is still in Greece. Or has finally decided to come back. Her cat won't recognize her. Or vice versa. Yesterday at noon he ran away into the park and refused to come out of the tree. The elm of my hell. Shaking his tin of food at the foot of the tree. Why are you doing this to me, Why? But you don't have to travel very far to find danger. Miss Rose's *Times* confirms it today: the doors of the Tower of London have been opened again to tourists. Where will the next bomb go off?) furrowing the surface of the blue lake with its shores of cottony fog, toward Twickenham, made me cross the lagoon of forgetfulness with the whistle of an arrow, Pfeilf! and the roar of that reactor on the Dummer that frightened the grebe we were watching from the canoe.

First kiss, underwater. Grebe-style. Our first kiss. Subaqueous. That Monday afternoon, again on the lake, standing next to the canoe. She and her friend had spent eight days on vacation and would leave on Friday morning. There was no time to lose. I took her by the hand, a little farther out, pronounced her Indian name, she caught my eye, hesitated for half a turn, and we submerged completely to kiss one another away from prying eyes. 1, 2, 3 . . . I could have counted to 27. When my undine began to dive, that morning, she could stay under for 27 seconds. But, gallant chronometricler, I told her 32 and shook my head as if I could not believe my own eyes. But then, in the canoe, we kissed until we lost count and, almost, consciousness. (By the following night we could do mouth-to-mouth like expert first-aid givers, though we never could avoid the chin-chin of our spectacles as thick as the bottom of a glass. Diligent students of lively tongues and living languages.) The clouds in the southeast accumulated like dusty sacks, the waves turned gray, and the trees violently shook out their wild hairdos. It was there, coming closer and closer, our daily storm. Racing, running before the wind!

Scenes of photographic clarity. My redskin mounted on the prow of the white canoe, hair wet and the line of her lips blue. A cool Tuesday morning. Her slender legs spurring the water on. I pushed her—Into the lake!—and she still smiled at me from the water. Instructions for lifting herself back into the canoe. Up you go! Oops! At the end of her holiday, or almost, I would take note of the various bruises, black-and-bluish green, that colored her thighs. Which did not stop me from resting my head on them.

Paragraph by paragraph, I try to remember her all over again. So that the brief summer idyll will never end. Though it could only last till Friday morning. She never had any illusions. On Wednesday, surrounded by foliage, watching a procession of worker ants, my provisional grasshopper acknowledged that what we had together perhaps could only have endured if she could have always been, every hour, every day, my redskin from another time, and if we could have lived our lakeside passion untroubled by fears of becoming pregnant, certainly a cogent etcetera. And I don't wish to leave till the end the tears that ran down her cheeks with the rain on Thursday. That Thursday afternoon, lost from view in an empty field. I called her by her Indian princess name and her tears came faster, her smeared little owl mask contracted, she cleared her throat, and out came the heartbreaking cry of a crow. (Lady into raven, Nevermore . . .) I pressed my face to hers, it was no laughing matter this sorrow of my spotted owl, and I rocked away her hiccrying and craving, cradling the nape of her neck in my palm. Early the next morning, at five, I walked with her to the bus that would take her away forever. I recalled her at other moments as I made the rounds of Richmond all afternoon. The bend in the river, visible on the far horizon from the heights of Richmond Hill, a great comma between trembling leaves, brought me abruptly back to the Dummer. First view, first morning, from Lembruch. Lake scenery painted with a palette knife by an Impressionist painter: blue, with smears of white and yellow (water lilies) and green splotches (islets of bulrushes). In a dream my red-skinned undine rises as tall and skinny and naked as a reed from the middle of the lake (giacomettic-skeletal, like the articulated wooden figurines the ancient Egyptians would pass around at banquets, crack! croc! . . . Eat, drink, and be mer—) and with head bowed she raised up from the water with both hands, dangling from a line like a large lead weight, a sun globe with serpentine rays. At this, the poplars along the wide path that encircles the lake became agitated and turned gray. In the center of the Dummer, beneath the globe of the sun, a canoe with two people paddling . . . And suddenly, a wall of fog. We paddle rapidly to cross it. And another one. We paddle even more rapidly, splashing frantically, but we cannot make our way out of the vast halls of heavy fog. And in the mazes around Richmond Green I saw us again on Wednesday night navigating in our S5 toward the nebula of Orion. Traveling light: a bottle of schnaps. As night fell I decided to try the smoky liquor in the brawling bars of Bayswater. When I came out of the station, the moon was a luminous parenthesis closing over Queensway:)

Quarters
and half-dollars . . . , she murmured, dreaming perhaps of her savings, the girl who for some time now had been nodding against my shoulder in the bus that passed among white cotton fields at nightfall.

And despite the mask of makeup, the heavy mascara deepening the blackness of her eyes and the red of her fiery lips, I should have guessed she was no more than seventeen years old and had run away from home.

Her skimpy white dress (sent as an Easter present by her eternally absent mother, I later learned, who had not yet realized that by now her little girl had grown taller than she was) had no more to give in spite of her repeated tugging, too short as it was for thighs like hers, and hours later, when she told me she had been working as a waitress in Memphis, I deduced that her body must have been a provocation even for the pimps who frequented the bars on Gayoso Street.

The bus stopped at the Texas border and she agreed to accompany me to the Look Motel in La Mirada (beneath the neon sign a great electric eye was blinking), no doubt because she had no other place to drop with exhaustion. And because she hoped—and was she right?—that I would leave a few dollars as a memento.

If when the night was half gone the cries of her nightmare had not wakened me and I had not taken her drenched with perspiration into my arms, attempting to calm her, perhaps she never would have told me the vicissitudes of her life.

She had dreamed again that her uncle was pursuing her in his car—the same tenacious Ford of other real pursuits in the Mississippi hamlet that was her home—through the fields while she tried to run faster with the heavy jangling bag that held the treasure (a bag filled only with small change) into the nearby woods; but her feet were caught in the tangled roots of a tree and her pursuer had almost reached her. She saw his devil's face with two dark curls like horns at both sides of his forehead and his savage smile as he opened his razor . . .

One might say he was Evil incarnate to his niece, who at first twisted her hands in anguish and as she spoke of him clenched her fists and her teeth, increasing the fury with the sibilant sound of her words.

Squatting on the bed in step-ins far too pink, from time to time she moved aside with a rough movement of her hand her dark hair to reveal the deep blackness of her hatred. Widening her close-set black eyes with fear, at times, or narrowing them hard with rage. And so with her head raised toward the ceiling or toward an invisible heaven, pleading and defenseless, for a moment I caught a glimpse of her eyes like the eyes of Goya's little dog half-buried in the sand or in the magma of an enigma.

She put on a black kimono pulled from among the clothes in her traveling bag, but in a few minutes, reliving one of her confrontations with her uncle, she began to slide it along her shoulders and the gesture left her half-naked again.

She evoked a stormy breakfast when her uncle accused her of delinquency and would have beat her with his belt if not for the intervention of the black cook who had also stopped her from throwing a glass of water at her uncle.

Her upper lip trembled with an insistent tic as she relived the scene.

I tried to quiet her, putting my arm around her waist and telling her in a honeyed voice to sit down, Sit down, honey . . . , trying to kiss her. That honey not made for the mouth of a mule because she began to laugh as if she were braying a sarcastic honey, honey, honey . . . and said the only person who called her that was the damned black cook. Damned, yes, that is what she said even though she told me the Negro woman had raised her since she was a baby with the greatest devotion just as she had done with her mother and her three uncles. In reality when her youngest uncle, the Benjamin of that tribe, bleated in fear or fury the damned old Negress still rocked him in her arms, a hulking man of thirty-three who had been her first playmate though sixteen years older than she (: in one of her first memories she saw herself in the house of the nephew of the black cook playing beside him on the floor with spools of thread that began to roll but her great overgrown uncle tried to take them away from her and made her cry), the drooling dolt of the family, and it started to sicken her watching him eat or rooting like a hog at the table clutching at a slipper of satin yellowing with age as if it were a crust of bread, the idiot.

Seeing her all painted like this and her no less vulgar gestures and sashaying, it was difficult to believe she was the last offshoot of one of the most distinguished families in the South, my miss from Mississippi, and the great-great-granddaughter of a governor of the state, great-granddaughter of a general, and granddaughter of a lawyer who declaimed verses of Horace and Catullus as he emptied glass after glass of whiskey and eventually sold to a golf club his last pasture next to his mansion with the peeling Greek columns to send to Harvard his firstborn son, who ended his first year of law school before he ended his own life, drowning for no cause other than the lost honor of his sister, and to marry his only daughter to a young banker from Indianapolis who then cast her off because his calculations of his approaching paternity did not add up.

And most definitely he also sold his family's last piece of land in order to continue his dangerous drinking because the doctor had repeatedly predicted that he was killing himself.

There is no old southern family without tares blighting its Tara and its bloodline, and she perhaps was attempting to escape, without knowing it and in vain, the family inheritance. Like mother like daughter . . . , as her determinist grandmother would say, that stiffly erect complaining white-haired lady with eyes as black as hers who had forbidden any mention of her mother's name in the house.

As for her father, she never knew him; and it is likely that her own mother, as promiscuous as she must have been, from such unholy oaks such acorns grow, did not even know precisely which one he was among the crowd of night beaux who breathed in the perfume of honeysuckle on the swing in the discreet corner of the garden where the daughter also swayed in the swing with commercial travelers, touring actors, and Don Juans who were passing through, for the local swains had all already swung their fill in that swing.

When the flashy suitor in the red tie appeared with the carnival show that had just come to the hamlet she could not help falling for the bait. And she was not afraid to be seen with him, even to walk in defiance in front of the farm-implements store where her uncle worked. When he saw the red tie, and the red-painted face of his niece, he saw everything red.

Fortunately he did not see the man with the fiery tie as he

was seen by his idiot brother and the black adolescent who took care of him, in the garden of the family manor swaying so elegantly with his niece and then making his magic passes. He put into and took out of his mouth a lit cigarette leaving the idiot and the black boy openmouthed and making his impatient beloved turn flaming red with fury. He was a variety performer this pitchman and also knew, among his other turns, how to pluck at a saw as if it were a banjo.

And he never saw, luckily, how his niece slipped through the darkness down the pear tree whose branches rasped against the window of her bedroom (the grandmother vainly locked her in every night) to meet the artiste with the red necktie in the swing in the garden, under the cypress trees, as she had been doing almost every night with her successive traveling lovers.

But her uncle was not as interested in what she did in the dark as in what she might seem to be doing in broad daylight and in full view of everyone, bringing disgrace to him and to his family.

And so when he saw her again with the man in the red tie speeding by in a car, stolen no doubt he told himself, that came at him head-on and suddenly swerved and sped away, he clenched his teeth and pressed the accelerator and began the pursuit.

He lost them in the outlying lanes of the hamlet and drove into the countryside. He even had to run on foot across fields trying to find them. He followed the marks of the tires, he plowed through the briers and underbrush of the woods tracking like a hunting dog. At last, under a sun like white-hot lead, in a sandy ditch, he saw the unholy Ford. As he ran toward it it started up and went off fast, the horn blowing like a squealing pig.

When he went back to his own car he discovered that to top

off everything they had let the air out of his tires. The last drop of gall that made the cup of his patience overflow, and the chalice of his passion, because the pain in his head was not to be borne, each throb a brier in his crown of thorns.

But his true chronic splitting headache was his niece. Even before she was born she had caused problems. It was that bastard child's fault that his sister was left without the banker and he without the job the banker had promised him in his bank. And the girl had even been senselessly baptized by her mother with the name of the suicide brother who had not only lost his own life but had made the family lose its last strip of land as well.

This was why he tried to compensate in part for his losses by taking the money sent every month by his prodigal sister over the past sixteen years for the support and maintenance of her daughter.

The proud lady with the white hair ritually burned every month the checks her daughter sent using the match lit for her by her Sole-Support-of-the-Family son. In fact they were counterfeit checks of no value which he had skillfully substituted for the real ones.

The day before her flight the bastard daughter had insistently demanded from her uncle the money her mother had sent in her last letter. She had to settle for the ten dollars he gave her but she knew he was robbing her again.

Why did she need the money with so much urgency?

She took it with her own hand on the night of Holy Saturday and when her idiot uncle and the fourteen-year-old black boy who took care of him, her former playmates, saw her climb down the pear tree as she had on other nights they did not know that it was her final descent down the Tree of Sin and that she was running away after breaking open a small metal box in the locked bedroom-sanctuary of her uncle and taking almost seven thousand dollars: four thousand that he had been robbing from her for sixteen years, month by month, and almost three thousand that her uncle had been hoarding, penny by penny, over a period of almost twenty years.

Rob a thief and be pardoned I almost blurted out without taking into account that the sentence might be for life . . .

The seducer in the red tie stole not only her heart but also, within a few days of her running away with him, the seven thousand dollars he had encouraged her to steal.

I have spelled out my Q for you looking for you in Kew Gardens, spelled just as it sounds. Quel Q! I hear you murmur, and yet I don't know if I should have come today to the gardens of Kew because this afternoon I saw you, I swear or could swear it was you, in the maze of old clothes stalls in the open-air market at Camden Town. I saw your hair, your hips swaying in pants as sheer as gauze. You disappeared among perverse Persian carpets behind which three unveiled odalisques were trying on ethereal garments.

I was still looking for you along Camden High Street but the noisy Greek Cypriot pro-Makarios demonstrators and their clashes with the supporters of the Greek junta blocked my way. In any case, better to see you here than to suppose you are in Cyprus.

Strolling beneath the vault of glass and palms, just a while ago, I thought of other, wilder palms and of the path that will be taken in life by my miss from Mississippi if she has managed to reach Los Angeles. She fled her uncle (his only option was to pursue her because he could not go to the police about the robbery that he himself had been committing for sixteen years) and looked for her mother while still pursuing her lover in the red tie.

The last known residence of her mother was Hollywood, where she lived with a moving picture producer and then divorced him three years ago in Mexico. And she did not forget that her lover with the red tie had ambitions to be a comic actor and his Mecca was Hollywood.

His number with the saw-banjo could be a success. If his wings were not cut first . . .

Sitting now across from the high Pagoda, unreal tower in this typically English twilight, I have become something of a Buddhist and tell myself that our lives are mere imaginary projections. Illusions of the Look . . .

I went so far as to wonder if she could be pregnant, though nothing was noticeable yet, and perhaps that was the reason for her asking her uncle so insistently for the money and in the end stealing it from him.

I never felt so miserable as I did in the Look Motel (I hope to God it is not the look of the Ubiquitous Eye) that morning. All I had was a fifty-dollar bill. I slipped away like a thief while she slept, and on the night table I left the little box that gleamed like a coin. A.M.B. Adieu Ma Belle . . . Still one rubber. But probably she wouldn't need it now. It was my gift and my theft. One rubber.

le Douanier could have painted her as the sleeping beauty in the tropical forest of the night, lying on a bed of bracken and ferns and surrounded by eyes burning bright as fruits hidden among the luxuriant vegetation.

Indeed, the so-called Customs Agent would have had to classify her as contraband on the murky frontier between different kingdoms.

Animal and vegetable: her pale temples, straw-colored like a fawn's, accentuated the perfume that her body exhaled of earth-flesh, fungi, the smells of captured forest dampness, moss and mushrooms in the deep woods.

Masculine and feminine: her broad, bony shoulders, her long feet, her figure as tall as an ungainly boy's, made the bitter smile of a lost woman even more troubled and troubling, more out of place on her childish face with its gently rounded chin.

Celestial and infernal: many churches in Paris were suddenly visited by the strange American believer, recently converted to Catholicism, who sometimes, kneeling in prayer, ended her orisons with impious laughter. A woman, one of her lovers, even accused her of trafficking with unholy spirits.

Angel or beast?: her short pale hair hung in the curls of a Renaissance cherub, almost on a level with the finely arched left eyebrow, and contrasted at times with the unqualified rage in the cruel iris of a wild beast that dilated the mysterious blue of her eyes.

I will not add other conterminous kingdoms in which to situate, in all her ambiguity, the girl, more a graceful creature than a beauty sleeping in the forest of the dark night of the soul, for there were hidden areas in her that could be penetrated only by a poet with a mystic vein, or perhaps one marked by madness.

I said sleeping, but in truth she was in a faint.

That is how I saw her for the first time, in her room, number 29, in a small hotel on the Place Saint-Sulpice, across from the church. One of those typical middle-class hostelries in the Latin Quarter that adds luster to its two stars with an illustrious-sounding name: Hôtel Récamier.

She lay sprawled on the bed, surrounded by a confusion of potted plants, exotic palms, and cut flowers.

I saw her at first as a painting by Rousseau, but immediately superimposed on the *naïf* vision was the fine illusion of a Magritte: the jungle of the Customs Agent was trapped in a bourgeois drawing room, its walls, even the ceiling, completely papered in plants and gaudy flowers on a garnet background identical to the red of the carpet.

And the face of the American girl (she was no more than twenty) was framed by her long, beautiful hands.

Her face seemed serene in her unconscious state, but I am going to concentrate now on her hands, for their sensuality at times astonished me (as well as her husband). She had the uncertain, intense touch of the blind. Her hesitant fingers would extend into a gentle touch that came to rest in resolute avidity. But again, tentative, trembling, silken, her fingertips would slide softly, exploring the surface of pleasure in a prolonged caress. And she had lavished her caresses equally on men and women.

No, not equally: with greater frequency—and I try to imagine the delicacy of her avid desire—on those of her own sex.

There she lay, heavy and disheveled, half flung off the support of the cushions, and her legs, in white flannel trousers, were spread as in an interrupted dance. But her black thick-lacquered pumps looked ready to resume the cakewalk again.

I would still be staring at her in stunned admiration if her compatriot Dr. O'Connor, who had brought me with him from the Café de la Mairie across the *place* to assist the fainted woman, had not urged me to slap her wrists. She woke for a moment when the doctor flung a handful of water into her face. She opened her eyes, "I was all right," and could not have been as well as she said because she immediately fell back into the pose of her annihilation.

The curved, bent figure of the doctor, partially hidden by the screen beside the bed, made strange passes, the movements common to an alchemist or a man of magic, and with the skill of a "dumbfounder" he slipped into the limbo of his pocket a loose hundred-franc note lying on the night table. She did not recover the bill but she did regain consciousness, after a while, and even recognized the doctor, who helped her recall that they had seen each other on other occasions in the Café de la Mairie du VIe.

A month after her fainting spell, more or less, she married one of Dr. O'Connor's friends; another patron of the Café de la Mairie, an employee of the Crédit Lyonnais, and allegedly an Austrian baron, he was a man twenty-seven years her senior named Felix, though she brought him little felicity. The Baron wanted a male child to carry on the title created by his father, an Italian Jew called Guido. Soon after she married, she could not bear to remain in the house, and she went out to seek independence and solitude. She would wander alone through the outskirts of the city, at times she would take the first train to the first city that came to mind, and once she disappeared for three days that seemed eternal to her anguished husband. She would come back at all hours, as if nothing had happened, and her flights also seemed to make her memory fly away. She ardently embraced the Catholic religion when she was already carrying a child, and she took to visiting the churches of Paris: Saint-Germain-des-Prés, Sainte-Clotilde, Saint-Merri, Saint-Julien-le-Pauvre . . . , hoping, perhaps, for a revelation.

She drained the chalice to the dregs, then looked for consolation—or revelation—in drink. The child grew like a tumor in her womb.

She was delivered at night—completely drunk—of the new Guido. The Baron must have told himself with satisfaction: I did it! But she, who gave birth swearing and cursing, could not accept the child she had never desired and once again took to the streets at night, a pathetic peripatetic who frequented bars and returned home at any hour. On more than one occasion her husband had to turn his back and pretend he had not seen that woman leaning on the bar, alone and laughing, her hair swinging over her eyes, staring into the void of her glass. My God, how easily the bold hands of other drinkers pawed at her.

And one fine day or fateful night she said to the unhappy Felix: I'll get out! dragging her cloak with the defiant swagger of a bullfighter, and disappeared from his life. The husband, perhaps, was not entirely unhappy because he kept his son, who, however, turned out to be mentally defective. But a hereditary blot is the best documentation for the purity of blue blood. As Dr. O'Connor told him, with his customary eloquence, madness is the last muscle left to the aristocracy. Surely he meant the tendon of its Achilles' heel. And the Baron convinced himself that he had not lost his wife because she was in Guido, and so, in his way, he had also kept her.

I believe that if I have fixed her in the painting of my first Rousseauian vision, it is to enclose her there so that she does not become yet another Fugitive.

From time to time I sat at night on the green bench across from the Hôtel Récamier, in the darkest corner of the *place*, spying, in the light of the two lanterns at the entrance, on the clients who gathered there.

She will return as she did in times past, I would tell myself, and the illusion became more intense if the two windows on the second floor were also lit.

Lulled by the murmur of the fountain, its skirts of water gleaming in the dark, festooned with stitches of foam.

The tall figure in the unbuttoned overcoat, hands thrust into pockets, who walked, feet dragging slightly, past the columns of the church and crossed to the hotel. She? No, a he, somewhat inebriated.

I thought I might find her as I made my nocturnal rounds, visiting the pubs and cafés on Fulham Road. Even when I came to the Small Café to look for you.

And for a moment I thought I saw her, in the gilt-framed mirror pitted with lunatic pockmarks, or fly shit, offering her slender neck to the female vampire in the tailored black suit. Do tribades come in triads? Now a third Grace joined them, wearing the kind of green hat with a feather favored by Robin of the Forests of the Night, her tiger eyes burning bright as the three women kiss and greet one another with enthusiasm.

The bonze mannequin—the bonzesse, as you would say—has not yet arrived. This café seems decaffeinated without her mad head gleaming like a billiard ball. A rasping kiss on her razored head. A sound like sandpaper . . . You wouldn't prefer, would you, a candy-sweet kiss on those large red lips?

Too much smoke and I fan myself with this morning's wrinkled newspaper. (Guay gobbled down the crossword. A crossword-loving cat catches no errata . . .) I trust you are not one of the forty thousand tourists trapped in the crossfire on Cyprus. When the bullet or bomb kills, who cares if it's Turkish or Greek? Fifty dead this afternoon, it seems, following the attacks on Famagusta by Turkish planes. Hotels were not spared in the bombings. Last night I dreamed you were with other refugees, most of them women and children, in a dusty ditch, perhaps along the highway from Nicosia to Kyrenia, and some soldiers, their faces covered with branches and leaves, forced all of you to dig a great trench. The firing woke me and when I sat up I saw your ghostly silhouette, yet it was only your English cloak that still hangs on the door to my room. I wrapped it around me and went down to the Green with the cat. Soliloquy au clair de lune of a streetlight. A repeated why or guay beneath the cape. I too could have meowed a pitiful *pour quoi*. The gentleman with the cat on his chest. All I needed was the hat to look like Sandeman.

She too liked to buy extravagant antique clothing, filmy silk skirts or heavy brocade tunics.

At the end of three or four months she returned to Paris, returned to the VIe, in the company of Nora, a compatriot some thirty years of age whom she had met in New York at a performance of the Denckman Circus.

They moved to an apartment in the Rue du Cherche-Midi, in an old house with a garden.

Gradually, in the years they lived together, her nocturnal departures acquired a slowly increasing rhythm. At first her lover attempted to accompany her, to participate with her as she went from drinks to drunken companions, from table to table, touching, from acquaintances to assignations, but Nora soon allowed her to go out alone because she knew she would eventually lose her if she curtailed her liberty, or libertinism, her instinct to be a nomad of the night.

One night as she waited for her, lying awake as usual, Nora saw another woman embracing her beside the statue in the garden.

She was a middle-aged woman, also an American, four times a widow and therefore wealthy, whose name was Jenny. Her beaked profile and thin body made one think of Olive, beloved of Popeye.

With tall Nora and tiny Jenny, she maintained for a time, though with certain ups and downs, the ménage or surménage à trois, or the stress, the tempestuous torments, of three-sided jealousy. But in the end she left Nora and went back to America with Jenny, who, in turn, tasted the torments of Nora as she paced the solitude of her room, caught on the treadmill of jealousy and pre-resentiments, while her love with the restless ass went back to her vagabond ways, prowling the stations, riding the trains, wandering the countryside.

Round and round in infernal ever-narrowing circles.

Until she drew near Nora's old family estate and the barking bloodhound that made her return to the pure animality of madness.

When I referred to conterminous kingdoms I forgot to mention animal and human. Where does the territory of the irrational begin?

In the ancient chapel that belonged to Nora's family, on a deserted hill, in that ruined whitened sepulchre, she went out one night to meet the dog face-to-face beside the altar; his hackles standing, his tongue like a tatter of blood, the dog moves back quivering while she moves toward him on all fours, barking and laughing, barking her laughter. And me, on another night not fit for a dog, the obscene bitch in heat made me growl and whimper, tremble with fear and excitement, shiver and sob.

S_{t.}

Martin's Lane will be lively soon, when the theaters let out, and I properly chose the Salisbury—the actors' pub—to recall one more time and with one more beer the memories of my English actress from Berlin.

An actress, and on top of that a singer.

The fact is I never saw her in any role, except when she played the part of her own vaudevillian life, and I heard her sing only once, badly but to great effect, in a small Montparnasse bar in the middle of Schöneberg, near a corner on Tauentzien-strasse.

Someone, I hear her voice again, husky, *exactly,* low, *like you,* and her brilliant lips inflate or inflame into a kiss.

She was attractive, and at the same time there was something irresistibly comic in her appearance: perhaps her dark little head with its very short hair looked too small for her body, like the head of a long-legged wading bird, or her great brown eyes seemed disproportionate in a face so long and thin, or were too light, as if they had been artificially implanted beneath the black fringe of hair and the heavy black pencil that outlined them. Or perhaps it was the dead-white makeup on her cheeks, almost like a clown's, that contrasted so with her long black silk dress.

She sang absentmindedly, *Now I know why Mother,* with a

carelessness and indifference that had a certain charm, her hands hanging limp at her sides.

Slender and nervous, they were streaked with veins like the hands of an older woman. But she was only nineteen, though I thought she was twenty-five when I saw her for the first time a few days earlier, on an autumn afternoon at Fritz's flat. Fritz was one of my private students.

The first thing I noticed while she dialed, in our presence, the number of one of her numerous lovers, was the emerald (heraldic vert?) or coleopterous green, I don't know what to call it, on her nails. Egyptian scarabs. Beetle nails . . .

And yellowish fingers much stained by heavy cigarette smoking.

I too smoked endlessly as I waited for you, full of hope, in the Torino, camouflaged behind my respectable *Times* (I trust, at least, that you haven't decided to travel to the north of India, because cases of smallpox are on the increase, especially in Uttar Pradesh: so far this year 22,556 people have died), looking from time to time at the fleeting faces on Oxford Street. I don't know why, but this morning Torino began to ring in my head. Not your favorite café. Unless it was the city. You always wanted to see the Holy Shroud with your own eyes. A holy hankering . . . I saw you crossing the street swaying on your high cork-platform soles, but the vision vanished next to the window I was looking through: she really was lame, and what I thought a backpack was her hump. Oxford Circus phenomena, and I continued to wait for the miracle . . . My patience and the pack came to an end, and I went to look around Soho.

As I walked down Argyll Street, I burst into laughter, annoying those waiting in line in front of the Palladium to see and hear, LAST DAYS, "Mama" Cass. I must have lingered over the line because you have, or had, a cassette of Cass, the Big

Mama, or, if you prefer, the White Mammoth . . . And we listened on your black box with batteries so worn it produced the bombilations of a baritone elephant.

I laughed because I recalled a New Year's dinner at the pension of Fräulein Schroeder, with all the other lodgers, when my charming "song-and-actress" announced with great aplomb that she had performed at the Palladium in London, undoubtedly in order to impress the landlady and in particular a colleague, a music-hall singer. But above all she told her lies, I suspect, so that she would believe them herself. There was an almost wild ingenuousness in her lies, as absurd at times as she was herself.

Frequently, and for no particular reason, she made me laugh. You're mad, she would tell me, as if that surprised her; but the laughter was contagious and we both laughed as if the two of us were mad.

Sheltered Soho Square does not even remotely resemble Wittenbergplatz, the central square open to all the winds of Berlin, and yet today, a little after a somewhat cloudy noon, as I chewed on a hot dog in front of the bewigged statue of Charles II, who looks as if he will continue his walk among the flowering urns on the square, I began to remember the happy sunlit days when, she with no contracts and I with no classes, we would spend our idle hours sitting on a bench, watching and commenting on the passersby.

There goes another Frau Frog-jaw . . . , who reminded us of Frau Karpf, her former landlady, when she lived on a remote street behind the last stretch of the KuDamm, near the Halensee. Frau Karpf came in, sagging toad-jowl atremble, to serve us coffee, and her lodger would purr pleasantries in an elementary German that was all her own, and even call her angel, curled like a cat on that broken-down sofa in her room.

And then jumped to her feline feet again to prepare her classic concoction: she broke two eggs into two glasses and seasoned them—it sickened me—with soy sauce and vinegar and stirred up the mixture with her fountain pen. Salt and pepper?

Look at the one with the ostrich head craning her neck there in front of the window of Ka-De-We. Frau Strauss . . .

We didn't need to go to the nearby zoo to admire the fauna d'après-midi.

But she did not realize, the inveterate watcher, that she was the principal attraction, with her yellow beret and an old fur coat that looked like the skin of a mangy dog.

She had great plans for us and asked herself in too loud a voice what all those passing people would say if they knew they were in the presence of the most extraORdinary WRIter, a future Nobel PRIZEwinner, and the greatest, most MARvelous, Damen und Herren, ACtress in the world. Great contracts would rain down on her like a shower of gold.

She knew nothing of mythologies, and it was not precisely a shower of gold that left her pregnant.

It was almost a Christmas present from Klaus, the little blond who accompanied her on the piano, and in other things as well, but not for long: in a well-timed arrangement he went to London alone in the middle of January to synchronize music for the films, and the little sneak dropped her for a compatriot of hers who was related to a lord.

She accepted her disappointment with a furtive tear and a raucous laugh. Troubles never come alone: just before her lover, she had lost her job at the bar.

Her parents sent her a monthly allowance that allowed the unemployed actress to survive in Berlin.

I was never sure if what she said about her family was completely true.

At first I thought her mother was French, which is what Fritz told me, but she later admitted that the story of her mère was mere invention, to make her seem chic.

Did she really have an angelic seventeen-year-old sister named Betty? Mr. Jackson, her father, was he the owner of a textile mill near Manchester? Perhaps, one improbability following another, her mother was a wealthy heiress with a manor house and land.

Her father, an accomplice or simply accommodating, had given her permission to leave school and go to London to begin crowd-work in films. Then she got a small part in a company touring the provinces. That was when she met Diana, another actress who was older than she, and they traveled to Berlin looking for opportunities that never seemed to materialize. Diana the huntress soon found a banker with whom she went to Paris, leaving her friend alone in Berlin. She too longed for a rich lover.

The early symptoms of her pregnancy were not yet apparent when we met Clive, a corpulent American millionaire whom I never saw sober. By breakfast, as he himself confessed, he had already consumed half a bottle of whiskey. And she did not lag far behind: she began to drink as much as he, though I never saw her drunk. Sometimes her eyes looked boiled, and the layer of makeup, which grew thicker every day, could not hide the devastating effects of her drinking.

But Clive came on the scene at just the right time because her parents, no doubt to force her to return home, had stopped her allowance, and she could find no work. The truth was she only talked about finding it, but made no other effort and spent the day in her room. On one of our rare outings, to the Troika bar, we made the acquaintance of the providential Yankee. Appropriately enough, the Troika was where our peculiar ménagerie à trois began. The capitalist, the chorus girl, and the cadger. He had promised to launch her stage career, a project that seemed more chimerical with every passing day, and frequently made plans for all of us to take fantastic trips, by land-sea-and-air, to Egypt, Tierra del Fuego, Tahiti, Singapore, Japan, the Everglades, wherever . . . And I would be his private secretary, with no duties except uninterrupted leisure. The good life is brief, and Clive vanished like a dream, leaving us a farewell note and three hundred marks at his hotel. That same night we blew fifty on a dinner—that didn't agree with her—and the rest, which she planned to spend on her wardrobe, would be used to pay for the *Schwangerschaftsunterbrechung*. Abortion is shorter . . .

At last it was spring and the cafés were bringing their wooden platforms out into the sun on the KuDamm and Savignyplatz. We rode in a taxi as if it were a hearse to the clinic. (You know all about it, what it's like. Unfortunately I couldn't go with you.) I will always remember her in that bed, without her makeup, looking like a good little girl.

Then we took separate vacations and she left our pension on Nollendorfstrasse to share a super modern flat with a German girl near Breitenbachplatz, in Wilmersdorf. That was where for the first time I saw her dressed all in white, and it suited her, but her face looked even thinner and older. Her hair was cut in a new way, what elegant waves. Her eyes avoided mine, and before the telephone rang twice—Erwin? Paul?—I realized her life was very busy again.

We barely saw each other after my visit, three or four times, I think, and when I began to miss her and thought about ringing her up, on the anniversary of our meeting, I received a postal card from her in Paris. Had she followed in the footsteps of her friend Diana? A month later she sent me another card from Roma. All roads lead to Amor? (I remember now that Fritz pronounced *Love* like *Larv* . . . The mask of love covering the face of my English girl from Berlin?) I never saw her again. But every time I went down into the subway at Wittenbergplatz and saw against the yellow and green tiles the huge poster of the redhead in the long yellow gown playing the Bechstein piano on the shores of a blue lake at dusk, *Now I know why Mother,* I would hear it again, her saddest song, *Told me to be true* . . .

There is one answer to all the questions that burn in my brain today.

Perhaps.

I begin—and do not end—with the most incandescent.

You? . . .

Was it or was it not you I saw . . . earlier when I was leaving the Earl's Court station? That is the question, that is the quest . . . as I continue to look for you in the labyrinth of London.

Another illusion? Lost?

In the precipitate five-thirty press of people.

Today are you wearing very white, very very short hot pants?

The darkness of your swift thighs glimpsed in that thicket of legs and trousers advancing up the stairs. The entrance to the station regurgitated us as it ingurgitated other harried hurrying travelers.

I lost sight of that dark thighness as I emerged onto Earl's Court Road. But to be sure, I looked in the news shop on the corner. Several long-haired types with sleeping bags in front of the bulletin board. Would you pay five pounds seventy-five pence a week to share a ramshackle house in Richmond with three other out-of-work tenants? Or would you prefer, for a few pence less plus doing the shopping, the lodging offered by an agoraphobic gentleman in Hendon? Still tacked to the board is the card of Madame Starzinsky, the clairvoyante of Earl's Court. I see a journey . . . Could the old woman be right? Not a chance! In the rear the usual leafers browse at the wall of magazines and newspapers. At one time I studied my ABCs there free of charge. Today, Miss Rose's *Times* is enough. I ought to put an ad in the personals. Will the dark swallow return? My swift bird of passage . . . Or I could write "Je t'aimes beaucoup," just like that, just like the man called Shaun, what a name, who writes comme ça to Pauline in the personal column. I you loves, you me loves . . . But I'll pass on to you the latest news that the newspapers won't pick up.

Reis returned almost a week ago from his vacation on the Isle of Guernsey. On the trail of traces of the lost Victor Hugo. Since his landlady the medium traveled with him, I suppose they even attempted to speak with the Great Spirit. Votre Honneur . . .

I can imagine Mrs. Askew crossing her eyes at each question, they and Mr. Reis's bald head radiant in the darkness. He had been talking for a long time about a trip to Guernsey. The sea breezes have brightened his face, his eyes are more mischievous than ever, but I'm afraid the inclement weather has made his asthma even worse. As a souvenir he brought back for the table an oilcloth decorated with multicolored marine motifs: an old salt with long white hair and beard who clenches a pipe between his teeth as he rows his boat under a sky almost obscured by seagulls . . . Two creels, an anchor, a heap of netting and a ball of twine on a rock . . . Sails on the phlegm-green Britannic sea . . . A gull resting on a reef . . . A tiny fishing village and a red-hulled boat sailing out to sea . . . A trio of mussels . . . A pair of superimposed starfish . . . The sun shining through the clouds onto the snot-green sea where a red sailboat heads toward sepia cliffs . . . Three creels next to a boat with hauled sails in a cove on whose most prominent headland there stands a lighthouse . . .

Last Sunday I had time to examine the oilcloth—spread on the table in my honor—while we patiently put pins in winkles and especially during the game of chess after dinner. I'm certain he bought the oilcloth because the old salt is his own caricature. When I pointed that out to him, he at first pretended not to hear, then he pretended to be surprised, and finally he burst into guffaws, laughing so hard he began to choke. I thought he was going to have one of his asthma attacks. But in fact he took advantage of my distraction to stalemate me. Coup de patte! And I swept the pieces off the board with my hand. Then we bent each other's ear, and our elbows, gin after gin, until very late. He was very surprised—and distressed—when I told him you had disappeared. La donna è mobile . . . and he shook his head in disapproval. Clenching his cold pipe between his teeth, he assumed a Sherlockholmesian air, perhaps asking himself where the devil you could have gone. Where are you risking your life?

(Although we all risk our lives. Yes, living is a risky business. In Maida Vale, as I was leaving Reis's house, a treacherous van almost ran me down in the dark. Vandal!)

The *Times* reports on the first page that yesterday a time bomb was found under a seat on a plane flying the Belfast-London route, and they had to make an emergency landing in Manchester.

But I don't believe you've gone anywhere near Belfast. Or that you had to give a concert with a certain impresario of prey.

La ci darem la mano . . .

Of course, it was also sung by a girl from Madrid who aspired to be a concert artist. And above all to be free, like her compatriots Don Giovanni and Carmen. Long live liberty!

Earl's Court is not Chamberí, but to remember her I came here to the Troubadour, a place she surely would have liked if only for the name. And here is where I am writing to you today. Every day on a daily basis—as she would say, so tautological—I write to you. I'm sitting at the table in the rear, near the bar, and from time to time I look up at the ceiling, where, like ex-votos, they've hung old coffeepots, rusted odds and ends, a jumble of junk that you always found fascinating. And, left dangling as I look for the *mot juste*, her mad image, poor dislocated loca, came back to me.

A maid made so postcoitally melancholy, so very triste? I should have asked myself when I saw her cheeks streaked with tears. A broken doll, dismantled and disarming, lying on the sofa, her clothes in disarray allowing a glimpse of certain intimate areas, her left leg, oh so white, resting between my thighs as I continued caressing, mechanically, her right leg stretched across the back, near the nape of my neck, a leg sheathed in the silky black stocking that ended in a bowknot, a tightly kinked curl at the end of her thigh.

And when she was completely nude, still sprawled on the sofa, her right arm across her belly and her left thigh resting on the stump of the right a little above the knee, still she had the presence of spirit—d'esprit—and black humor to brandish the leg sheathed in black as it rested on the back of the sofa and offer it to me: her ugly stumpling . . .

The naked bulb hanging from the ceiling went out, along with the dream vision.

In darkness, once again she shone brilliantly with all the splendid features of Catherine Deneuve.

Even paler, as white as paper. The incredible whiteness of Japanese paper, her body gleaming and slender, her elegant hands, her cheeks. With her hair pulled up in a high chignon, and wearing that purple dressing gown, she bore a resemblance to the highborn ladies in old Japanese prints. There's no reason to describe her as she really was, with her dark hair, flashing black eyes, pouting red mouth . . . because I always see her as I saw her in the dark—an oniric or ironic displacement—with the beautiful face of Catherine Deneuve. The actress robbed her of her face forever . . . She, who would have also liked to be an actress!

With a few bits of clothing and a sheet she would create costumes in my studio and improvise a diversity of roles, diverting little sketches, a multiplicity of characters, a minstrel show with a thousand faces, guises and disguises. Her mimicry made me weak with laughter. Her best imitation was of senile old Don Juan, her tutor. Or, rather, her corruptutor. (She also invented words . . . Constantly and with all the freshness of her rustiquicity, to use one of her terms. Words are such poor things, she believed, that she attempted to coin new ones so that everything, without exception, could be said.)

She would stroke an imaginary goatee and contort into an obsequious posture, part courtier and part dirty old ogler. Her senescent tutor seemed to have stepped out of *The Lances* by Velázquez. That porcupine Espínola! Along my spine the hackles bristle when I recall that thorny subject, more painful than the thrust of a spear.

At first I believed, as did other residents of the Chamberí district, that she was his daughter. And then, though he was in his sixties and almost three times her age, her husband, which is what I was led to believe by the wizened witch, her servant and go-between.

She was walking along Ríos Rosas with that dark virago on the sunny Sunday afternoon in October when I laid eyes on her for the first time, while she compassionately contemplated a group of sightless children. And she did not shrink from my gaze. Is love truly blind? Two days later, at dusk, the three of us saw one another again on Quevedo Square. I followed them, and when we were almost at her house the skeletal procuress took wing and left the way clear for me to approach her alone, the girl who acquiesced and did not dissimulate and agreed to everything with an impassioned yes, yes, yes!

You? Is it you? My first words as if I had met her last year in Marienbad or, more anachronistically, in another life. (I remember now that she did not care for the afterlife, had no interest in the next world. Or in the transmigration of souls. Long live my body! She had no wish to be dust, enamored or otherwise, enamored as she was of this mortal life. Let them give me back my fresh young flesh, she would say, along with all the kisses you have already given me and will give to me in the future . . .)

We began to see each other half-secretly, and little by little she told me a little about her brief life of twenty-one years during our long excursions to the outskirts of the city: hugging the edge of the Lozoya canal, Don Juan was her parents' closest friend and she an orphan, watching how the setting sun drew a veil of Velázquez blue across the horizon of the Sierra, her mother went half-mad when she was widowed and died two years ago, walking confidently in her short coat into the cool wind blowing hard against her shapely body, and on her deathbed she regained her reason and entrusted to her dearest friend, Juan López Garrido, her only child, her little girl of only nineteen, and we would separate—tear ourselves away—at nightfall, near the old reservoir, beside the little horses of the carousel with their front legs raised and bent under them in an interrupted gallop.

On other afternoons we would drive out of Madrid to the leafy glades of El Pardo, to lie down on the nettled carpet and search for the needle in the pine grove. We never got to the point . . .

Loves That Bind

Until at last she decided to confess, as she held me in her arms, that Don Juan was not her husband but only her tutor. Her seductutor! Within two months of taking her in, the list of women seduced by the inveterate Don Juan grew longer. Mille e tre . . . in Ispagna, as if we were keeping count.

Days later she also decided at last to come up to my attic, next to the lightning rod, which might protect us from the wrath of Zeus but perhaps not from that of her lover-tutor, who was increasingly jealous and zealous. His pride would not permit him to put in an appearance here, she reassured me. And she became increasingly reckless, defying the inquisitorial looks of her aged lover, his questions and reproaches. She wanted to be free. And she aspired to a liberated love, perhaps indoctrinated ad hoc by her libertine tutor. And she did not wish to marry the man she loved. Long live independence! Which is why she so lamented the state of dependence in which her tutor kept her, not having gone to school, not having a profession. She had to make up for lost time, and her mere desire would instantly transform her into a language teacher, or a painter, or even a member of parliament, with her silver mimic's tongue . . .

After that day when she first climbed to seventh heaven, to my attic so close to her house, we took no more walks. But we devoted ourselves not only to amorous exercises but also—and with what passion—to intellectual ones. She believed there was still much for her to learn. And soon. How easy it was for me to teach her to prattle the *bel parlare*. I read Leopardi and hear again her bel canto:

Che fai tu, luna, in ciel?

I still ask myself the question. And above all, we read Dante. She, my Panchita my Frasquita my Paquita da Rimini, was especially moved by the episode of Paolo and Francesca. On that day we read even more. *Diverse lingue* . . . And Shakespeare, or *Chaskaperas,* in her Babel parlare. *Unsex me here* . . . , she declaimed to the heavens, like a typically Spanish Miz Macbeth. And between bulky tomes we made the beast with two backs. She could be bold without vice or corruption.

I attempted to practice the art of Apelles in that attic—it was my smeary period, as she so clearly put it with more than a grain of Attic wit—and she became so imbued with the ambience— she even relished the smell and touch of the oil paints—that when I placed the brush and palette in her hand, she began to emulate me, taking risqué risks. Appel à la révolte . . .

We lived in such great artistic and erotic exaltation, almost in a mystic communion of all our senses, and all our nonsenses, babbling in our private language, a potpourri or bubbling pot of parolas from various lingua francas, that when I had to leave, because of pressing family problems, for the Mare Nostrum, which was never really ours, we both unconsciously accepted the separation as a respite. We never imagined then that it would be permanent. I did not premeditate the break on the shores of the Mediterranean; but it came gradually, like an imperceptible tide, slow but inexorable, eventually washing away the footprints we had made.

In her letters she gave free rein to her increasingly unrealizable plans: she would be an actress, writer, concert artist, painter . . . We would both devote ourselves to art, body and soul, and communicate platonically with one another from our respective ivory towers. More and more tepid in her letters, perhaps on account of the pains in her leg; definitely tired or bored with relations at a distance that seemed more ethereal with every passing day.

A black dot, that charming black birthmark on her right

knee, was in reality a period. The end. Barely a callus at first, around the little mole.

I will cut short the pain and grief she suffered before they cut off her right leg.

They didn't cut her leg, they cut her wings . . .

Her character and ideas changed, she let go her ideals, let herself go. She, who had aspired to not depend on anyone, not even on the man she loved, found herself reduced to the most complete subordination. A prisoner forever of the aging Don Juan—oh sad victory—who now aspired to be a true father. When I returned to Madrid, I visited her from time to time, always with the consent of her tutor; but from the very first my presence disappointed her, she viewed me as a stranger, I even suspect she thought my conversation vulgar, and I decided not to force upon her this ritual that was forced on both our parts. I can see her still, as she looked when I could hardly recognize her, collapsed in her chair, as pale as death, her fine translucent hands crossed on top of the afghan.

Comply, comply . . . : the clump-clump of her crutches in the house still resounds in my ears. She rejected the perfect artificial leg that no one would ever caress for a pair of crutches, which eventually deformed her shoulders and chest. Three years after the operation, so pale and wasted, she was a mere shadow of what she had been. At twenty-five she looked older than forty. She began to spend her time in church and in the end infected the old sinner with her faith. The love of music that still remained she nourished in church, and she played the organ at solemn ceremonies to the great contentment of the congregation. All her esthetic enthusiasms were sublimated into the delicate craft of pastry-making, the art of the tart . . . regaling the gluttony of Don Juan, who married her in the Church to put an end to their reprehensible out-of-wedlock union.

Were they happy? They ate little buns—buñuelos—as light as air.

Her story—really the saddest of all—illustrates the old saying: Woman's place is in the home: break her leg if you have to. Just one? Unspeakable.

Un

peu trop de monde, my schoolmistress or maîtresse from the Midlands would have said in her English accent if she had found herself in this pseudo-Cockney tavern in Piccadilly, so suddenly full of French tourists.

(All I could understand, in the blare of voices at the bar, was that they were repeating Toulon, Toulon *tout court*. You wouldn't have gone to dances in that port, I trust, where—according to today's *Times*—the night before last disturbances broke out between North Africans and French sailors. A twenty-year-old sailor was stabbed to death. The fighting began, the newspaper says, in certain dance halls. Arguments over *filles* . . .)

French had been one of her favorite classes, along with botany, and I remember that she remembered her first French grammar book, a gray grammar, as clearly as the pear tree that bloomed like a foaming wave next to the house in the Nottingham countryside where she spent her childhood and then her adolescence. There was no containing her contentment when it was time for exercises at the state school in Nottingham and she was attempting to write correctly in French: "I gave the bread to my younger brother." (To Billy, who was four, or to Tom, who was only two . . .)

She was fairly shy then, and would hide her bitten nails in embarrassment. And four years later, when she was already a young woman of sixteen, she also hid under the bed a box of sweets and ate them all herself, when she went to bed, and when she woke in the morning. It was her solitary pleasure, her shameful secret.

And her most shameful secret—though no longer solitary— a short while later, when Miss Inger, a rather beautiful, fearless-seeming schoolmistress with an athletic bearing, so expert in what she did and twelve years older than her pupil, had her taste other secretive sweets.

But I am playing havoc with the logic of chronology, because even earlier, months earlier, she'd had her first love: a fine officer in the Royal Engineers, twenty-one years old and of Polish blood, as his name—Anton Skrebensky—revealed, a friend of her family, who were Polish, too, on the maternal side.

A few days after they met, as he was seeing her home on a warm July night, at about nine-thirty, she recalled it so clearly, under the ash trees on Cossethay Hill, the soldier could not resist the allure of the splendid dark-haired girl with her golden skin and golden eyes, her thin white dress (she liked to wear white in summertime), and he touched her lips with his lips and she opened her lips to him, drew him nearer her firm, slender body to receive, soft and deep, soft, oh soft, yet oh so softly deep, her first kiss on the mouth.

I still feel her lips tightening, gradually hardening for the duration of the kiss. Indurating both mouth and body, which was her convulsive way of kissing.

I was one of her lovers before she married a school inspector, and I prolonged my emotions—perpetually vicarious— with the emotions of her earlier loves.

At times, when I remember, I cannot tell what I lived and

what I was told. I remember, in any case, concentrated experiences.

It was Skrebensky who took her to the fair in Derby, but I am the one who sees myself in his place, climbing with her into the swingboat that I prefer to call a flying ship, rushing higher and higher, her dark mane of hair flying, her face radiant with excitement, shining as brightly as the golden light in her eyes, laughing, screeeeaming, falling terribly back into the abyss then flying up again on the apex of a wave of air into another time, when she was very small and her father would take her in the flying ship, higher and wider and wilder, and people looked on disapprovingly at how the young man made the little girl, gasping and grasping at her seat, go flying through the air. Afterward he would take her by the hand, she as pale as a ghost, to have lemonade, and ask her not to tell her mother that she felt giddy. And when she got home she was violently sick behind the parlor sofa. (Just like Why this afternoon with the herring bones I bought him ex profeso at the market in Shepherd's Bush.) She was the oldest of eight children, six girls and two boys, and as a child she was always her father's favorite, the child of her father's heart. Sometimes he called her Milady. The tiny mite of a lady and the farmer, who had tried to show her (at the age of four?: it was one of her earliest memories) soon after dawn one morning, when a cold wind was blowing, how to set potatoes. A pathetic lesson, really, because the clumsy child made her father lose patience and she ran away from him to where a little water ran trickling between grass and stones. She found herself alone in her blue overall and her red woolen bonnet.

She was a dreamy adolescent who read legends and tales of romantic love, and at night she would lean against the frame of her bedroom window with her hair hanging loose on her shoulders, and gaze at the silhouette of the nearby church, which was a turreted castle, and imagine herself the maiden imprisoned in the tower, waiting for the knight who would—and then one of her brothers was knocking, kicking at the door until finally her mother told her to unlock it.

Skrebensky appeared on her horizon as an exotic, romantic figure, more aristocrat than soldier, and he actually was the son of a Polish baron.

A glory of golden legend surrounded their romance, which would be sealed with a clasp of gold. I mean the Rhine gold ring. Before he left for darkest Africa he offered her a ring that they dropped into a glass of Rhine wine and both drank as if it were communion wine; then she took the ring from the bottom of the glass, tied it to a cord, and hung it around her neck.

Another of Skrebensky's gifts was the enormous box of sweets—he sent it to her shortly before he left—that she kept under the bed for herself alone.

(Sweethearts' sweets . . . More bitter the peppermints her uncle Tom bought from a vending machine at the Nottingham station, as the two of them watched the train leave that was carrying Anton Skrebensky away.)

The enormous box of sweets lay hidden for some time, though it was empty by now. Why did she refuse to share them? she continued asking herself for a long while afterward, ashamed.

Soon she would hide with even greater shame her relationship with Winifred Inger, her teacher. When they were together in the classroom, a magnetic attraction existed between them, an attraction that became concrete for the first time during the first swimming class. She trembled in her tight bathing suit at the side of the pool, waiting for the class-mistress to appear: as firm-bodied as the Diana she had seen in books, and her knees—she saw with admiration—were as white and polished and proud as marble, separated in that way. She dived into the water after her mistress, who immediately challenged her to a race. She swam eagerly, longing to reach her; but Winifred, swimming with easy strokes, arrived first, swung herself round, caught her round the waist in the water, and held her for a moment against herself, the bodies of the two women in laughing embrace.

In time, Winifred asked her to come to tea on Saturday, to a lovely little bungalow (a shanty, really) on the banks of the Soar, and the pupil thought she had found earthly paradise. There they had tea, in delicious privacy, and the talk was led, by a kind of spell (cast in her own interest, I suspect, by Miss Inger), to love. Miss Inger maintained that all men were impotent, incapable of really taking or making love to a woman.

When night fell, despite the rain, Miss Inger suggested a swim in the river. They undressed together in the shadow and walked out holding hands. The maîtresse led her in the darkness, their naked bodies pressing close. The rain turned into an ice-cold shower, and they ran for the shelter of the bungalow, shivering with cold. And inclination.

They became inseparable. When they weren't at Winifred's lodging, they sought to lose themselves among natural surroundings. And they spent many delicious afternoons on the river. Winifred was very fond of water—of swimming, of rowing. And her pupil had a true fondness, since the time she was very small, for running water. As a girl she spent her idle hours watching the flow of streams and rivulets. She would never forget the magic moment of bliss when she saw the blue flash of a kingfisher.

(I remember her on that windy night in March, in Nottingham, when she proposed going down to the river. Her radiant expression, on the banks of the Trent, an almost savage brilliance in her eyes as she watched the river's silent current flow through the wide night.)

The long vacation came, and with it separation: Winifred went away to London, and she was left in Cossethay. Gradually their love began to languish, passion gave way to pessimism, the eyes of memory did not always bring her pleasant images, at times her mistress looked ugly, her hips growing big, her ankles and her arms too thick, her whole body cleaving heavy like moist clay.

I don't know if it was calculated, but the pupil found the way to convince her uncle Tom, a bachelor who managed a colliery in Yorkshire, that it was time for him to marry her teacher, the lover she was growing tired of.

A while ago, in Piccadilly, I was looking at the statue of Eros, heels in the air, great wings, transformed into a rara avis—the phoenix?—taking flight. Suddenly the waxing half-moon came out from behind a cloud, as if it were painted scenery. I thought there was something lunar about my mistress, and that I remembered her in phases.

At the age of sixteen she kept a diary in which she recorded her irreflections, her most spontaneous thoughts. One night, after admiring the moon, she wrote: "If I were the moon, I know where I would fall down."

If I were the moon . . . —perhaps she wanted to lose herself in the moon, to become one with the moon in communion.

She desired that communion on the night of a full moon, the first night she spent with Anton Skrebensky after the wedding of her uncle Fred at her grandparents' farm, when the moon looked so large and white over the hill. And she offered her breast to that whiteness, she filled herself with moon. And Skrebensky wanted to take her away from there and he covered her with his cloak as they sat and he held her hand until she asked him to leave her alone. She threw off the cloak and walked toward the moon. There was more music and he followed her and they danced again. He caressed her, holding her against him under the full moon; but he was the one who felt the emptiness while she kissed him ardently, deeply. I believe she frightened him. He took her home in silence, and she ran to her room and went to the window, raising her arms, offering herself up to the brightness in the sky. An image that she may have seen in one of the books filled with Merlins and Lancelots that enlivened the nights of her adolescence.

Skrebensky returned six years later, when she was twenty-two, and they resumed their bittermoon—one might call it that—during a few days' holiday with a group of friends in a bungalow on the Lincolnshire coast. It was the first week in August, and they had fixed their marriage for the twenty-eighth of that month. They left the bungalow at night, in the moonlight, and walked along the sea hearing the run of the long, heavy waves that made a ghostly whiteness and a whisper. The scene demanded an embrace and he, as her fiancé, had to provide it; he ran his hand along the blue silk of her dress, electric fire that slid along her hypersensitive skin (one might say she was missing a layer of skin), along her thighs and belly, and he entered her with so much excitement that she dropped to the damp sand and continued looking at the luminous clouds while he breathed heavily with satisfaction and she felt as cold as the sand upon which she lay.

One evening they went out after dinner, across the low golf links to the dunes and the sea. The sky was decorated with small stars, as dazzling as diamonds. A great whiteness glared across the sand and they confronted an incandescent dune, a moon flooding them with light. The surface of the sea flashed in silver scales (if you allow me the luxury of this description) and she plunged into the water, giving her breasts to the moon, her belly to the waves. She turned to face him and cried: I want to go. Where? he asked, as I would. And she said: I don't know. But he knew where to go and he led her to the dunes, to a dark hollow. No, here, she said, and went back to the moonlight. She lay motionless, with wide-open eyes looking at the moon. He came directly to her, without preliminaries or prologue, he made love as if it were a fight, a struggle, until he succumbed and seemed to swoon, his forehead buried in her hair and his chin in the sand. He saw that she was still looking at the moon. But a tear glittered and ran down her cheek. A tear fell in the sand . . . I assume. The following day, the day they were to leave, they barely spoke. But they knew it was finished. Fourteen days later he married his colonel's daughter.

She went home to Beldover—the town, a little farther north, where her family had moved three years earlier—and told them she had broken off her engagement.

One rainy afternoon in early October when she was walking in the countryside, she thought she would die beneath the hooves of some runaway horses. She climbed a great oak to reach the other side of a hedge that would separate her from the horses, but in the end she fell. The violent fall induced a miscarriage. Fate is fond of cruel symmetries: she had made love with Skrebensky for the first time, months before, under a great oak on the outskirts of Beldover. I don't suppose it could have been the same tree.

In reality, her engagement to Skrebensky had been a weakness; I assume she had confused compassion with passion. He pressed her constantly, he wanted to know when they would marry, and she answered always with new evasions. Until one day—and it happened here, in London—along the golden

Thames of Richmond at sunset, after eating supper on the terrace of a hotel on the river, she told him she would never marry. He began to weep, with syncopated sobs. Tony, no . . . The other people were staring. It was eight in the evening but still brightly light. They hurried away and she decided they should take a taxi. They were driving through Kensington Gardens and he was still crying. It was too painful for her, wiping his tears with her handkerchief, it was wet through with tears, and she had to take his handkerchief from his pocket and dry his face and his lachrymose mustache. My love, she called him. I can imagine the self-contained expression of the driver looking in the rearview mirror at the gentleman crying like a baby.

I believe she was happy with him on only one occasion. And it was here, in London, months before they broke up, during an Easter-week vacation they spent in a Piccadilly hotel.

(A few hours ago, I went into the Ritz, looking for writing paper. My *Belles Lettres* tablet is coming to an end. I intended to write to you from this luxe, calme, et discrétion, but finally decided to come here to our noisy tavern in Piccadilly. Toulon, Toulon, those two boors in their Scottish tams are still at it, raising two empty glasses to the redhead in the abundantly packed white silk blouse behind the bar, Two . . . , making a V for victory with their fingers until she understood that they wanted two large whiskeys—two long . . .)

They usually had supper in their room, and often at dawn they were still awake watching from their high balcony as the rosy fingers dispersed through the dark trees of Green Park and drifted toward Victoria Station and the growing light on the Byzantine tower of Westminster Abbey, while the sound of traffic round Piccadilly grew heavier. The air was cold and they went back inside. They bathed before getting into bed. We bathed, I mean.

I recall that she liked to leave the doors to the bathroom open so that the bedroom would heat up. She watched me bathe from the bed and I, my hair still streaming into my eyes, saw her golden face and dark hair against the stark white pillow, brightening the yellow flame in her eyes, as I toweled myself dry and the room was reflected, blurred and unreal, in the mirror. I walked to the bed and her arms encircled my waist and she breathed in the scent of soap on my skin. We slept entwined, sunk deep in the same deep sleep. Until noon . . .

I saw her for the last time, six years later, in a small station in the Austrian Tyrol (on her honeymoon?), walking away, wrapped in furs to protect her from the blizzard whirling in snowy vertigo.

Voluptuous little volute, voilà, of her short white skirt. What trim hams when she's up on her toes, what taut calves until she serves. Playing tennis this morning with a little friend here in Brook Green, the pretty girl in the miniskirt I saw in the Rendezvous Café, let's see now, was it ten days ago? Vicky! She tossed her racket in the air, gave me a coquettish look, and made a V-for-victory sign. Admiring her through the wire fence until the game was over. Schoolgirls ready to fly, fluttering their wings . . .

And then I came down to the river to look for you in the Embankment gardens, a misguided spy hiding behind his *Times*. Until he gave up in gloomy despair . . .

Going up Villiers Street along the left bank, near the tunnel beneath Charing Cross Station that leads to Craven Street (ah, I can still detect the fluvial effluvia), there was the pub where my magic master revealed to me: Young man, all great dreams are born in London.

I had met him barely an hour before in Bedford Square—chance or fate?—and now I was his assistant. Monsieur Sosthène de Rodiencourt, Engineer Initiate, one of the many titles printed on the business card he handed me. A strange man, very short and well over sixty (though he admitted to only fifty-seven), disguised as a Chinese in a kind of gray silk soutane. Rather than the French consulate, he seemed to have come from some exotic room in the British Museum on the other side of the square. It appeared I was initiatable.

Though for the moment I was untutored and knew nothing of the Tara-Tohé.

The Flower of Dreams! Of the Magi! Of the Secret!

Say no more. And it had to be plucked at the roof of the world, shh, Sherpa! in Tibet.

The journey of initiation actually began in that pub, the Singapore, between dark and light beers that my master ordered from the robust redheaded barmaid who turned a deaf ear to his exclamations—Stout! Bass!—and the calling out or cawing out of faraway names: Mahé . . . Karikal . . . Swoboly . . . Penwane . . . Lhasa . . .

The journey would be long and hazardous, but during the expedition we would have the opportunity to combine devotion and business by placing in Tibetan monasteries the automatic prayer wheel—thirty-seven mantras per second!—an invention of the great mystic engineer.

In reality we would travel not to Tibet but, nothing to it! to the fourth dimension. The open sesame provided by the Tara-Tohé. The seven-petaled flower of seven colors. We would walk perpetual snows, Everest for ever . . . from peak to white peak until . . . —oh!

We have grasped it, the flower opens in the palm of the hand—ah pneuma!—the body becomes light as a feather, as foam, va! p'tite mousse!, as light and transparent as air . . .

To pay for our journey, the Master Inventor consulted the classifieds in the *Times* (one must read the *Times*! he said), the ads for engineers and inventors, until he providentially came upon the one placed by Colonel O'Collogham, himself of the

Royal Engineers, who gave us bed, board, and a laboratory for our experiments in his mansion in Willesden.

In that mansion I truly entered the fourth dimension.

In his garden, farewell to Tibet!, I found the Flower of Dreams.

And I deflowered her? . . .

Colonel O'Collogham's little niece, virginal, and martyr because of my maxima culpa.

(Was she really his niece?)

The blue-gray-violet of her eyes, what iridescence, depending on the light, and her dazzling smile. My blond bit of silky lace, my tender little spangle, her well-turned thighs with their long agile muscles, her little pleated skirt so minimal, made even briefer by the mischievous little leap that punctuates her calves so firmly, another half-turn, what boldness, so lightly brightly flitting! She is a flowerbird, what a fluttering of petals, a winged sprite of the forest, what pounding what palpitating pit-a-pit in her little bird's breast . . . I thought her no more than twelve or thirteen, an adolescent nymph! in my first vision of the Eden of Willesden.

Was she a golden dream? An infantasy of fairyland, my little golden girl? Did she escape from the painting by Richard Dadd that we looked at so often, tête-à-tête at the Tate? (And I will go back now, for the retrospective—careful! I may catch you spying on the wee woodcutter holding his hatchet high over the huge hazelnut in the forest clearing . . .) A creature from the court of Titania, Queen of the Fairies? I ask myself as I sit on our bench in Leicester Square under the prodigious thundering of the dark cloud traveling so tempestuously above the treetops (does that still frighten you as it did in this very spot on another July afternoon?) on this isle of shipwrecked sailors and vagabonds, in front of Shakespeare, his head snowy with pigeon droppings, his hand on his goatee, and only God or the devil knows what he is plotting.

Here, before the bearded bard, wily Shakespeare, my pretty little playgirl and yours truly made our first stop on that journey to the end of the fifth circle of hell. I had to make some purchases for the colonel and my master, valves, burettes, bellows . . . and the colonel's niece was to be my London guide and guard. To keep me from erring in my errands or wasting their wealth.

From the top of the bus as it reached Trafalgar Square, I had already caught sight of certain dangerous former colleagues, some women of my acquaintance plying their trade nonstop, and a man who also worked the sidewalks behind the National Gallery, a Picasso of the pavements sketching the Eiffel Tower in chalk: I pointed him out from a distance to my curious colleen, who wanted to walk closer and see. I wondered about stopping on the steps of the church of St. Martin and finally opted for the oasis of Leicester Square. It was five in the afternoon, and as we could see from our bench, some women were already at work in Leicester Square. They came and went en cascade, French girls run by a French pimp I met when I came to London.

We have things to do, let's go, but she wanted to go on watching, as curious as a cat.

(Of course, Why has escaped. Guay. It must have happened yesterday afternoon when I left the door to Miss Rose's apartment open for a moment to go to my room to find a can opener. I've put up a photocopied notice on almost every tree in Brook Green, the same one I've attached here for you: "Lost, large black tabby. Answers to/with Why? Contact Emil Alia. Phoenix Lodge Mansions." I hope he comes back before Miss Rose does. My chaotic schedule may have turned him wild. Yesterday at noon he was very nervous—and perhaps hungry: I had forgotten to feed him since Wednesday—and he almost left me without a *Times*. Semi-*Times* was what I had left, just a few pages. Two or three days ago, when I took him out to the Green at night, he climbed a tree again. Why are you doing this to me again? Guay. So now you're not the only one I'm looking for.)

I was too weak and gave in to her: we would spend a while longer at our observatory. In fact I only had eyes for her, I was captivated by her thighs and their golden down. And suddenly, a murmur in my ear, and Bigoudi appeared before me. Her face garishly painted, her gold bag swinging, as brazen as ever. What do you know, he's seducing babies now, and she approaches my sylph, touches her skirt, I don't know if to lower it or raise it even higher, for it was already up where her thighs begin. After reproaching me for never falling by Leicester Square, she turns her attention to the girl, it was Miss this and that, cavorting and cajoling, beguiling her. She sits, insinuating herself between us, stroking her, stealing her?—feeling her. How pretty, how really really pretty, and she smooths the little skirt, fondles it, her eyes suddenly ablaze like burning coals with an inane idea: Why don't you lend her to me? she says, no doubt she'd had too much to drink. I promise we'll be back to see her another day, now we have errands to run, and we continue on our way. I am aching with jealousy. Don't you find her disgusting, distasteful?, at every corner I am assailed by another doubt, another presentiment, I wanted to know everything, what did she think, what did she feel, did she find a slut like that likable? Answer!, but she doesn't answer, she is indifferent to my torment, walking so pertly at my side, ah, so blond and so young she looks like an angel, with heaven in her eyes, but maybe she's a fallen angel, with perversity and the devil in her flesh, her body so supple, so suggestive.

As we pass a dark doorway I push her deep inside the den, put my arms around her, fondle her, breathing faster, I want to kiss her, I drool on her a little; she resists, twists, slippery as an eel in a dim corner, but I hold on tight, kissing-kitchy-koo, I make her moan, I am hard on her, kisses avidly sucking at her face, and then my left hand runs up and down, down her belly, her little tummy taut as satin, frantic I rub and rub against her, her Anglican groin as smooth and seductive as silk, up and down, along the sheer muslin of her thighs, up and down, coming and going and going and com . . . ing!, going away, slipping away, and I throw myself at her neck, grrgrrgrr! I give her a bite and she unexpectedly slams me pow on the chin, ay, she leaves me in chaos and I turn on her and return kapow the caress. Pow kapow! I hold down her arms and crush her against the wall, what a bind, the poor thing's between a rock and a hard place, and I kiss her all over again, in libidinous libation to my minia-ture miniskirted rose, I lavish her with kisses, I shake her and sense her assent, her head falls to my shoulder, she staggers and collapses in my arms, poor thing, I rode her too hard, I rub her temples, I kiss her again, I shake her to and fro, I place my ear to her little tits, tit-tat, she's breathing, she stammers something, Let's go, my girl, I encourage her, Upsy-daisy, I tell her we have to go, we couldn't stay there, people were coming, Walking, she at my side and I the pack mule dissimulating, hauling the bits and pieces of our earlier purchases on my back.

We turned onto Wardour Street and went into an arcade filled with curious old curiosity shops, almost a museum of exotica and oddities from every latitude, stuffed and mounted albatrosses and sturgeons, astrolabes and starfish, carnivorous plants and herbivorous animals, vipers in jars and copper cobras from India, mute maps and photographs in shrieking colors, and I invented fantastic stories for her, absurd histories about the contents of the store windows, another and then another, she always wanted more, and suddenly the pangs of jealousy again, was the colonel her real uncle?, I imagined him, a huge man with a head like a billiard ball, playing with my little girl, violating her? raping her in rapture? And in Leicester Square I had seen how well she got on with Bigoudi, the two of them cooing like lesbian lovebirds . . . Damned little degenerate, come on, I drag her along holding tight to her hand, a vile vixen, my baby my baby's breath my lily, libidinous!, I pull at her even harder . . . Office workers were leaving the office buildings, everyone was looking at us. I went along long-gone, like an ignominious somnambulist, pulling her by the hand, holding tight, I didn't want her to get away. I walk like a man hallucinating, love is hallucinogenic.

Books in a shopwindow, perhaps it was to escape that we ventured into that French bookstore. Suzette suce . . . She read French very well, I move her away from dangerous readings, from Kamasutras, Pornosutras, and livres cochons d'Inde, toward marvelous maritime travel books, we will prove all the pleasures on all the seas, from the Baltic made balmy to the melliferous Mediterranean, from the tantalizing Atlantic to the passionate Pacific . . .

At full sail, my little wind vane, full speed, my pirate princess, full speed ahead on Oxford Street. She enjoyed the long trek and trotted happily at my side. We could have taken the carriage of the golden charioteer there above the marquee of Selfridges on our right.

I've been retracing the itinerary of that hallucinatory trip, and I stopped for a moment at the old green wagon filled with fruits and vegetables on the corner of Old Quebec Street, across from the Cumberland. We are almost in Cucumberland, the kingdom of Pepino the Short, and my mouth began to water at the sight of some yellow melons from Spain, twenty-five pence apiece. Other fruits, all of them forbidden, come to my over-heated mind. A grenade exploded last night in a nightclub in Salisbury and six people were injured. But I don't believe you need to go that far to put your life at risk. Four bombs exploded yesterday in Belfast.

Nothing better for another halt, when one is hiding from indiscreet glances, than Hyde Park, a green magic carpet. I wanted to escape with my enchanting fairy girl, where? let's fly, on our way to the sea. We crossed from Marble Arch to Speakers' Corner. It wasn't Sunday but that afternoon there were orators perorating and protesting their opposition to all things human and divine. And then on top of everything it began to rain. She is soaked and shivers in her minidress, I warm her with my body, I embrace her, my freezing little frippery. I have an idea: I untie the bundle, remove the canvas, and put it over our heads, it covered us. Like a man listening to the rain I listen to the golden-tongued English-speakers. It was teeming but that didn't prevent their words from streaming out. "The rich must pay" . . . Pay or play? . . . The rich man's leisure is the labor of the poor. But I really didn't listen, I looked only at my girl and her visionary eyes, my capricious little girl who has lost her good humor and turns petulant; but I don't let her go, I take advantage of our canvas covering, it covered us, and I cover her with caresses, I discover her little by little, I sip and kiss the little drops at the tip of her little nose and chin, I lick and lick again her pretty face, as on that afternoon in Willesden when the tiny tip of her little chin trembled, trembled brilliant with tears, and I was her little lapdog frolicking to amuse the poor little orphan . . .

And again I lick and lap at her, ah, let it rain let it pour for forty . . . as long as I have her here against me trembling with cold, my little sparrow . . . Will you come with me to Mare Nostrum, will you come with me to southern seas? No I won't, and you can swim there! she said mockingly . . . Still she was shuddering, I kiss her, I whisper into her curls, I nibble her ear until I hear her complain . . . I could bite her harder, moving down her neck (. . . ah, nectar . . .), and again a corrosive jealousy gnaws at me and I am in a rage. You don't go after girls, Bigoudi, in front of everybody in the middle of the day in the middle of the square. I see her again, that vampider, ready to take advantage of my pretty girl. The best thing would be for us to get away to my forgotten little island far away. Soliland? I tell her endlessly about better worlds where butterflies are as big as birds and birds the size of flies and brightly colored fish fly over the mirror of a perpetually calm sea . . . But I think I heard a stomach rumbling, my God, where's my head, You must be starving, it's eight o'clock. She was hungry and cold. Stand up. And I saw how her eyes widened with fear. What do you see? Aghast, she didn't hear, and she let out an aaah! of abject terror. There, standing before us, that strange-looking stranger. But she seems to have recovered, perhaps a touch of vertigo when she stood suddenly, she stares at the creep and smiles at him. And he jabbers at her in English and French, an incomprehensible Anglogalligobbledygook, I understand nothing, I'm the one struck dumb, and my little girl chatters away animatedly with that scarecrow in the black tattered suit, stuck firmly in the ground in the rain while the two of us are still under canvas. And the two of them talk endless streams of gibberish, they laugh, and she is bewitched while he blusters on with the quavering baa of his goatish voice. Baastard! I don't understand what my girl sees in him because he's uglier than sin. The fact is that his face like a skull and his skeleton's body remind me of something. Can he be the one? That bum I saw fall to the tracks, hit by the train, in the Baker Street station. Resurrected? And he offers me his hand, cold, like iron, like ice! and it freezes my arm, my heart, and he mutters his myriapodish last name. Mille-Pattes! And my voice trembles, too, I'm an ice-bound idiot. And my girl breaks the ice, she suggests getting something to eat, did she really say, Shall we go to lunch? Instead of supper. And I'd swear Big Ben struck six. It's at least eight, I estimated, but time must have slowed, become so retarded it doesn't even know where the Greenwich meridian is.

Chop-chop! Hurry up, she urged us on. To table, gentlemen, allons. He had a strange bittersweet smell, a putrefying smell, agh, didn't she notice it? My little girl skipped along so merrily, showing off her thighs, so provocatively pirouetting for him. The ragged, rotting slug was slobbering, everything coming up roses for him: You are our rose in the rain . . . And they pranced along arm in arm, so cocksure I could barely keep up with them but heard them coquettishly cooing like a pair of turtledoves.

We would have needed more than a compass rose to guide us in the wind and rain through the labyrinth of narrow streets where we found ourselves lost. And I was still burdened with my backpack of junk. We walked straight ahead, following our noses, and mine still out of joint, until we came to the Corridor, that restaurant de luxe with its profusion of candelabra and brocade. Brocade and cordon bleu . . . Despite the shreds and patches in his tattered tux, he strutted like a costumed actor playing a beggar prince or chimney sweep. The maître d' bows, the best table for us, with a centerpiece of roses. But the place doesn't smell exactly like a rose, there's a rank stink of wax and grease all reeking together. My baby girl twitches her turned-up nose, like the bunny rabbit in the habit of sitting on her lap there in the garden at Willesden, but she doesn't detect the foul odor, from beyond the tomb, perhaps, she adores the luxe of the restaurant, she has a good appetite, the best, for caviar, shrimp, olives . . . Between appetizers she tells us of her jaunts to Paris with her dear uncle . . . And she also drinks, Chablis, muscatel, our pert little miss gets pissed. She pours her own champagne. She begins to talk more than she should, about our plans, our travels to the Maracaribbean Sea and its Virgin Islands . . .

The scarecrow, too, knows how to play the clown, he imitates Buster Keaton, he makes her laugh, makes my baby imbibe even more.

The champagne flows like wine, pop, and I drink as well, especially to forget the smell, and how my cruel girl forgets me, forgets herself, laughing hee hee, shrieking eek eek, letting herself be tickled between the thighs by the corruptor who stinks of the grave and glows like phosphorescent larvae, glowworms, fireflies, ignis fatuus in his skull, his deep eye sockets.

And suddenly, an especially loud cork popping? an auditory illusion? an explosion in the middle of the restaurant.

Was it his work? Did he hypnotize us?

We rushed outside, his laughter guides us in the dark, let's go, come on enfants de la patrie, he takes us to a nightclub, the Twit-Twit Club, snaps his fingers like castanets, sending out a glowworm's glow and a swampy smell at each step, to lead us luciferously to the fifth circle of hell, down by the docks, the Avernian depths. Finally we stop at a door black as night, he pounds at the portal, and after a long pause it partially opens: Voi ch'intrate . . . we plunge into a flood tide of light and heat and odor (verbena in the evening?) and thundering noise. The chants of bacchantes, epileptic dances, electrifying spasms, maniacal music, we are in the middle of an orgy. Back, vade retro . . . I have to save my virginal girl, where, where is she?, not a trace, I can barely see the masses of faces, the mirrors whirling and dizzying dancers twirling touching each other on the illuminated floor. I can barely make out the scarecrow who sank into the tumult with my darling . . . Incubi and succubae drunkenly cavorting on the floor, the red roar of a millipede beast . . . ah, there in the surging tide of asses and bellies my little girl caperspinsleapshakes laughing Oh-wah-ooh mews my crazed little kitten. She and I fly through the air on the crest of a wave of disjointed bodies that join and disconnect, ah, there in the vertiginous convulsive gavotte of the mirrors I see my ballerina again with her skirt blown high by the great hurricane of the cancan, hands up and your feet, too, ah the little rogue giggles pawed by a hundred hands pressed by a hundred bodies, wallowing crushing cruelly delighting in my girl, my girl they manhandle my girl they contaminate and I bellow and sob and ride my rage on another wave of bodies. No end to the bacchanal, anal and genital, the sexophoning of fauns and satyrs and uterine Furies, a mirrored saturnalia until the terrible sound of a drum, vrom! VROMM! marked the entrance of a tall gaunt bearded man disguised as a graveyard guard (though I can't make out if the silver letters on his cap spell CEMETERY or SYMMETRY) who came to bring the orgy to an end and to take away, to the sound of the drum and as docile as a lapdog, the pestilential Lord Mille-Pattes, so-titled by my angel. And I take advantage of her surprise to drag away my rebellious angel, kicking and screaming. I force her out of the club and into the night of Niagara Falls. We seek shelter in a dark doorway. My baby is soaked to the skin, almost naked, her clothes in shreds. She retches, she doesn't hear my harangue. She vomits, I hold her, my hand on her forehead. Leave me alone! and she shakes me off after heaving up her guts, telling me to leave her alone, her savior who pulled her away from the clutching hands and feet of that frenzied mob. I lift her up, I kiss her, Don't cry, I plead, I press her to me, I warm her, again I see scenes from that fiendish orgy, how she permitted herself to be pawed, her lascivious wriggling and waggling, ah, I bite her on the jugular, she wants to wiggle free and I hold her even tighter, I squeeze and pinch the cheeks of her sweet little butt and push her up against the dripping wet wall. The rain pours down and I drink from her mouth, her mane of hair, my little vixen, more than vice-ridden, I want to know if she liked the foul-smelling slug in rags and the bitch Bigoudi, Tell me, I shake her, it enrages me that she doesn't respond, and then she said my name, sweetly, like honey, her breath intoxicates me, she kisses me, yes, she does, and then she bursts into laughter . . . surely she is mocking me, I hold her even tighter, I caress her hard little nipples, I press her even harder against the wall, I put my knee between her thighs, I bite even harder, my mouth against her shoulder, and she yields, moves to my rhythm compassionately? forgive me my love, now the motion is perpetual, no one can stop me, that's-it-move-faster and she lets her legs go limp, she isn't kissing now; she slips down and I hold her up against the wall. What have we done, what have I done, a handful of rain in her face. I drape my jacket over her shoulders, I revive her and start her walking. Let's go now, what will the colonel say, and suddenly, damn it, I realize I left the backpack of purchases back in the restaurant, the Corridor, and it could be anywhere now.

The outcome would be pretty peculiar. Colonel O'Collogham lost no time in disappearing without a trace. His mind went blank at times, it seems . . .

My precocious little pet, who in fact was fourteen, almost fifteen, got pregnant that night. It wasn't in my nature to be a father.

Not at twenty-two or at thirty-three. Ecce homunculus . . . (Ay, I've just had a terrible foreboding. The cruelest month that you've spent so far away, is it to reflect, to reach, calmly and without pressure, a life-and-death decision? To be or not to be, to abort or to let sprout . . . You always forget to take your damn pill! Is that why? Could I be the future progenitor? Are you up to your old tricks? When I met you, you didn't have a passport, you'd left it as security at that cynical clinic at King's Cross. Crisscross? Double cross? And they didn't give back your passport until you'd made the last monthly installment. Once, when we touched on the thorny topic of the rights of the hypothetical father, who also had a right to decide, you almost scratched out my eyes. Qu'il décide? and you were so furious you actually said Kill the seed! Really? If you lie, then non è vero. Si le grain ne meurt, lest the seed die . . . But what pappagallish prattle I'm spouting. I can't imagine you as a sweet mamma. It isn't in your nature either to be a mother.)

But she would disappear suddenly, too, like her uncle the colonel. After my rash attempt to sail away to the silvery La Plata. When you're twenty-two all that glitters is gold . . .

My treasure's tresses. Shaking her ringlets in the sun . . . And her brazen little belly. My voluptuous little girl. The last time I saw her she was holding my arm, laughing at the break of day, walking into the wind near London Bridge, and from time to time I tried to keep her little plaid kilt from flying up to her face. We had spent the night at Prospero Jim's new pub, down on the docks, with almost all my dangerous London friends, the dyed-in-the-wool drunks guzzling away on that resounding isle, full of sound and . . .

Sometimes I've wondered if my evanescent dream girl was really a fairy queen, an angel, or the succubus of my nightmares?

I have invoked her on a bench in Regent's Park near the outdoor theater where they are playing *A Midsummer Night's Dream*. Now the hungry lion roars, and I swear to you from the nearby zoo there came roars—of a hungry lion?—that made me doubt the words I heard. I crossed the park, heading north, and sat on the grass beside the entrance to Gloucester Gate. A man with red hair has just run past wearing a white sweatband round his forehead, a red T-shirt, white shorts. And then a bare-chested boy carrying a baby in his arms walks by with the brunette elegant in her long pink skirt and green vest. Night begins to fall and I doubt the reality of the moment. No more words. I assume the lotus position and concentrate on the Flower of Dreams in that garden of delights in Willesden.

arning,
and I almost take away with me the board at the Notting Hill exit warning us again against suspicious packages. Last night a car bomb exploded at Heathrow. Make a note of that if you fly home. And last night two bombs went off in Paris. And the *Times* has also picked up the fact that in the middle of the night there were two fires at the Marine Hotel in Llandudno. I can see you with the other 119 guests running out of the hotel in pajamas and nightgowns . . . The *Times* mentions only the shortened name of that never-ending village in northwest Wales. Ever since we saw it written out with all its letters on a wall on Pentonville Road, you've wanted to visit the place, if only for a few hours . . . the shortest vacation in the longest village . . . Where are you?

We were walking here, your hand—gloved—in mine, on that cold Saturday in February when you approached me in Paddington Station. All my life . . . I should have said that was how long I had been waiting. A nice phrase. Imagine, it seemed to me I saw you again, playing with the old organ-grinder's monkey; but you vanished in a flash in that flood of people. I thought I saw you again at the entrance to the Electric Cinema. Can I be hallucinating? We spent so many nights there in black and white.

But I came to Portobello and went into the garden of the Westbourne Grove pub, where we once took refreshment, to drink and remember another Saturday that was something less than Holy.

A weekend of whiskey and roses with thorns, in that Florentine villa in Hampstead. To play the minstrel passion, laughing, I allowed my face to be crisscrossed, struck with a bouquet of bloodied roses. Her fiery hair flying at each blow behind the veil of blood. I saw red, everything was red, whirling red, in that red chamber. They help me or force me to drain a glass—is it broken? Blood on the glass, and the blood-red mouth bites my mouth. Another drink and a few slaps to revive me. Whiskey and sodamasochism . . . because we'd had too much to drink and I could barely stand.

When I woke, after a disturbed sleep, I found myself turned into Gregor.

But she, the opulent redhead in the fur coat, had been no dream. She was standing there still, la belle dame sans merci, at the foot of the great bed with its canopy of red damask where I lay spraddled, belly up. Naked. And unable to move, for my hands and feet were tied to the four bedposts.

I saw again the emerald blaze of her eyes piercing me with a glacial glance. She made a contemptuous movement of the head, and the fur slipped down to her forearms and the ringlets of her hair flamed against the snow of her shoulders and full round breasts. She was nude beneath her coat, which fell partly open, and I glimpsed through the dark fur the marble whiteness of her loins finely veined in blue. She pushed her sleeves up to the elbows with the energetic movements of a fighter, and from the mantel over the fireplace she took down a whip coiled like a cobra.

Wait! Wait! I implored in my impotence when I saw her brandish the whip decisively in my direction.

I relived that moment a while ago, in the tobacco shop across from the Notting Hill Gate station, when I saw the cards on the bulletin board at the entrance offering all the severities and services of the English vice, all the disciplines of Anglican culture, la culture anglicanne: SEATS RE-CANED, with firm caning on the bottom . . . ; CORRECTION SPECIALIST, a strapping young woman . . . ; WHIPS & WEEPS, for the wayward . . . ; GERMAN GOVERNESS, drilled in discipline . . . Miss Bottomlay continues advertising in her hard-hitting way, as does the blackjack player with the poker face, the chatelaine of chastisement . . . but I did not need any of these merciless mercenaries to flay my hide in order to crawl inside the skin of the poor devil called Gregor.

Coming down the Portobello market, I recalled that other cruel Saturday in February when I fell into the hands of the dominant madonna in fur.

I recognized her immediately, the lush redhead wrapped in her ample jacket of scarlet satin edged in white fur, reclining on the red velvet ottoman at the rear of the antiques shop in Westbourne Grove. In reality, I saw her portrait first, a large oil painting hanging just above her small red-haired head: a nude white as pearl among dark furs that she holds against her breast with her left hand, leaning in her indolence on her left elbow on the same red ottoman. She was just as Gregor had described her to me, and of course she holds aloft in her right hand a whip like a scepter. And her naked white foot rests carelessly on the shoulder of a slim, somber young man in black, lying there like a dog, grrgrr, poor Gregor . . . and gazing up at her with the eyes of a whipped greyhound or martyr.

She realized that I recognized her, or at least recognized her scarlet *kaẓabaika,* and her left hand began to flick the cord of her jacket as if it were a whip. After looking me over from head to foot, she asked if I were Greek. Not Greek, not griego, not even Gregor. But it seems I was destined for her, since she lived in upper Hampstead near Spaniards Road and the pub The Spaniards Inn, where I once recounted to you the new adventures of Dick Turpin and Black Bess . . . ; however, the quasi–country inn was not where we had our first drinks that Saturday, but the crowded mare magnum of The Cruel Sea, at the sharp turn of Heath Street, which allowed me a few easy compliments: the cruel sea of your eyes, my martyrdom . . .

That same night, with an ironic smile:

"Do you want to be my new Gregor?"

The name she gave to anyone who served as her factotum, her servant or—to call things by their right name—her slave.

We were in her Hampstead villa-museum filled with antiques, a replica of the one she had rented in Florence during a winter of passion.

When I reached the wall that surrounded the garden of her house, there in the chiaroscuro of the moon, I thought I was on the Via San Leonardo. The aura of Florence on the hills of Hampstead. Now we will walk in the darkness along the walk white with camellias. I thought with a shudder of the garden of delights and torments in her villa on the left bank of the river, di la d'Arno, across from the park of the Cascine, a garden that Gregor had cultivated with painstaking care and watered with his own blood. Is there no Florence without thorns? At the bottom of the garden, pinching her left breast with her right hand and covering her mons veneris with her left, the white Venus appeared like an apparition. *La Venere* . . . And he had an Italian or Latin air, the sallow, emaciated old servant, somewhat sinister all in black, solicitous as he took his lady's coat, humbly accepting her dry reprimand for not having lit the fire in the dining room.

I walked through the villa with the strange sensation that I had already seen it, already heard it, in my real life. The bedroom completely covered in blood-red damask (floor, walls, drapes, the canopy of the great four-poster bed), and on the ceiling the painting of Samson, his hands tied, lying at the feet of the red-haired Delilah on a red damask ottoman . . . ; the winding marble staircase leading from the bedroom to the sumptuous circular bath, the great marble basin in the center bathed in the sanguinary light that fell from the red crystal dome . . .

She was my cicerone and at times I could complete her remarks as I slowly remembered.

I was, once again, Gregor. Poor Gregor with no resources who agreed to go to Florence with that rich, young, beautiful, and capricious widow who enslaved him. And as he, with pleasure, allowed himself to be enslaved, he corrupted her. He molded and shaped her to fit his desire. The slave is born but the master is created . . .

I see the journey by train from Vienna to Florence (he, in third class—thank the Lord she could find none lower—and in first class the great lady wrapped in the fur greatcoat she used for traveling) accelerated, as if in a silent film: at each stop, Gregor jumps down from his car and runs to his mistress to receive his orders. In the Stazione Centrale he was the porter, carrying the heavy luggage of his mistress to the taxi. In the Grand Hotel of Florence she stayed in the two best rooms, with a view of the Arno, and Gregor slept in a tiny unheated, windowless cubicle on the fourth floor. In spite of this, the hotel staff soon began to whisper that she—the Russian, as they called her—was having relations with her servant.

More hard work on the streets in the center of Florence, finding the signs that say CAMERE AMMOBILIATE, climbing up and down stairs and more stairs, looking for an intimate, comfortable flat while at the entrance she awaited the results of his search. It was just as well that, finally, his mistress decided to rent a villa—more discreet for her plans—and ordered Gregor to walk around the city until nightfall.

He went (along the Via de'Servi?) to the Duomo, perhaps he thought he could float away in the immense emptiness of the cathedral; then I see him hurrying down the Via dei Calzaiuoli to the Palazzo Vecchio; in the Piazza della Signoria he shuddered before the statue of Judith cutting off the head of Holofernes and thought again of the verses from the Book of Judith that he had read so often: "To punish him, God smote him by the hand of a woman." Unless he thought of them standing before the Judith painted by Cristofano Allori, in the Galleria degli Uffizi, or before the drawing of Judith by Mantegna in the same museum. Or it may be that in the museum he only had eyes for *La Venere dei Medici,* object of all his veneration, displayed in the Tribuna as if in a chapel. And it is likely that at this time he also visited the Palazzo Pitti, in particular to stop at *The Torture of the Eleven Thousand Martyrs,* by Pontormo, and upon seeing that forest of torments, he probably evoked the terrible pleasure produced in him as a boy when he read the lives, or rather the deaths, of the martyrs, above all if they were illustrated. And finally he went down to the Arno (I imagine him walking along the Lungarno Corsini in the direction of the Cascine) and spent some time on its banks, not suspecting that a few months later he would want to drown himself in those waters, in the steely reflections there by the Ponte Vecchio . . . And in the distance, among the red roof tiles, he must have seen the Campanile and the Cupolone like a pale Don Quixote and blood-red Sancho Panza, tutelary gods of the city. And he contemplated the surrounding green hills with their cypresses, olive trees, palaces, cloisters, and white villas scattered in the distance, not yet knowing that in one of them he would find, at one and the same time, paradise, purgatory, and hell.

How would I like her to dress for dinner?

She showed me, or I should say she displayed, her lavish clothes, or costumes, for this was a wardrobe for a theater of cruelty, and I looked at each item of apparel that Gregor had described for me down to the last detail:

The filmy white *déshabillé* in which she presented herself to Gregor on the terrace, one stormy morning, appearing for the first time as his flesh-and-blood neighbor after he had taken her, the previous night, for a marble Venus in fur.

The white satin dress and scarlet satin *kazabaika* edged in ermine that she wore when she beat Gregor for the first time, after he begged her to on his knees.

The ermine Cossack hat that she wore on the night she ordered Gregor, after whipping him, to kneel and kiss her on the mouth.

The formfitting riding habit of black cloth and the jacket trimmed in dark brown fur that she wore during the first train ride with Gregor, when she amused herself by placing candies in his mouth or smoothing his hair with her fingers, as if he were a lapdog.

The negligee of fine white muslin and lace in which she received her slave Gregor on the first night in the hotel in Florence, as well as the coat of dark brown fur she wore over her shoulders and compassionately removed in order to cover him, caress him, kiss him on the divan just before she said that he bored her and slapped him so hard that she made him see stars and hear their explosion as they shot past.

The jacket of velvet, green like her eyes, trimmed in furs that caress her throat and bosom against which she suddenly pressed her slave Gregor, drowning him in kisses, during the first night of passion in the recently rented villa in Florence, before she had him write out a suicide note: "Weary of existence and the deceptions that accompany it, I have put a voluntary end to my useless life."

The long gown of silver satin that clings to her body with each stroke of the whip as she lashes Gregor, bound to a post of the canopied bed by three black Graces, the cruel, newly hired serving girls and dispensers of disgrace who untie him so that the slave may kneel before his mistress and kiss the white foot that peeks out from beneath her satin hem.

The dress of black velvet with a wide ermine collar in which she attends the Teatro della Pergola and spends four hours in her box receiving visits from her "chevaliers servants," while her servant Gregor stands guard at the door.

The high-heeled shoes that, on their return from the theater, Gregor, kneeling at her feet, could not manage to remove and replace with her velvet slippers until she presented him with a lash of the whip. And then a kick as an added present.

The coat of black velvet with which she covered herself, and the dark *bashlyk* with which she covered her head when she went out at nightfall, escorted by Gregor, to meet a German painter in a leafy corner of the park of the Cascine.

The dress of violet velvet adorned with fur and the Russian boots of the same material that she wore when, in the park of the Cascine, she succumbed, in the presence of Gregor, to the charms of an elegant Greek officer.

The dress of blue moiré with deep décolletage and the coat of white fur draped over her naked shoulders, exactly as Gregor sees her from the parterre of the Teatro Nicolini while she in her box devours with her eyes the handsome Greek in the box facing hers.

The heavy dress of sea-green silk that reveals her arms and

bosom and swish-swishes with sweet satisfaction as she dances until dawn in the arms of the beautiful Greek at the residence of the Greek ambassador, their every move followed by the tear-filled eyes of Gregor in the anteroom for lackeys.

The sleeveless deep-cut dress of silver-gray silk that traces her magnificent form as she lies on the ottoman, in the warm glow of the fire, caressing Gregor's brow as he kneels languidly at her feet, kissing her eyes, until she shakes off her languor and tells him she is going to whip him a little to make him show a little more passion. Then she lashed him to a post of the canopied bed, put on the ritual *kaʐabaika,* and asked if he wanted to be truly whipped.

"Yes."

Then, from behind the curtains of the canopy, there appeared the dark curly head of the Greek, who began to whip him savagely while she laughed and packed their bags.

She put on the ample fur greatcoat that she wore for traveling and walked down the stairs of the villa on the arm of the Greek and climbed into the car that would carry her far from Gregor, tied to his pillar of torment.

The dining room must be even colder, she said, scrutinizing the coats hanging in the large closet. Didn't I care? she asked with a gleam of complicity in her eyes as she placed the brown fur coat in my arms. I draped it over her shoulders and caressed the nape of her neck as I arranged the fiery ringlets on the collar of the coat. She lightly tossed it back, brushing my face, and in the soft fur I sensed the warmth and perfume of her body.

An intimate candlelit supper served by the old servant in white gloves. We soon grew warm and our jests became more daring. The servant came and went with an increasingly somber air. As he refilled my glass he spilled the Bordeaux on the tablecloth and spattered the even whiter bosom of his mistress. Now

I ought to give you a real slap! she exclaimed, and we both began to laugh. The servant seemed disconcerted, in suspense, until he withdrew, as red as the Bordeaux wine.

After the cold repast, torrid passion: as we kissed, lying on the white bearskin in the firelight, I discovered in the red shadows at the back of the room the watchful figure of the old servant. He likes to see me enjoying myself, she said, and burst into laughter against my neck.

Sometime later, without anyone having called him, he reappeared, carrying a tray with glasses and a bottle of whiskey. It was not his night, it seems. As he kneeled to serve us, he broke a glass. Then she did give him a slap that echoed throughout the entire house. The old servant remained on his knees, meekly gathering up from the floor the pieces of broken glass. In that posture, as he raised his head toward his mistress (I thought for a moment that he would offer the other cheek), I suddenly recognized the face, much older, wearing the identical expression of gratified humiliation, of the young man with the greyhound's profile lying at the feet of the lady with the whip and the furs in the painting (a copy?) I had seen in the antiques shop in Westbourne Grove.

I understood later—too late—that the old man was not really a servant and that I had been invited by his belle dame sans merci to that villa or museum or theater of cruelty only to make him suffer even more.

And then I would replace him, the scapegoat or scapestud? (The whipping playboy? . . .)

We'd had, or I'd had, too much to drink the night before and I could barely put my thoughts in order . . . Whiskey, laughter, roses . . .

Her full, very red mouth, parted, panting. Her temples damp with perspiration.

After crisscrossing my face with the bouquet of roses that now were red.

She allowed me to carry her to the great red bed.

Her preposterous proposition that we could make love only if I first let myself be lashed with a real whip.

Wait! I shouted when I saw the whip in her raised hand, trying to gain time. You can easily guess what I chose.

It was cool in the garden of the pub in Westbourne Grove, so close to where that strange curiosity shop was located, and I took refuge in the smoky saloon. I looked again, over the bar, at the advertisement showing huge fingers seizing the glass of sherry or sun, which reminds me of all those commercially comestible or potable letters I dashed off so correctly. Rectally and righteously. In vino veritas. In vain . . . At least someone was reading them.

The whip remained on high, I can't forget it, and I remember that before I made my decision I tried to imagine the pain, the bite of the whip, a whiplash and another whiplash—another whiPLEASURE!—and in a single swallow I finished this bad sherry that you call xérès.

enophobia
and racism in the United Kingdom . . . Superiority of the black race . . . Greek atrocities in Cyprus . . . Turkish atrocities in Cyprus . . . Mr. Nixon mixing it up, or the incessant tangle of tapes . . . Mr. Wilson and inflation . . . Why there is a sugar shortage now . . . Krishna and the expansion of consciousness . . . Esperanto for peace . . . The Apocalypse has already commenced . . . among other topics that I followed in fragments this morning at Hyde Park Corner as I went from group to little group, looking for you. I thought I saw you (why do I go on creating illusions?) near our old scrounging friends who after so many years still sustain and support the same placard, the same ultimatum: THE END IS AT HAND. A happy ending?

The same one we saw here the first time we woke—so late—together. It must have been your idea to come to Speakers' Corner. And we ate, almost at the Spanish supper hour, a supposedly Spanish omelet at a café on Edgware Road. The omelet was your idea, too. I recall everything and resent nothing.

The Antichrist in the pale djellaba is back again, the one with the long blond curls, vampire fangs, cadaverish white skin; sometimes we saw him behind Brook Green, too. The blue of noon in his demonic eyes. Poor devil . . .

The black man in his everlasting navy blue pinstripe suit,

his thumbs hooked in his vest, will once again make his predict-
able banal joke about Jamaican bananas at the expense of whatever lady happens to be passing by. I also saw the drunk with
all the dead leaves on his fly. And the poète—a coquette—with
the high pompadour and the ring in his ear who resembles the
young Ezra Pound.

As I watched a group of young men and women with shaved
heads hymning and haranguing Hare Hare, I was shaken by the
singular (nonsensical?) idea that perhaps you've joined some
sect—or a commune of squatters? It takes into account your
weakness for mystics, madmen, and all manner of marginal
types. When we passed the Buddhist monastery on Haverstock
Hill with its announcement that on Thursdays at seven they
offered a talk and meditation session, you were ready to push
me inside. To put an end to doubts if not the redoubtable
Buddha.

I saw myself, once, at Speakers' Corner (in another avatar),
arms extended and hair covering my eyes, standing on three
Express boxes, repeating over and over again in Sanskrit: Of all
forms of illusion, woman is the most important . . . You bet.

Then I went to the booth that sold drinks, sat in a deck chair
striped in all the colors of the rainbow, and had tea and the *Sunday Times*. The news of bombs in Messina almost made me
jump out of my seat. As I did in the small hours last night. You
were strolling so stunningly in the port, with grape leaves as
your fig leaf and a scythe in your hand that gleamed like a moon,
listening to whistles, applause, and remarks for every taste. And
suddenly everything began to tremble and the houses fell in on
you amid clouds of dust. I don't know if it was a tremonitory
(*sic*) dream, I hope not, or one of Sicilian revenge . . .

Then, on Bayswater Road, I slowly walked past all the
bric-a-brac-abracadabra-batikmantic-magic-flyingcarpet-pop-
pourri-dalineations of post-hippie crafts and arts that were pre-

post (preposterous rather than absurd) along the park railing, recalling the more or less annotated visits we made there on so many Sundays. In reality you regarded the objects with interest, you sometimes stopped to chat with the artists and even took what they said seriously. The red-bearded giant and the giantess with short green hair and skirt are still sitting in their folding chairs beside their van. Van Gogh and Magog . . . , and I remember you were not at all amused by the nickname I gave them. (Lack of respect for the artist? Every day I look at the postcard of the blue old man who weeps, sitting in his chair, his fists covering his eyes, that you pinned to my Chinese screen so long ago. Nothing sadder than seeing an old man cry . . .)

I ate rather late in our favorite Chinese restaurant on Queensway. Sitting before the tower of covered dishes, I was recovering memories, relishing past moments that do not soon go up in smoke. On the other side of the window, life flowed by. In some couples I could see the couple we had been, drifting without a care along Queensway. In the small church across the street an occasional woman went in or came out, her head covered. I imagined you as devout. Covering your face . . .

Maison Pechon doesn't open on Sundays. I would have liked to sweeten my memories.

I fell asleep in Holland Park after watching over the wild games of the squirrels. I woke to a chorus of peacocks and the zooming of airplanes. I kept looking at the blue sky. A blue eye among the clouds. Presentiments . . . in a ship's wake that unravels across the sky. I was feverish again. (It's that damned Why's fault, I caught a chill the other night looking for him in Brook Green. All for nothing.)

As night began to fall I ambled along King's Road until I went into the Picasso to tell you about my demoiselle d'Avignon, a compatriot of yours whom I met when she was almost

X-ed out in a bar in Barcelona. In a bar on Avignó, almost at the corner of Escudillers, filled to overflowing with fools that night early in October. A group of French tourists were gabbling and cackling in confusion about going to a bar named for an artist, it sounded to me like Gargallo or Chirico. Their table was covered with empty wine bottles and I thought she was with them, the very pale brunette in an elegant dress of navy blue silk with a wide white collar, who was gulping down red wine and blood sausage with all the voracity of a peasant girl, or as if she wished to give the part some veracity. And made up as heavily as a whore from the Barrio Chino. Merely an actress? A demoiselle de Paris, living in the lap of luxury and leisure for whom—if life is not a dream—all the world could be a stage.

We started up a conversation as soon as her kiriko-korusing compatriots decamped. Between glasses, which she had me fill with some frequency, she proclaimed her ideas—communist commonplaces.

I asked her please to lower her voice.

(A mountain of years have just fallen on two anarchists sentenced in Barcelona. Forty-eight and twenty-one! At least it's not the ghoulish garrote, the sentence handed out four months ago. The *garrote* . . . another universal Spanish word. So that no one can say we haven't invented anything . . .)

She was drunk, I realized too late, with her hair disheveled, *en bataille,* and her pallor intensifying as she guzzled more and more red. But she went on making her marks, Marx and more Marx . . . Typical of her. She traveled to Barcelona in a sleeping car with *L'Humanité* for a pillow. But she didn't come to Barcelona because of her communist ideals, I later learned; she was drawn there by a compatriot vacationing in Barcelona who sent a telegram to Paris asking her to join him immediately.

She soon made her first scene, what she wanted to be our first scene together. She sat looking at the almost Olympic rings of red wine on the paper tablecloth, placed her fork in my right hand, held it, and slid it, under the table, along her silky thigh . . . At first I didn't understand, but beyond any doubt she wanted me to dig the fork hard into her thigh . . . Then she pushed back her chair, rose to her feet, and raised her dress to see the wound. People must have thought she was a tipsy tourist who wanted to dance or sing flamenco. *Cante rondo,* as she called it . . . Her underthings were pretty. I liked her sky-blue step-ins and especially her naked thighs. I couldn't waste a second, I had to go down on my knees and put my lips to her thigh, swallow the few drops of blood from the wound that existed solely in her overheated imagination. Carving up her thigh was not my specialty. She was drunker than I had supposed and kept crying, leaning on my arm, until I filled her glass again with red wine and made her drink it.

The fault lay with a certain Tropfmann—or some such name—who had made her hurry to Barcelona for nothing. At almost the same moment that the passion of his life appeared out of nowhere, a cadaver, one might say, a true walking skeleton, that fatal blonde in whose embrace one could find Eros and Thanatos simultaneously. He was, no doubt, an intellectual. And this Truppman could not or would not interpret her playacting. Nor did he wish to strain himself with his ménage à trois in the Hotel of Four Nations, which is what both women lustfully desired one nightmarish night. Perhaps he wished to save her from the clutches of the skeletal blonde. Or desired the perverse skeleton for himself alone, the possessive obsessive bridegroom of death. Was he not impotent only with death?

Trembling with excitement before the corpse of the old woman who was his mother, he took off his pajamas and began to masturbate . . . Necrofilial. Enough! Trop c'est trop, Troppmann. Were these horrors true, or was he trying to *épater la bourgeoise* who read de Sade? Though she was no ass-licker. She knew, as did all of Paris, that he had an abnormal sex life, but she thought a degenerate deigns to do what he does because he suffers. And she wanted to save him, above all from the dangers and temptations of death. She began caring for him. She went to see him when she learned he was ill, and as a way of demonstrating how docile and solicitous she was, she drank the white wine he longed to watch her drink. Then she kissed his hand, stroked his brow, kneeled beside his bed, kissed his brow, and let him slide his hand under her skirt and up her legs and along her buttocks, so fresh . . . And yet, they never went as far as making love.

She wanted us to go out to breathe in the Barcelona night. But we still drank wine in another bar on Escudillers. We sat on a terrace on the Rambla de Capuchinos and out of the blue she took a notion to walk through the Barrio Chino. She staggered, holding my arm and stumbling at every step along Calle Arco del Teatro, and on Calle Cid she insisted that I help her find a transvestite nightclub called La Criolla. I finally convinced her that we should go back to her hotel, on the corner of the Rambla. Was that man Troppmann still there? She asked me to accompany her to her room. In fact I had to help her to her room. It was hot and I opened the window. She asked me if I heard shots on Calle Fernando. Only a backfire. No doubt she was delirious. Now you'll ask me to drink some more and sing . . . Before I could open my mouth she opened the armoire and took out a bottle of champagne that was almost full and poured herself a glass. It was lukewarm but she drank it down in almost one swallow. And another, quickly, without offering me one.

Standing, looking down at the carpet, she began to sing in a solemn voice:

Loves That Bind

J'ai rêvé d'une fleur
Qui ne mourrait jamais.

She stopped suddenly, walked over to the door to lock it, and asked me to lie on the bed.

And slowly, one article of clothing at a time, she undressed. She left on only her stockings. Lighter than her thighs. Her body was more attractive than her face.

She began to sing again, in a husky voice, her head shaking:

J'ai rêvé d'un amour
Qui durerait toujours.

Her sobbing stifled her voice. She came, weeping and naked, toward my bed, kneeled down, and buried her tear-streaked face in the pillow.

"I'm drunk," she said.

The bottle and glass were empty on the night table. And I could see her in the moon-shaped glass of the armoire across the room. View of Barcelona with full moon. She got into bed with her white shoes, bottom upward, and buried her head in the pillow.

I spoke into her ear and could feel her breath as she muttered something incoherent. I have a clearer memory of her winy breath than of anything she said. I have a clearer memory of her ardent, solemn voice than of her words, incomprehensible at times.

"Aren't you afraid of death?"

She jumped up to close the window and came back to the bed to announce:

"He can't get in."

(Troppmann or Tropfmann?)

She didn't hear me. As if she were walking and talking in a dream:

"Are you afraid of Frascata?"

She stretched out alongside me, naked, motionless, very pale, like a dead woman, or assuming the appearance of a dead woman.

It was a farce, surely, but I didn't understand its meaning, its lack of meaning.

Had she said Frascata or Frascati?

For the flu, nothing's better than booze. Flush out a fever with drink. I was still recalling my drunken chantactress in the drugstore in Chelsea: a go-go girl with white stockings and sturdy thighs was moving to the lento beat I was humming to myself, hearing the solemn, ardent voice that will never be erased. A flower that will never die. Always alive. Immortelle . . . And afterward, in the Trafalgar, dernière bataille, last bottle. Brandished at the bar by a drunken boy who wanted to cut off the discussion. Nothing to do with me. Swill and let swill . . .

My burning forehead against the tiles. Distant blue tiles d'antan . . . I miss her cool hand on my forehead. As I relieved myself in the lettrine of that pub, I read a message (can it really be true?) in large letters on the condom-dispensing machine. I'll copy it out for you:

SOMEONE

SOMEWHERE

WANTS

A LETTER

FROM YOU

Yang

has returned! I mean Guay. Why. His pitiful wail this morning,
very early, when I was beginning my first yoga exercises, down,
head down (to see if my fever went down in difficult equilibrium: Y, probably for Yggdrasil . . .), in the wild garden in
back. Why. I thought he was a black bag fallen down beside the
trash can. Turned into trash, literally, half his fur gone and a red
flap where his left eye had been. My purblind puss. Mon gros
chat châtié. My cat's atrophy. Catastrophe. What will your mistress say when she sees you? A letter from her waiting for me
since the day before yesterday, a letter from Ithaca (in New
York, not Greece, as I had thought) announcing that she will
return next week. Everyone is beginning to return. And you?
Will you return to me, too? Is Why your black herald? This
morning—at seven!—a dove woke me at the window of my
dovecote. Your messenger? The mask of some alar spirit? Alas!
Rapid alate flutter. I got up immediately, to put my best foot forward on this melancholic-alcoholic Monday? Let's go, on your
way! This morning I played the old cassette from the old days
over and over again. *Trátala con cariño.* Treat her with affection.
Almost without batteries, as usual, our black box. As if she were
moi . . . , I can still hear you singing along. Now Why sings the
accompaniment. As he went back and forth from my room to

Miss Rose's apartment. He followed me all over the house. You see what happened when you followed your yin . . . Went after your pussychatte . . . Went chingando over the hot yin roofs. The price of freedom. An eye. Why, oh Guay. Just as well they didn't castrate you. Chat châtré . . . This reminds me that you left behind a black Penguin edition from the Swiss Cottage library: the letters of Abelard and Héloïse. Belles lettres . . . My only love, she calls him, her poor castrato. The love of all loves . . . Why's wail more and more insistent. But I had no tins left. And I brought him a saucer of milk. What greedy lapping. Tantalizing taste as important as the tantras, eh? What tonguing. So eager he overturned it. Little by lit . . . Poco a popocatepittle. Now. Meow. A little via lactea along the black tiles in the kitchen. Milky Way. Milchstrasse. La ruelle de Saint-Jacques . . .

All roads—most especially those in heaven—lead to my star escaping from Hollywood. Who also studied astronomy in her native land. At the University of Hawaii.

One of the first images—almost photographic—I have of her: lying on the bed, her tan arm hanging over the edge of the bed listlessly, her palm turned up as she reads an astronomy magazine whose cover displays the domes of an observatory. Other domes attracted the attention of this observer: the swell of her breasts glimpsed in the dark décolletage of her night-gown slightly pulled aside.

I still smell the aroma of her light-tobacco cigarette (Camel?) that she had just put out in the porcelain ashtray shaped like a swan.

The first photo, bella vista . . . in my memory, she is overexposed: standing, dazzling in a flood of morning sun, at first I saw clearly only her slim dark hand holding the strap of the red bag at her hip. She wore an elegant slate-blue dress.

Her brown hair, somewhat bleached by the sun and the chlorine in the pool . . . Her small ears, visible through the curls . . . Her heavy eyebrows and warm, candid brown eyes . . . Her amusing nose a shade too tilted to be Greek . . . Her wide full-lipped mouth . . . Her slightly weak chin . . .

As dark as a Moorish girl from Granada. Brown as a pomegranate, I mean. Good-looking, tan, and young. An ageless beauty, though she was thirty.

And when she settled on that green daybed, crossing her long dark legs, I could appreciate her exquisite curves. And her almost aristocratic bearing on the broken daybed . . .

I also remember her that same day in the afternoon, dressed all in sun, in yellow slacks and yellow sandals. And I do not grow weary of watching her brown neck and arms, and the trembling of her breasts that stood up under the fine blouse embroidered in green-feathered birds with long brilliant tails, and red flowers, and gold pyramids. Probably a souvenir of Cholula.

And I continue to contemplate her yellow walk and the graceful swift movements of her sandals in which she seemed to be floating.

And I also remember her on that last day walking barefoot, almost on her toes, like a Pavlova in a white swimsuit at the edge of the cobalt-blue pool that was her swan lake.

She was, to generalize, one of those North American women on her second divorce, slender, of average height, who rode like a graceful Diana the Huntress of the Far West, her face radiating health, as brown as a Boy Scout's, her hair always clean and shining, though carelessly hanging down, as if she were doing an ad for shampoo.

Youthful, or ageless? That same afternoon (a little while before we went to that brutal rodeo in Tomalín: of course, I, a poor Spanish fool, would learn that in Hawaiian, cowboy and

Spaniard are the same word: *paniolo*) I noticed the fine lines around her mouth, an expression of fatigue I had not seen in Paris. Or in London.

(Each time I went into Cosmo Place, to my job in that dusty basement as a proofreader of galleys in Latin—Facilis descensus Avienus . . . —I thought of her. Of our cosmopolitan hotel in Bloomsbury. Where our love lies buried. Bloomsbury days . . .)

London . . . Paris . . . Granada . . . Los Angeles . . . Was there a Hotel Los Angeles in Granada, or was that a convent? All roads lead me to her, but at times the constellations of labels on her luggage of a lady errant leave me light-headed.

Hilo Hotel in Honolulu, Villa Carmona in Granada, Hotel Theba in Algeciras, Hotel Peninsula in Gibraltar, Hôtel Manchester in Paris, Cosmo Hotel in London, Hotel del Canadá in Mexico City, Hotel Astor in New York, The Town House in Los Angeles, Hotel Mirador in Acapulco . . .

There was also a Hotel Fausto . . . where? And labels from hotels in Reno (she divorced her first husband there), Santa Barbara, Nazareth (Hotel El-Nasira?), and other holy and unholy places that I've forgotten.

But I digress. The Hilo Hotel, in Honolulu or Hilo? Her father, a native of Ohio, had a pineapple plantation or halakahiki in Hawaii, near Hilo, where she spent her childhood. She always carried in her handbag an old photograph of her father as a young man, in the uniform of an army captain, with her same candid eyes beneath thinner brows, and a similar sensual, sensitive, full-lipped mouth under his black mustache.

The uniform did not become Captain Constable, or he—despite his name—did not become the uniform, and he left the army to undertake riskier campaigns that would make him long for the old martial days.

It was not easy to amass a fortune with the *Ananus comosus* plantation, but nobody would have thought of manufacturing synthetic hemp from the pineapple tops, and nobody would have even attempted to harness the energy from a nearby volcano to run the hemp machine. Misunderstood, like so many other inventors, the captain consoled himself by sitting on the lanai, the covered patio of his plantation house, and sipping okolehao and awa and singing plaintive Hawaiian songs, Aloha oe . . . , while the pineapples rotted in the fields and the native help gathered round to sing with him. She had vague memories of the plantation at the foot of the volcano, but in the labyrinth of memory she still could hear the glissando guffaw of her father, who did not have much reason to laugh. When she was six, her mother died. And thanks to her mother's brother, Uncle Macintyre, a wealthy Scotchman with financial interests in South America, Captain Constable was named American consul to Iquique. Of the four or five years they lived in Chile, she especially recalled her father's brooding expression, his isolation greater than Robinson Crusoe's, which would bear new fruit, like a pipe of his invention, insanely complicated, that one dismantled into seventeen pieces for purposes of cleanliness, but that only its ingenious inventor seemed able to put back together again, though he was not a pipe smoker. In that pipe he burned up all his energies, neglecting routine consular business. And since misfortunes never come singly, a short while later, when the hemp factory in Hilo also went up in smoke following a rather suspicious fire within only six weeks of its completion, he returned to his native Ohio to work for a wire-fence company that soon went bankrupt. He decided to return to his old ways, his pineapple days in Hawaii, and the dementia that detained him in Los Angeles was not precisely a delusion of grandeur—though he discovered he was penniless—but the one called delirium tremens.

At the time she was suffering her own delirium. The terrors she would relive in recurrent nightmares. A heavy hand clutching her shoulder through the dark doorway . . . Two hundred horses stampeding toward her in a ravine . . . The shots, *pow-pow*, fired by the villainous *paniolo* or cowboy . . . Starting when she was only thirteen, she had supported her father for five years as an actress in "serials" about the traffic in white slaves, the tricks of gangsters, the truculent battles of gunfighters. Her adored daddy was her manager. The Holy Father on his throne. Until his death returned Uncle Macintyre to the scene, and he shipped her back to Honolulu to pursue her studies far from the Hollywood studios. First he hired a private tutor to make up for lost time, and then he sent her to the University of Hawaii, where she took a course in astronomy. Contemplating the tropical night above the Manoa valley, she dreamed of becoming the Madame Curieuse of astronomy who spies on the firmament through the eye of a telescope. But a future husband soon blocked the view . . . : Cliff Wright, an overgrown and not very intelligent millionaire, who, with the help of that bawd the Hawaiian moon, easily persuaded her to leave college and marry him. The wedding did not receive good press because of the bride's past as a precocious actress. Yet her youthful charm conquered everyone. Youth is the opiate of the people . . . But she soon realized he was not the blue-ribbon catch he had seemed—pugnacious, adulterous, inept, an infantile giant . . . —and divorce would come inevitably two years after the birth of her only child, named Geoffrey, who died of meningitis at the age of six months. Uncle Macintyre washed his hands of the girl, who was, after all, a Constable through and through, and who had inherited the wild and reckless character of her father's family. After the divorce, when she was twenty-four, she left Hawaii and returned to Hollywood. Her agent increased the glamorous publicity. The young Hawaiian siren is back, a serenely sensational woman with an air of mystery and that deep light in her eyes left by a tear-filled past that has prepared her for great dramatic roles. Her body is more sensual and sculptural than ever. A honey-colored Venus newly emerged from the sweet waters of Onomea. Venus de Hilo, born of the sea . . .

Would some opulent producer, his wallet as bulging as his paunch, launch her into stardom? Shortsighted producers tend to have short memories.

She had been a precocious star, and now, with more grief than glory, her swan song . . . , she would be a shooting star shining only in that selva oscura as she walked alone down Virgil Avenue, a burned-out star who had nothing left but promises and pretty words.

This frustration—and nostalgia for the heady Hollywood days—would lead her five years later to be first the colleague and then the lover, though in an ephemeral way, of Jacques Laruelle, a forgotten French movie director and childhood friend of her second husband, who had passed, as she had, through Hollywood and dreamed of filming his own *Faust* one day. What a marvelous Marguerite she would have been. Radiant, ardent . . . (But one must not throw pearls or even marguerites before the public.) Only with Laruelle could she talk about Hollywood—and from words they moved to actions.

And if she had another brief affaire with the stepbrother of her second husband, a good-looking English boy named Hugh, it was perhaps because he reminded her—more or less unconsciously at first—of the cowboy star in Hollywood with whom she had made three pictures when she was fifteen. Though by the time Hugh showed her that he too could be a real cowboy or *paniolo* and take the bull by the horns and ride it up to the clouds—there in that rodeo in Tomalín with her cuckold of a husband sitting as a horned spectator beside her—they were no longer lovers. Or to be completely fair, and not become entangled in the branches of that forest of folly or fodder or jealous foreboding: the reason for her infidelity lay not in Hollywood, nor in her passionate nature, but in the passion that had just conquered her second husband.

I too would have liked to be with her in Hollywood. I mean in the Hollywood Bar in Granada.

This *paniolo* would have liked to have known her in Granada, as her second husband did. That is the place. That is where they met and married. All things are possible in Granada. There they thought they could be happy, thought that paradise was theirs. Perhaps she told him her story in the gardens gardens gardens of the Generalife. I imagine them sitting for a moment on a rough green bench against the high green wall of a hedge. Perhaps she went on with her story in the bar of the Hotel Washington Irving. Unless it was in the Alhambra. I see him following her words as he looked up at the marvelous stucco traceries. And with his hand he covers his mouth open in admiration. Near the Alhambra they had their first date for their first supper; but she understood *in* the Alhambra and they did not meet . . . (Two years later, in Mexico City, he was the one who could not remember the name of the restaurant on the Via Dolorosa where they were supposed to have their last supper, their farewell supper . . .)

He would look for her hungrily—and thirstily—in the Alhambra, and around it. I see him standing for a long time in front of the Puerta del Vino . . . The Englishman with the little goatee and the rebellious blond lock of hair falling over his blue eyes (or over his dark glasses?), clenching his pipe. Did she ever come that night? They were happy and ate chicken with tomato that was not yet spectral. Or a Sacromonte omelet not made with divorced eggs . . . A portable Granada in a series of snapshots that they would look at again when happiness had been left behind. From the heights of the Silla del Moro they promised eternal love. In those ruins she might have told him about the ruins of her past. About Geoffrey, her dead child, who had the same name—isn't it remarkable?—as he. About her dead father (wasn't it surprising that he had the same profession and habits as her father?) redivivus in the person of this consul for Great Britain in a Mexican city with an almost unpronounceable name, Quauhnáhuac (that QUAUHNAHUAC whirls almost like a drunken Ferris wheel at a fair), at the foot of two menacing volcanoes that were even more unpronounceable, Popocatepetl and Ixtaccihuatl, apocopated into Popo and Ixta, which would make her recall her difficult childhood on the island with five volcanoes, especially Mauna Loa with its crater Mokuaweoweo.

And she would speak to him, finally, about Cliff, her first husband. Cliff: precipice . . . But the one who really went over the edge into cantinas would be her second husband. Steeply inclined to drink. And she, to the end, attempted to save her marriage. Through fire and water. Firewater to the very last drop of raving drunkenness and into ravines . . . This new consul, like her father, also turned to the bottle. (Consul . . . Qu'on saoule . . . Let's get drunk . . . , that's how it would sound more or less to the guilty ears of Monsieur Laruelle, the name the Mexicans gave to her childhood friend, poor Old Bean, whom he—though he had put horns on him—would have wanted to save from his un-Faustian, unhappy fate. A drunk, a hopeless drunk . . . a chorus of angels in that inferno would repeat.)

It is likely that the Consul also spoke to her in Granada of his past. Of his parents, who disappeared when he was a boy. His father vanished mysteriously into the peaks of the Himalayas. Mal haya . . . Evil to him who evil thinks . . . Of his wild childhood with distant cousins in the northeast of England. Of the first time he asked for whiskey in a pub, just imagine, when he was still the boy Old Bean, as if we were to call him the black garbanzo of the family, a Johnnie Walker that would lead him to explore from that time on all the drinks there were to drink in the world.

And he would speak to her in particular of his mother, who died in Kashmir when he was very young.

Looking back on the past of both orphans, that marriage under the spell of Granada was destined to failure that had its roots in an incompatibility as tragic as it was absurd: the Consul was looking for a mother, and she—but she found him—was seeking her father's double. He was thirty-nine when they met—twelve years her senior. In spite of his age, he would identify with the dead Geoffrey—his namesake—but she could not become his mother again: she was too busy becoming a wife . . . And it isn't necessary to go on with circoanalytic acrobatics—you either catch on or you fall—to see that he drank in order to die, to rejoin in that besotted rodeo—an unbroken round of cantinas—his dead parents.

At that time Quauhnáhuac had fifty-seven cantinas, all of them barely enough to quench the thirst of the Consul. He loved his wife deeply, but alcohol ranked a few degrees higher than love. Or, to be more precise, only in the spiritual seclusion of chapel-cantinas, in communion with the divine spirits of contradiction, could he express all the intensity of the love he felt for his Beatrice. His Ophelia. His Dulcinea. The love of his life. El amor de los amores . . . He even wrote her drunken verses as he reeled from cantina to cantina. Chanting cantinas in praise of Our Lady . . . He liked the mix of mezcal and poetry.

The alchemy of vermouth and the verbum. The double Christophanic enigma of the XX on Dos Equis beer. He was an alchemist searching for the magnum opus he would write one day about the hermetic sciences. He knew that a great work, like genius, lay hidden at the bottom of the bottle. In the cantinas of Quauhnáhuac, when he contemplated the bottle of Anís del Mono (but to his hallucinating eyes the monkey on the label was no mono but a demon holding a gallows in his paw instead of a bottle of Anís del Mono ad infinitum . . .), he could not fail to see that this was the Wise Monkey . . . And other such mysteries well known to one initiated in the occult sciences. It is the best . . . But he lost his powers, an exhausted ex-Faust, and he could not commune again with the dark forces. He would pretend that all the glasses were communicants . . .

When did communication with his wife really break down? They separated after two years of marriage; they said good-bye in Mexico City, in a hotel portentously called the Canada. How many times she had dreamed of an idyllic shack by the sea and at the foot of the snow-covered Canadian mountains, though the closest she had ever been to Canada was Niagara Falls. The shack between the ocean and the forest . . . That Eden would be theirs and they would live as frugally as Adam and Eve before the Fall. But how could she convince the Consul to leave Quauhnáhuac and Tequila? An ominous black manus with an accusatory index finger pointed the way. Orlac in the region of the great lakes? The Consul preferred to keep circling (Laczem) the arctic-cathartartaric circles of his own Inferno.

I too dined on steak tartar tonight in Paradiso-E-Inferno, our Italian restaurant at the corner of Southampton Street and the Strand. Minos the terrible, unless it was Cerberus with his red burning eyes and prominent belly, assigned places at the door. Because I came alone I was given Inferno, to the right, next to the door. Through the window I watched the rain and the people hurrying past along the Strand to see if you were among the damned. No one is alone? Still sitting on the sidewalk with his cap-cum-collection plate is the hefty young man who, when winter comes, takes shelter in his cardboard house. It is as long as a coffin. The case is altered. One night we talked to him. He had been a boxer. You don't like boxing either . . . I don't know if he's been in jail again. His head is shaved and now he has a bloody cross of adhesive tape on his head. Da capo linéaire . . . Poor shorn compañero . . . Looks terrifying with all that blood or Mercurochrome on his cranium . . . I recalled that she could not bear the sight of blood either. That dog bleeding to death, streams and arroyos of blood running along the empty road in Hilo or Honolulu in illo tempore, and she fainted before she could give him any help. But you're worse: you just need to hear the word blood. That white night in the Electric Cinema, when we went to sit down and you pinched your finger in the seat. Is there any blood? And when you heard blood in the darkness you became dizzy . . .

I was so alone in the Inferno that I reckoned up my accounts on the back of the check I handed to you:

 ו ו34 51 ו

Writing numbers that no one will decipher. I settled my account this morning looking down. Seven? . . . That is the real number of the beast. Writing letters that no one will read . . .

All those letters she wrote to him after she left. Beautiful letters . . . At least she could send hers.

To Calle Nicaragua . . .

Where are you? If at least I knew where you were.

In this silence that unsettles me, I imagine all kinds of horrible things happening to you.

The *Times* goes on feeding my fears. Nine new deaths from

cholera in Portugal. Floods in Bangladesh and northeastern India have caused fifty fatalities. And the afternoon papers are not far behind. The placards for the *Evening Standard* and the *Evening News* at the entrance to the Charing Cross Road station. The poor girl beaten to death in Belfast. The police still don't know who she is; they estimate that she is between eighteen and twenty years old. Today a letter bomb blew up in the face of a woman in a tobacco factory in Bristol. And another death in larger letters. "Mama" Cass found dead today in her London flat. I will play her cassette as a requiem. On the Day of the Dead as well. And the *Times* reports that last night a ten-pound bomb was found in the Prince of Wales pub on Lillie Road. I pass it almost every day. Except yesterday. One must drink dangerously? Today I planned to follow the route of seven, from pub to pub, from the phantasmal Fitzroy Tavern at the edge of Soho to the George and Dragon in Acton.

To recall the belle of Hawaii, I should have gone to a pub near Elephant & Castle with Hawaiian decor and music, where in days gone by I met a real hula-hula girl who tried to teach me the sweetness of her tongue. Honi kaua wikiwiki. (Kiss me fast. Kiss me, fool.) Oh honey! Honey was not made for the mouth of a poor fool . . .

But I went instead to Lord Chandos, behind the Paradiso-E-Inferno and almost directly across from the National Portrait Gallery, where, in an inspired moment, I once tried to write a letter to Francis Bacon signed Lord Word. And next door, the tacatacataca of Flamenco. Granadan zambra, crafty carousing. Almost enough to make you order a fino sherry. But I asked for a Highland Queen, to honor my half-Scotswoman. (Ancestors in Highland castles in icy air who did not pass on the genes for Loyalty, Order, and Thrift . . . To the stars by the most asperous road . . .) I clear my throat. Strong, this whiskey. Odor and taste . . . Once again in Lord Chandos abstract words fell apart on my tongue like rotten mushrooms. Trompettes des morts. Dead words that fall to dust. Here we revived that poor lover half-dead with love who collapsed in the doorway of the post office as we passed. Can't one live without loving? Or without love? I love, therefore I am. I exist. I insist. I thought he'd had an attack. Half-bald but very young, dressed in a dark suit like a clerk from the City with his umbrella and black briefcase. Sprawling on the sidewalk, whimpering. We kneeled beside him. Call a doctor? Tears on his eyeglasses. And drool on his chin. You gave him your handkerchief. Whimperembling like a whipped dog. I don't know how long he'd been walking, he could no longer stand, and he fell. Days without food. Without sleep. We were the Good Samaritans. We brought him into Lord Chandos. Do you remember? A little before midday; but he didn't want alcohol or food. A cup of tea trembling in his scratched hands. By his own nails? Great scratches, on the backs, covered with blond hairs. Do you remember him? Sniveling so much we understood nothing. Some relative or friend. He scribbled a telephone number on the paper I handed him . . . The number of the Beast? You made the call and spoke to a very pregnant woman who came to pick him up. After half an hour in a Volkswagen Beetle. As young as he and in her sixth or seventh month. She looked at us in embarrassment, at you and me and at the poor sniveler. She didn't want anything to drink. She stood and waited, next to the table, until he got up. With an expression of doubt, or fear, or perhaps disbelief, as if he couldn't believe his own eyes. She came back. She came to him. And when they left, you declared (what did you base your opinion on?) that she was not pregnant by him.

I'd like to do the same now. Throw myself on the ground, along with my bag like a postman's sack filled with unanswered letters. But I don't have your number. An address where I could send an SOS. Call her. For God's sake. Let her come back to me. Even if only for a day. I'm not alone. Call Valparadiso. Edenburgh. 7734 514 51 345. Hello! Hell-o! No, no answer . . . Is this the right number?:

$$7734\ 514\ 51\ 345$$

Don't worry, I'll stop doing my little numbers and go on . . .

Did I drink more than my share in Lord Chandos? I sat for a while to enjoy the air on the steps of St. Martin-in-the-Fields. In the fields of cotton clouds. An optical illusion in Trafalgar Square? Nelson the stylitic at the top of his column had turned his back to the river and its bridges to scrutinize Tottenham Court Road with a spyglass. On a clear night you can drink forever. Morelia or Moriles? More or less. Spy, afar, glass, forever . . .

Then I was in Fulham. First in the bar on Hollywood Road across from the Pekingese restaurant with that huge painting in black lacquer and gold at the entrance which had you sailing through the Yin night and the golden afternoon of the Yang-tse. I ought to write these names for you in Chinese characters with my enigma-writing machine. Ma Chine infernale! . . . But the best thing would be to make confetti out of all these papers with no consignee.

I crossed Fulham Road toward the brick bulk of St. Stephen's Hospital. Our protomartyr. Cousin Stephen . . .

I recall that when she came back to him—because after a year she came back!—a little before disembarking, she was greeted in Acapulco Bay with a gust or shower or iridescent hurricane of butterflies that fell like multicolored heartrending love letters. Shreds of paper into the sea . . . Beautiful love letters . . .

In reality, as soon as she left the Consul to return to the United States, she sent him a postcard from El Paso in which she asked herself and asked him why she left him and why he let her leave. *Why did I leave? Why did you let me?* And signed it *Y.* But that postcard sent to Mexico City, after traveling to Paris, Gibraltar, Algeciras . . . reached Calle Nicaragua in Quauhnáhuac a year later on the same day as her surprise arrival, the November 2 that would be their last day together. Too late. Guay. The delinquent mails of fate, that was the true infernal machine. Though the Consul doubted that those words arriving in time, before his rancor rankled, could have saved them. Saved their love.

His stupid goatish pride . . . , and I drank whiskey, too (though not Chivas . . .), in his honor at The Goat in Boots. Flocks of people all the way out to the sidewalk. 1882, on the white plaque at the second story. A good year. I thought he was an advertisement: beside the door, the dandy wearing a white suit and a goatee who watched with Machiavellian eyes, leaning on his cane, as the dark girl in the poppy dress, red shoes, red bag, pressed against her boyfriend. Beautiful poppy. Amapola. I don't know if he's going to assault her or strip her naked with his eyes. Ah, those spying old goats . . .

And I was about to go into the oh so típicamente Spanish tavern next door, as clean and pulchritudinous as a whitened sepulchre with its little black lantern. Strong dishes. *Cabrito al horno.* In the capricornian style of Cape Horn . . . I walked along Park Walk to the end: The Man in the Moon.

A pale clair de lune behind a cloud. Silent friend. In the contagious silence of the night. Today is her day, the moon's day. Lunes.

How she liked the names that the ancient astronomers gave to the seas of the moon. Mare Serenitatis. Ora pro nobis. Mare Nubium. Ora pro nobis. Mare Humorum . . . I lost her among the clouds. I have an idea you'll return in four or five days, when the moon is full. Just as it was when you left. A bright idea?

Tempted to spin the wheel of fortune on the bar. Will you come back to me? The Quixotriste figure mirrored in the bottles looks at me. Round black glasses like the ones John Lennon wore, black hair and beard, even blacker ideas. In mourning. Rigorous. The man in the moon. If my astronomer from Hawaii were here, she would explain what the Man in the Moon is made of. On clear nights, on the plantation in Hawaii, the girl would contemplate the Man in the Moon. His head is the Sea of Rains; the bundle of twigs in his arms is the Ocean of Storms; his right leg is formed by the Sea of Tranquillity, his left by the Sea of Fertility, his outstretched hand by the Sea of Crises . . . Mare Crisium. Ora pro nobis . . .

The bottles are duplicated in the mirror.

Babel of bottles. Babel of glasses. Glass tower to reach the stars. All kinds of liquors and cocktails. Sherry Spider. Arakhné. Scorpio . . . To continue my orbit of the consterna-tions. I imagined a tall round Babel of inverted glasses piled one on top of the other. Crystal screams to raise the pitch. And now instead of a gallows I raise my Y. Another glass. I cannot ask for mezcal. And they don't have Anís del Mono. No mo' anise? Marie Brizard. (Does he want Breezy María? Quiere María?) Pernod to beg your pardon. I've had too much to drink. I couldn't decide if I should have a 7Up or a White Horse. I ordered the whiskey so I could weep with hippocups for my heroine. Like the crack of a whip. Hit me again . . .

Giddap, horse, down the via dolorosa.

Arre, jaca, to Oaxaca? Where the Consul went when she left him. A serape from Oaxaca on the bed where she lay . . . I too can write the saddest names on this sad night. Oaxaca, or to Jaca? The casket to Jaca. The casket will come. By express.

Pony express. To the endgame. Checkmate. Checkmate kills. The little quarter horse branded with a 7 on its hindquarters. Horse of the Apocalypse. To open the seventh seal of seventh heaven. Kicking up a row, that devil's pony. The day she returned to Quauhnáhuac and the Consul, they both saw him under different circumstances: in the morning ridden by an Indian, early in the afternoon grazing peacefully near that same Indian dying by the side of the road to Tomalín, and at nightfall on that longest and saddest of all days of the dead, the Consul saw him tethered at the door of the last cantina and untied him. And set loose fatality, because that was where some killers shot him dead. (Fate played its card with her letters, too, because the Consul defended them as if they were treasure from those killers who tried to snatch them away in the last cantina, and gave carte blanche to death.) And the untethered horse, maddened by the storm that followed, would later kill the Consul's wife, who was lost in a dark wood.

They sketched a Y on their last day: a stretch of road together, then bifurcating to their respective deaths.

The letter of divorce. Ours? Guay. A stretch of road together. Nel mezzo del cammin . . . And then we each go our own way. To our destiny . . . She looked up the word divorce in a dictionary on the boat that took her away from the Consul. From divertir. Divert . . . But she went back after a year. Still wearing her wedding ring. Of course, her divorce from the Consul had not yet failed. The ex-Consul, because he had resigned . . .

No one will be able to take away from you all these letters that I put on the table. *Belles Lettres.* Registered trademark. I fill both sides of the tablet with the little black letters of my roundelays. Little black ants. My Greek E's are horned. Like the Consul's. And like those of that other great cuckold Señor De la Flora. And each Greek Y like a scorpion. Your sign. Mine, the calligraphic loops that adorn the cover of the tablet. A labyrinth. Like my goings and comings. A Gordian knot of love. It is true there are loves that bind. More than once on the point of forgetting it in a pub. A way of dealing them out. And not losing them, at least until I play the last card, the last letter. Almost like a deck of cards these cardboard coasters with the signs of the zodiac that you like so much. Yours isn't among them. I'll set my glass down here. Sagittarius.

I settled into the empty seat here at the table by the door that opens onto King's Road, to finish writing to you with another White Horse. Hyhnhnm!!!

Spectral white horse in the dark and stormy afternoon, in the brilliance of a lightning flash, beneath the sky flaming white as a winding sheet. And in one shooting flame and one shrieking neigh the horse and the terrified woman were fused. Mare of the night bolting, runaway nightmare?

Sagittarius is agitated.

A lightning bolt, a luminous arrow in the dark sky.

The constellations whirled, all the planets of the zodiac, and she ascended in a fiery dream.

Closing time. Lighthearted farewells at the door. Everybody's happy. Am I happy, too? I went out into the night to contemplate my astronomer elevated to the highest altars, Antares and le altre stelle moved by love.

At the corner, above the well-lit display window of the retro clothing store, the hands of the mad clock whirled rapidly in reverse. A joke to help us forget that time does not move backwards. The true infernal machine. Designed to destroy everything. Everything. Impossible to go back. Ahead of me, so happy-go-lucky, the long-haired man with his pack on his back. His bed, his house on his shoulders. Shaggy compañero. Is there a constellation of the Snail? Remove the horns from the moon. Horned sister . . . There in front, in the light of the lantern, the sign of the old man with the scythe sitting at the side of the crossroads that points to FINIS. Not yet. Walking toward World's End, I was assailed by a doubt: Do we always have to meet our fate? I thought that on her last day in Quauhnáhuac perhaps she could have saved herself if she had followed a very different path, one where the horse of death did not go galloping . . . A few hours after she arrived, she suggested going to the zoo instead of going to Tomalín, do you understand what that means? But they paid no attention to her. Why don't we go to the zoo?

Z z . . .

at first it was the buzz. That didn't let me sleep a wink last night. My fault for leaving the window open. It was one of those Dutch mosquitoes that always buzz Zuider Zee . . . Zuider Zee . . . And when I turned on the light, it hid, I don't know where, probably beside the papered-over fly on the wall. Zz . . . when I turned the light off again. Zuider Zee . . . Zuider Zee . . . A buzz or a faux bourdon musical. At times as refined as a violin. At other times, hoarse as a horsefly. Or a comic-strip gadfly. Zz . . . I remembered with some regret the horsefly at the Horse Guards which wanted to feast on the piquant freckled peccancies of the little Belgian we found when she had lost her way in the Piccadilly station. She had wanted to see the changing of the guard, and all she got to see was a pissing horse. C'est pas mal . . . I fluttered my hands in front of her face, trying to frighten away the fly, and it stung me instead.

Doux Cupidon taon!

Unless sweet Cupid fly had already let fly his arrow in Piccadilly. Curious, and not at all alarmed when we showed her the emaciated zombies going into Boots pharmacy. C'est la vie . . . , she said when I showed her Eros taking flight over the fountain of life. But she lost interest in Eros and turned, pointing across the square at the advertisement on high: CACOCALO! Worst of all, we had to buy a bottle ipso flatus. It amused her that it was called Coke. C'est marrant . . . Like the drug. Just outside her school in Malines they also sold it. Coco Chanel, oui. The adorable way she had of taking a drink, then the pause that refreshes and three little burps that almost ended in coitus-inter-eructus. She wanted to go in to see that Piccadilly peep show. C'est du catch. Luckily she didn't think to ask for a dyspepsi loca cola . . . Then, in raptures over the photographs in color of naked women with feathers at the entrance to the FESTIVAL OF EROTICA in the RAYMOND REVUEBAR. C'est de la barbe-au-cul, Raymond!

It was still buzzing.

Wham! Got it at last. Le moustique est mort . . . But still I couldn't sleep. The telegram! It was because of the telegram I received that afternoon.

A zombie or semisomnambulist walking in slow motion down the stairs of the Hammersmith station toward the platform of the Piccadilly line. About to doze off as soon as I settle into the only empty seat in this smoking car, nodding next to the moon-faced Buddha, who also nods his assent.

HAM, letters that awaken my appetite. A ham sandwich wouldn't be bad right now. Alas, poor York . . . A figure dark as Hamlet hides the rest of the letters. What can he be reading? Letters letters letters . . . That I can't read. French? Must be some cheap novel, un roman de gare ou de garce . . . Or an exotic novel by Perroquet Loti, there's a green parrot on the cover. That speaks to me. The dirty old herbalist you worked for when you first came to London, always so well versed, so well perversed, always ready with insinuations and innuendos, and in the back room he kept a dirty old green parrot as repulsive as he was, who invariably repeated in French Psitacosis, psitacosis . . . No laughing matter, but it amused him that the only thing the parrot knew how to say was the name of a parrots' disease. Psitacose, psitacose . . . the only word he could say. La verve dure . . . yes, hard as his beak. Le pervers! This train will never move. I'd swear I've seen that guy in black somewhere. In Brook Green? Through the door—and for an instant I thought it was my own reflection in the glass—the dark skinny man with a beard and round glasses like John Lennon's went on reading his book, sitting on a bench on the platform in front of the circle crossed with the name of the station.

HAMMERSMITH

And in the upper part of the white circle, the mark of Zorro, twice, in black spray paint.

Zz . . . belles lettres for representing sleep. Mine. Even I, sly as a fox, have a right to doze. Not a wink the whole night because of the mosquitelegram. The sting of your telegram. Really yours, love? Or a morbid joke? Amorous or humorous? I turn it over and over. Finally the train pulls out and the zees dance. Or are they lightning bolts? Two bolts from Zeus ex machina? Zees for writing Zip-zap! a sudden blow. The telegram is a real lash of the whip. Dizzying zees that represent my nightmare. You've gone to Zanzibar, or Zaragoza, or Zwanze? I still can't believe the telegram. Trembling here in my hands. It's no joke, really? You used to laugh at my reversible or viceversicle telegrams, a method of my own invention for sending twice the text for half the price. Here's my most recent gratuitous one, from the back of a camel: APARTA SACO CARACAS⇌SACAR A COCA SATRAPA [Set aside sack from Caracas—Satrap taking out coca]. Or this one for cleaning up dirty money: SERA LODO LO SACAS⇌SACA SOLO DOLARES [Mud if you take it—Take out dollars only]. And even for gambling: ALLI TOCA PARTO LIMA⇌A MIL OTRA PACOTILLA [Fix is in am leaving for Lima—Bet another thousand]. Any city seemed to pose dangers for you, I thought, and every day I zigzagged through the *Times* looking for the place where the fatal accident would occur. But now I wonder if I could have been wrong about your sign. That well-known appointment can await us in any city, not only Samarra. Were you born on November 22 or 23? Today the city is Karavas, the town in Cyprus bombed by the Turks. In today's *Times*. I remember once when I was doing the crossword the Egyptian city that you zigzag to came up: Zagazig.

BARON'S COURT

Here's where we spent a few infernal hibernal days, in that frigihorrific room with a view of the cemetery in Palliser Road. They're worse off than we are. Where there's life, there's hope. Life is the last thing you lose. Those were my Baron de la Palliser days . . .

I'd need much more than a month to visit all our shared-in-commonplaces. Zigzag . . . all over London, to so many of our spots, for the past three days. Since Tuesday. But not writing to you. I decided I'd write Z as an epilogue, an ending, happy or unhappy, whenever I heard from you or knew if you were coming back or leaving me. I planned to write Z at World's End, in our pub where the old man with the scythe skulks beside a skull (calvariae locus) at the crossroads called FINIS, so close to The Man in the Moon, where I began my calvary. But your telegram has changed my plans. Man proposes and God disposes. In mysterious ways. And wavering lines. Like mine now. The shaking train makes my writing look like an old man's. Senile lines . . . My feelings, too, because of the telegram.

The supreme moment approaches. For good or ill. On Tuesday I looked for you in north London. I was about to go into the

Buddhist monastery on Haverstock Hill to ask if you had become a bonze. Buddha here beside me has turned into a bonzai. Curved and twisted in his seat. Still assenting with the zenza-zen swaying of the train. Another doubt assails me: could I be his dream? You know, Chuang Tzu, who did not know if the philosopher dreamed the butterfly or vice versa.

The sign on the monastery says there is a *bhikkhu* available on Thursdays. You liked the sound of *bhikkhu* more than monk. But it was only Tuesday, and I persevered on my pilgrimage after reading the good words: PEACE TO ALL CREATURES! Poor mashed mosquito. Mors necessaria . . .

Finally I sat on the wooden bench next to the station at Belsize Park, where we were so happy on so many afternoons. The bench with the inscription "My husband liked to sit here." It began to grow dark and I burst into tears. Yes, I am ashamed, I won't do it again. I felt bankrupt. Brokenhearted on a bench. You'd never dedicate a bench to me, would you?

EARL'S COURT

Here I met Rimbaudelaire, our pensioner poet. Who was also looking for a handout. You never believed his story about the war wound. He was almost a baby when the bomb exploded in his garden in Liège. An American bomb. You thought he was pulling your leg. He wasn't born one-handed. And he didn't lift his hair to show you the hole in his ear. It was the wind. When we were shivering with cold in his decrepit convertible Fiord as we drove to Victoria Station to pick up the rusty old trunk or *cantine* that your Armenian grandmother sent you from France. The jokes Rimbaudelaire made at the expense of that *cantine*, a tavern containing no bottles of rum, unfortunately, but weighing more than if the dead cantinero himself were inside. What was in there? The customs agents asked the same question. And Rimbaudelaire, incontinent with laughter: The *cantine* comes from the Continent . . .

GLOUCESTER ROAD

The sound and light of broken glass every time I hear the word Gloucester. And the screech and crash almost at the same time. That summer night when we watched the accident from the window. The motorcyclist thrown onto Gloucester Terrace, his crumpled bike beside the black Morris with the license ORO. Gored by the bullion . . . Shards of glass shining like stars on the asphalt. And people at their windows as if they were boxes at the theater. The biker covered with a blanket, and moaning. But nobody could touch him. Until a little while later, when the ambulance arrived. Nights later I dreamed I was the groaning cyclist on the ground and you stood at the window with other people (probably a party) and talked about the accident with your festive friends and the neighbors in the other houses, while I wriggled in the night among twinkling stars, like a worm. A glowworm. A frantic firefly . . .

SOUTH KENSINGTON

The Chinese doll, her legs bowed like a frog's in tight jeans, stands reading a picture book, *Alice's Adventures Underground*, next to the middle-aged traveler with the briefcase who reads a Maigret novel in French, clenching his pipe between his teeth (this is not a Magritte . . .). She slithered out just as the doors were closing, reminding me of our slippery little Belgian eel. After seeing the changing of the guard and the horses, who brush away horseflies with their tails, we had to help her find her friends. All of them were going to Carnaby Street. Schoolgirls in Malines must think it is a street of fashions still in fashion. Her little friends were nowhere in sight and we went from shop to shop, for nobody could understand that Franglais or Frenglish you speak when you go shopping. She decided she had to buy jeans. All her little friends were going to buy them. The gaullimaufry began when she picked out the most perverse, les vices américains . . . but I only knew about English vices. The Indian vendor viewed with approval as she tried them on. True, they looked very good on her, her rump nicely rounded in Levi's . . . But the best part came when it was time to pay. The head of the school had all her money. If we paid now, when we took her to the station she'd repay us. You were the one who took pity on her when she started to cry. We had to dig deep. The second time she had shed her crocodile tears for us. Though she wasn't buying Lacoste. It was another brand . . . to my cost.

KNIGHTSBRIDGE

All we could do was figure out who would wear the pants . . . She refused to take them off, and out she sauntered, so smug in her Levi jeans. And to prove I'm not a rancorous man, I decided to take you both to that pub on Carnaby Street where the genius of Stratford stares out the window . . . Do you know who the man with the little beard is? Her categorical response: Dr. Freud! But it turned out she did know who Shakespeare was. C'est l'auteur de To be! Toubib or no . . . No doubt the kid had a well-rounded education, and what a well-rounded shape she had, too. And despite your objections, I invited her to try English beer. Did she like it? C'est dégueu! She preferred la gueuze . . . But she immediately turned her back on the bitter to

listen to the Beatles on the jukebox. Les Bittels, les Bittels . . .
she shook her hips in excitement, almost crashing into the jukebox. It's true those levicious jeans looked ravishing . . . Yesterday, yes. And you were annoyed when I got up to wiggle with
her. Why don't you stop acting the clown?

The white-haired lady who just came into the car carrying a
green shopping bag from HARRODS FOOD HALLS is galvaniz-
ing all my gastric juices . . . Nothing to eat this afternoon. Why
wolfed down the one slice of ham I had left. A piece of it still
dangling from his mouth when I lunged for him. Lunch waving
bye-bye like the patch I put on his eye. Pretty comical, this pan-
tomime puss. Mon chat pitre! And he dispatched it, bon,
farewell ham of York.

She was very much a chauvinist, gastronomically speaking,
our little Belgian glutton. With no moules frites to be had, we
invited her, at your suggestion—and with my last money—to
have fish-and-chips at the Church Street market. No use trying
to explain that in this market American vices cost less but lacked
a label. It was the label that interested la belle . . . She gobbled
down chips, using both hands, but the poor thing's brains were
fried . . . She hadn't slept at all last night on the boat, singing
with the other songbirds. It was her first trip on a ship. And her
first to England. I suggested taking her to my room for a siesta.
The expression on your face was forlorn. You won't try . . . But
she didn't want to sleep, she wanted to go to the museum of
Madame Tussaud. Where all her little friends probably were by
now. Hopefully.

HYDE PARK CORNER

The bearded man gets off playing the harmonica, his camouflage jacket showing more grease spots than grass spots, the

same man I saw last night, sleeping so soundly in the fetal position at the entrance to a shop on Beauchamp Place, that the bobby couldn't wake him—Get up! Get up!—nudging him with his foot. Don't wake . . . Who was the first person to say that life is a dream . . .

You paid for the tickets to Madame Tussaud's. It was the first time for me, too, in that horrific wax horror show. The museum's hyperrealistic crimes. But it wasn't the monsters or the murderers or the more or less glorious battles that attracted the attention of our curious young Belgian. She stood in front of Picasso, sitting in checked trousers on his rattan chair, and after a moment of mature reflection she murmured: C'est un clown!

GREEN PARK

Green was the paradise of our love. Lost. Though our Belgian was not as verdant as the grass she rested on. We were in Regent's Park. La verdure et la verdeur . . . She chattered on about all the dirty old men who always wanted to show her their *zizi* . . . That's the only reason the old coots invited her to have a Coca-Cola. There was even one who followed her: "Viens ici, ma cocotte, je te passerai à la casserole! . . ." That's just what he said. He wanted to pass our little chickadee through his grinder. But Maman showed up just in time and split open his head. With so accurate a blow of the ax that Maman was left a widow. A widow alone in the world with her little girl. I couldn't believe my ears as I looked into the distance at the tower or spire of the Post Office. Mat de Cocagne. The Eiffel Tower of London. And phallic, too. I asked her if she had been to Paris. Just for three days. And, it seems, there were old men there, too. She told us in three little words what she did: I grew up. A precocious old woman . . . Who also wanted to stay in school until she retired. She wanted to teach the three R's. And not spare the rod. I imagined her at sixty-five teaching the rule of three to the most intractable children. Teaching ABZ to the young morons of Mont-Saintron or Montresain . . . But our little rook was tumbling again into sleep. She'd be better off taking her siesta at home before we took her to the station.

PICCADILLY CIRCUS

This is where, in evil hour, we found her lost beside the map-clock—WHAT'S THE TIME?—that shows the time all over the world. In the tumult and commotion of the station she had become separated from the others, all her little school friends from Malines. Because, because . . . , she tried to explain in her reiterative English. Because, because . . . is the only thing she knew how to say. On parle français. You suggested taking her straight to the police. Do you recall? She burst into tears. Her one day in London. She had just arrived. And she wanted to see what her friends would see. Piccadilly, the changing of the guard, Carnaby Street, Madame Tussaud, the zoo . . . An entire program. A tight schedule. Before boarding the 18:60 train at Waterloo for Bournemouth . . . She was still crying, and a bobby gave us a suspicious look. That's all we needed, to have them think we were kidnappers. Littlechatterboxnappers. The first misstep was mine. Well, your friends are probably still in Piccadilly Circus. Yes, the circus was about to begin . . .

The Marquee poster, here on this wall, made me take off my glasses and rub my eyes: ZZEBRA. In big capital letters, just like that, with two Z's, and beneath it, in smaller letters: Plus Guest and Mark Poppins. Was there a singer named Guest? El convidado de piedra, the Stone Guest, that would be a nice name, he rolls his own rock . . . Un drôle de zèbre, with two Z's. But if you look carefully, it's fine, the word seems more zebrine. Of Spanish or Portuguese origin? From now on I'll always write it with a Z. And our little Belgian wanted to go and see the zebras, the tigers, the chimpanzees, the penguins. Not to the zoo, no, I absolutely refused. If you think, *fillette*, that I'm going to . . . But you took her part. The other girls were probably there by now. I was assailed by a terrible suspicion that should have passed through our scattered brains long before this: where did this creature come from? And what if the sly *maline* was lying and there was no school in Malines, no other Malineses or whatever they're called? But for the moment she was still crying. Insisting on the zoo. Just as well that after her little temper tantrum she started to doze off again.

Finally you agreed it was a good idea for us to take her to my room for a siesta. She didn't have to be at the station for another three hours.

LEICESTER SQUARE

The bonze is still nodding. The time is twenty past one. A train passed, going in the opposite direction, its destination BOUNDS GREEN. Bounds, boundaries. Forbidden to go beyond reality. But how is one to know where it begins and ends? I grasp at the burning straws of what I see. And touch. This telegram singes my fingers. WE ARRIVE . . . Who? With whom? I've just seen spray-painted in red on the wall ROSE AGAIN! Miss Rose must also be arriving today or tomorrow, I think. But she was in Ithaca, New York, and your telegram came from Edinburgh. Edinburgh! Could you have gone back to the hotel that had old photographs of women on the walls of the hallways, the stairway, the rooms? Your double in the sepia photograph at the first landing. Or one of your earlier incarnations . . . You thought you recalled rows of footlights and bursts of applause. I believe you want to be an interpreter because you can't go back to being an actress. You thought you also recalled a tragic ending. Before the curtain fell. Why did you go to Edinburgh? And with whom? Are you really arriving on Friday?

Everything seems so unreal to me, so like a dream, that I have to clutch at concrete details. Gray switches dangling like pears from the ceiling of this car. Swaying back and forth. Not ripe. Pears peras esperas espoirs Babelle belle hell . . . Yes, hell has no boundaries.

The Indian in the white turban wrapped like a bandage reads the *Standard*. BOMB IN THE EAST END. A bomb from the Second World War. Time is a bomb . . .

COVENT GARDEN

Our wild little animal didn't like my lair. And she didn't want to take a siesta. She wanted to go to the zoo. Sniffing, wrinkling her nose as soon as she walked in. Did it smell of tiger? Of skunk? Of old clothes? Of stale cigarettes . . . She went over to the table and the ashtray filled with the butt ends of Gitanes. And made a face. How could anything smell so bad.

Doukipudonktan.

One can't pronounce well holding one's nose. Checking every corner of the room like a cat, looking at all the images on my Spanish-Chinese screen, some not very edifying . . . And especially interested in my hookah. She wanted to see how it worked. To amuse her I wrapped a towel around my head and a blanket around my shoulders like a cape. She laughed but didn't want to sleep. I would have been better off throwing a blanket over my head and myself out the window . . . Do you know who I am? (I should have said my namesheik . . .) Haroun al-Haschisch! And she laughed as I simulated a sneeze. You went to the WC for a moment and when you returned you went through the roof. Our silly little simpleton was laughing like a loon after each little puff. It's just to make her sleep . . . and you almost broke the pipe on my head.

HOLBORN

Polyglot polyphony. Foreign languages. Adios amigos. Alors au revoir, les gars! Ciao . . . The group of effusive tourists making their farewells as they leave the car. Nothing like a knowledge of languages. A gentleman from the City seems to nod his assent. Most interesting . . . We always got off here to renew our green cards. Foreigners a little less joyful and self-assured going to be interrogated . . .

Our little imp finally slept like an angel. In the heavenly choir.* Our little songstress from the choir of Malines. The music sounded sublime from Miss Rose's apartment. Forma e matera, congiunte e purette . . . A cherub lulled by the music of Cherubini. ZZ . . . Snoring like the angels.

But you shook her awake, roughly, because we didn't have much time to get to Waterloo. We made it, but only by a hair. And it turned out that the girls' choir did exist. Le chœur de Malines! Shouting encouragement from the windows of the train as we practically dragged her along. The train pulled out immediately, and I began to laugh, probably with relief, remembering that she got just what she wanted and didn't pay us for the Levi's.

I also nodded and don't know where the waking Buddha got off. At Holborn? The train is stopped now between two stations. A contagious silence. An angel has flown over . . . A dan-

---

* Seraphim (serafin)? You might have pressured me for precise details. And I would have told you, happily: It will end (Será fin) . . .

gerous association reminding me that I was going to King's Cross. The telegram was almost a formula: WE ARRIVE KING ✕ 2:14H. FRIDAY 2. There is no two without three? We arrive? A majecstatic plural that threatens the stress of a ménage à trois?

At two which two arrive? King's Cross is the last station. We emerge from darkness into light. I too hope for enlightenment. At last we arrive.

RUSSELL SQUARE

The doors opened and closed and opened . . . The doors of the car opened and closed five times, at least. For the past three stations. And for . . . almost a century. I wrote it down but crossed it out. With an "At last we arrive," I cut short my notes from the underground. Too nervous to write all the way to King's Cross. It was one-twenty-six when I arrived. A twenty-six-minute trip. Or almost twenty years. The two-day-old *Standard*—

BOMBED THEN
BOMBED AGAIN

—that somebody left on the seat beside me, almost makes the infernal machine move backward. Two bombs exploded yesterday in Manchester. Fifty wounded. Blood in the streets. Now the photographs in color.

KING'S CROSS

Say it with words. The huge sign on the way to the escalator. SAY IT WITH WORDS. As if that were so easy. I preferred, when I ascended almost to the clouds, to see the little square with the words "When I dream . . ."; when I dream, my dreams are not always pleasant. Like life itself. When I looked up, the brightly lit metal beams of the station ceiling, like gigantic letters suspended in the night. Belles lettres . . . Because it is night. Today it is night. A cold December night.

I reached the station with enough time to calm down and write down a scene that seemed to be a good omen. At almost the same time that I did, a couple arrived carrying soft-sided dark brown bags. He is tall, thin, white-haired, about forty. She is younger and shorter, also thin but attractive. Going on vacation, no doubt. I saw them arguing, though I couldn't hear why. He became angry and let one of the bags drop to the floor. Then she did the same with another, turned, and strode out of the station with a determined step. He stood in the middle of the platform, in the middle of his suitcases, not knowing what to do. Finally he decided to pick up the bags, and he began to walk slowly toward the train. She changed her mind, came up to him, and took one of the bags. Then she dropped it, threw her arms around his neck, and they kissed . . . At the time it seemed a happy ending. But now I'm not so sure. In any case, there are no final endings . . .

You were about to appear, as if by magic. Your dark head at the train window, next to the white-haired one. We arrive! And then I saw the dark-haired man with the slim mustache. My heart stopped. No, not Mandrake. The Great Karman! Your uncle from America, your mother's brother. The son of your Armenian grandmother. I always became entangled in your family ties. A magician, but he'd been a practical nurse prior to that. He had worked at many jobs, an unsettled life in America. You'd gone with him on his last tour. Almost a vacation. In Scotland. Zig jumped into my arms. Or was it Zag? The plush one (the one the Great Karman used for ventriloquism or ventralism while the flesh-and-blood dog howled his bowwow) had stayed in the steamer trunk. That I had to help carry to the cab. We arrive . . . It would have been better if you'd greeted me with the two doggies in your arms while the Great Karman barked at me and rained on my parade. But he was very ill, despite his healthy appearance. The doctors had given him only a few months to live. And you had decided to go with him to Los Angeles. You are his only family. Of course, I understood . . . Though now I doubt I really understood anything then. WE ARRIVE. At King's Cross . . .

Couples sometimes separate, reunite, separate again, the ties loosen, tighten, until they break forever. But that's another story . . . the one that never ends.

In reality you were just passing through London, and would not spend any time with all those indecipherable scrawls that I scribbled in the tablet you gave me. *Belles lettres* . . . Almost twenty years later I decided to transcribe them—Ma Chine infernale—on the typewriter of time.

There was another scene of jealousy and misunderstanding, if I remember correctly, because you found Vicky in my room as I was getting ready to correct her Latin exercises. Peccata minuta . . .

When I still believed it was possible to begin again, I had thought about ending Donjuanesquely with a list of all my belles. Madamina, il catalogo è questo. Questo è il fin. Albertine. Her death was the great tragedy of my life. Bonadea . . . But there's no need now. Now all my belles lettres are yours as well. You are letters. And so am I. In a way. And I recalled that old postcard on my swinish Chinese screen: the head of a man composed entirely of naked women. Arcimbold face . . . Homme à femmes. Man born of women, literally. And now each one, a letter. A man of letters. The rest is. Silence. Mute here at the end of the world. Of worlds. Finis. I came from King's Cross to the place where I wanted to end the last letter. To our tavern at the end of the world. But they've changed the sign. The old man and his scythe and the skull and the FINIS are gone. Now it is a ship of madmen or fools who go with lowered eyes through the world that no doubt turns. And here in the cold of the night I return to that other night when darkness fell on the kingdom because of a strike and we went into the warmth of this pub lit by candles while a chorus of old men and women sang old songs from the war. Fine words, nice lyrics . . . Recalling nostalgically some blackout or other . . . The choir of old choristers. Who did not sing like angels. I aged, too. In Spanish I could write it for you in four letters. But I'm not here for rebuses. I'll take the 11, as I've done so often, almost at eleven. Not at all placid this December Saturday. And now the soccer howligans walk by, here in World's End, waving their scarves. I saw them before (or aren't they the same ones?) in Trafalgar Square. Chanting their victory. But they certainly don't sing like angels.

A NOTE ABOUT THE AUTHOR

Julián Ríos was born in 1941 in Galicia, Spain. He attended university in Madrid and has lived in London, Berlin, and Strasbourg. At present he lives in Paris and Madrid. Ríos is on the editorial board of a number of magazines, contributes to journals from different languages, and has edited several fiction and essay series. His previous books (the first two with Octavio Paz) include *Larva, Poundemonium,* and *Kitaj: Pictures and Conversations.* Collaborating with visual artists, he has produced books and—in his own words— "painted novels."

A NOTE ABOUT THE TRANSLATOR

Edith Grossman is the award-winning translator of major works by many of Latin America's most important writers, including Gabriel García Márquez, Alvaro Mutis, and Mario Vargas Llosa. Born in Philadelphia, she attended the University of Pennsylvania and the University of California at Berkeley before receiving her Ph.D. from New York University. Ms. Grossman is the author of *The Antipoetry of Nicanor Parra* and of many articles and book reviews. She lives in New York City.

A NOTE ON THE TYPE

This book was set in Fournier, a typeface named for Pierre Simon Fournier fils (1712–1768), a celebrated French type designer. Coming from a family of typefounders, Fournier was an extraordinarily prolific designer of typefaces and of typographic ornaments. He was also the author of the important *Manuel typographique* (1764–1766), in which he attempted to work out a system standardizing type measurement in points, a system that is still in use internationally.

Fournier's type is considered transitional in that it drew its inspiration from the old style, yet was ingeniously innovational, providing for an elegant, legible appearance. In 1925 his type was revived by the Monotype Corporation of London.

Composed by North Market Street Graphics,
Lancaster, Pennsylvania
Printed and bound by The Haddon Craftsmen,
an R. R. Donnelley & Sons Company,
Bloomsburg, Pennsylvania
Designed by Virginia Tan

DATE DUE